Praise for the novels of
Cassie Edwards

"Edwards consistently gives the reader a strong love story, rich in Indian lore, filled with passion and memorable characters." —*Romantic Times*

"Excellent . . . an endearing story . . . filled with heart-warming characters." —*Under the Covers*

"Cassie Edwards once again shines as the master of Indian folklore, history, and romantic intrigue."
—*Rendezvous*

"A fine writer . . . accurate . . . Indian history and language keep readers interested."
—*Tribune* (Greeley, CO)

"Edwards moves readers with love and compassion." —*Bell, Book, and Candle*

"Edwards puts an emphasis on placing authentic customs and language in each book. Her Indian books have generated much interest throughout the country, and elsewhere."
—*Journal-Gazette* (Mattoon, IL)

ALSO BY CASSIE EDWARDS

Sun Hawk

Thunder Heart

Silver Wing

Lone Eagle

Bold Wolf

Flaming Arrow

White Fire

Rolling Thunder

Wild Whispers

Wild Thunder

Wild Bliss

Wild Abandon

Wild Desire

Wild Splendor

Wild Embrace

Wild Rapture

Wild Ecstasy

WINTER RAVEN

Cassie Edwards

A SIGNET BOOK

SIGNET
Published by New American Library, a division of
Penguin Putnam Inc., 375 Hudson Street,
New York, New York 10014, U.S.A.
Penguin Books Ltd, 27 Wrights Lane,
London W8 5TZ, England
Penguin Books Australia Ltd, Ringwood,
Victoria, Australia
Penguin Books Canada Ltd, 10 Alcorn Avenue,
Toronto, Ontario, Canada M4V 3B2
Penguin Books (N.Z.) Ltd, 182–190 Wairau Road,
Auckland 10, New Zealand

Penguin Books Ltd, Registered Offices:
Harmondsworth, Middlesex, England

First published by Signet, an imprint of New American Library,
a division of Penguin Putnam Inc.

First Printing, December 2000
10 9 8 7 6 5 4 3 2 1

BUFFALO

The buffalo is our brother,
He was given to us by our sacred father.
He is all we have left,
Why should we keep him from his rest?
He has brought us so many things,
For which he should be praised.
He is our last connection to what we hold so dear,
His purpose in life is so very clear.
He is an animal not which to fear,
From his shaggy head to his ample frame.
His spirit no one can claim,
He is the last of the free roaming herd.
We shall save you, I give you my word.
You were sent to save us those decades ago,
When you disappear, our spirits will be low.
The buffalo has a spiritual power,
We shall draw from that, until his last hour.
For now he is the last of his kind,
We shall help you until the end of time.

—Cassandra Olinger,
poet and friend

I wish to dedicate *Winter Raven*
to Tammy Russotto, a dear friend
with whom I share much on the Internet!
(Please check out www.cassieedwards.com)

In friendship,
Cassie Edwards

1

The angels most heedful,
Receive each mild spirit,
New Worlds to inherit.
—WILLIAM BLAKE

Kansas City, Missouri, 1859

It was late spring. Wild geese had flown from the South to nest on the tops of dead cottonwood snags in the groves along the streams that branched from the Missouri River.

A weeping willow tree graced the hillside, its limbs gently shimmying in the breeze, as Holly Wintizer stood in its shadows over a fresh grave.

Tall and willowy like the tree behind her, her golden, waist-length hair hanging in waves down her slender back, Holly couldn't believe that her mother lay in that grave. Putting on the dreadful black dress and the black veil this morning had been perhaps the hardest thing she'd had to do in her life. The clothing made everything too real, declaring that she was in mourning.

Holly choked back a sob and reached beneath

the veil to dab at her eyes with her lacy hand-
kerchief.

"Mama, how can it be that I will never see your
smile or hear your laughter again?" she whispered, alone now that the other mourners were
pulling away from the cemetery in their black
buggies. "You weren't sick *ever*, before."

A dark, angry frown creased Holly's brow as
she thought of who she blamed for her mother's
untimely death.

"Rudolph Anderson," she hissed, the sound of
his name as it crossed her lips causing a familiar
bitterness. She always felt this way when she
thought of the man her mother had been married
to for such a short time.

Holly still couldn't believe that her mother had
been taken in so quickly by the drifter, actually
marrying him only one month after having met
him in Harrison's General Store in Kansas City.

As her mother had explained it to Holly, she
had been trying to reach a bolt of cloth high on
a shelf in the store when, out of nowhere, a large,
strong hand reached up and got it for her.

When her mother turned to the man to thank
him, his blue eyes seemed to hypnotize her, and
his red hair glowed like sunshine as it lay neatly
at his freshly starched white collar. And when he
spoke to her, in a voice so masculine and deep,

her mother was swept clean off her feet and was never the same afterward.

"And then there came those days shortly after the marriage when you complained about not feeling too well," Holly whispered. She bent to a knee and placed a single long-stemmed rosebud on the fresh mound of dirt. "I wish I had suspected then what I suspect now, Mama. Just . . . maybe . . . you would be alive today."

She hated thinking about how fast their lives had changed after her mother married Rudolph Anderson.

Oh, Lord, was it really only two weeks after they had been married in the beautiful white Baptist church in midtown Kansas City that he had wiped out her mother's bank account and left town?

Yes, that was how cruel and heartless he had been, and it was on the very day that her mother had discovered the truth that she had died.

Doc Adams had told Holly that the shock of having been duped by a con artist had caused her mother's heart attack, killing her as surely as if the swindler had been right there sinking a knife into her aching heart.

But Holly doubted the doctor's observation. Her mother had always been a strong woman, with a strong heart. Holly could not help but believe something else had caused her death. She had requested an autopsy, but thus far she had not heard the results.

Holly gazed heavenward. "Mama, I love you," she said quietly. She swallowed hard. "Oh, how I will miss you." Hanging her head in utter despair, Holly went to her horse and buggy and rode away from the cemetery. The thought of going back to the house that had once been filled with her family's laughter was almost unbearable.

She was now alone in the world.

Through the years, her mother and father had often moved from place to place, and Holly had lost touch with her relatives. She didn't even have grandparents to fall back on. They had died before Holly had been born.

"It's all up to me now to make a life for myself," she said aloud, thinking about how she would find Rudolph Anderson and have him arrested for what he had done to her family.

It wasn't because of the money, either. Her need for revenge went deeper than that. It was because of her mother. No man should ever treat a woman the way Rudolph Anderson had treated Kathryn June Wintizer.

Wintizer. Holly believed that her mother had entered the portals of heaven with that name, the name she had received from her beloved first husband. The name Anderson was never truly meant to be a part of her mother's life, and it most certainly wouldn't be a part of her death. "Wintizer" was being engraved on her mother's headstone, not "Anderson." Holly had seen to that with almost the last cent of her and her mother's money.

Sighing heavily, she tried hard to shake off such troubled thoughts, knowing she had to have a clear mind to make decisions about her life. She drove along a cobblestone road through town, not even aware of horses and buggies or men on horseback riding past her and alongside her.

She didn't pay any heed to the lovely day with its blue skies and sunshine, not to the women in their lovely hats and dresses strolling along the board sidewalks before the two- and three-storied buildings of midtown Kansas City.

Holly was thinking hard about what she was going to do with the rest of her life.

She had never been forced to make her way, to work.

But now everything was different. She did have to find a way to make a living.

"At least I still have our house," she thought as she turned down a street that soon revealed a residential area with charming white frame houses on either side of the road. "As long as I'm there, I will still have a piece of Mama with me."

While there, she would be able to close her eyes and envision her mother sitting in her rocking chair, knitting, embroidering, or reading while Holly put together a puzzle on the floor beside the warm fire in the fireplace or just relaxed beside her mama and read a book of fiction.

If Holly thought about it when she was home, she might even be able to smell her favorite cinnamon rolls baking in the oven, and hear her mother humming contentedly.

Until *he* came along and ruined everything, Holly thought. After her mother married Anderson, Holly had not seen her laugh much anymore. She no longer sat and sewed and hummed contentedly beside the fire.

Holly hadn't been able to find it in herself to ask her mother why she had chosen to marry that man.

No, she hadn't wanted her mother to realize that she noticed the changes in her behavior, in her happiness. She felt that her mother had realized the mistake she had made though she had not yet worked her way out of it. In time, Holly knew, her mother would have booted the cheating liar out of their lives.

But she had not done it quickly enough, and he had run off with the family's wealth.

Holly's heart skipped a beat when she pulled her horse to a stop in front of her two-story white shingled house. Its wraparound porch, filled with wicker furniture, was where she and her mother had sat on drowsy summer days. The maple trees that Holly's father had planted around the house with his own hands had grown large enough to create a canopy of shade that Holly's mother had loved.

Holly blinked over and over again, not sure if what she was seeing in the yard was true, or imagined.

She stared disbelievingly at two large trunks, and then at boxes piled high with clothes, and then at the lone rifle that lay with her other things on the ground. Her saddle, with its saddlebags and gunboot, was flung down amid her other belongings.

"What's going on here?" Holly wondered, cold inside as she looked at her belongings sprawled on the ground. The shock of seeing them made her unable to move from the buggy.

When she heard the squeak of the front door as it slowly opened, she lifted her eyes to the porch and gazed in total surprise as a man and woman came out of her house and stood on the porch as though they owned it.

She looked from one to the other and soon realized that they were strangers, not friends who might be there to welcome her home from her sad moments at the cemetery.

Friends certainly would not have gone into her house and taken the liberty to rifle through her personal belongings. And friends especially would not have moved her possessions outside on the ground!

Inhaling a quavering breath, and finally finding the strength and courage to leave the buggy, Holly went and stood at the foot of the steps beside her things.

"Who are you?" she asked warily. "What is the meaning of this—going into my home uninvited? What do you think you're doing, putting my things out here on the ground?"

The man, short, squat, bald, and dressed in a dark suit, stepped away from the woman into the sunshine. His gaze was steady as he looked down at Holly. "This house is no longer yours," he said, his voice tight. "I purchased it, and everything in it, from Rudolph Anderson a few days ago. Me and my wife were civil enough to allow you to live here until your mother's burial. Today, while you were at the cemetery, we took possession."

He nodded toward Holly's belongings. "I went through your things," he said. "I've been kind enough to give you what I feel you need to get a new start in life."

This terrible news was so devastating to Holly, she felt as though someone had slammed a fist into her gut. Her stepfather had not only robbed her and her mother of their money but he had also had the gall to sell the house and everything in it. Except for what was lying on the ground beside her, Holly now had nothing!

"You can't be serious," Holly finally was able to say. "You can't do this. It's not—not ethical. It's criminal."

"I have the deed," the man said, lifting his chin boldly.

He looked over his shoulder at his wife, who was equally short and squat, and whose eyes were widely set and pale colored. Her black hair was pulled back into a tight bun atop her head, and her cotton dress strained at the waist and bust. She was nervously wringing her chubby hands.

"Edith, go and get the damn deed," the man growled. "Seems we've got to prove the purchase to the lady."

Holly watched the woman disappear into the house, then return again with a folded paper.

Holly stepped closer as the man waddled down the steps. Her hands shook as she took the deed and read it, her heart sinking when she saw that it was legal.

The house and everything in it were no longer hers. Her stepfather had sold it before he left town, and gotten even wealthier with the money from the sale.

Now that she knew she no longer had a legal right to the house, she realized she was too dead inside to argue anymore with people who didn't care how she felt. She loaded her belongings into her buggy and rode off toward town. She was stunned to realize that now not only was she penniless, she was also homeless.

"Jana," she whispered as she removed her black veil and laid it on the seat beside her.

She knew that she could go to her dear friend in a time of trouble, yet she hated to impose for even one minute on Jana and her husband, Frank. They had two children and were dirt poor.

But Holly had no choice.

She didn't even have enough money in her purse to pay for one night's lodging at a hotel. And she knew Jana well enough to believe that she and her husband wouldn't have it any other way. They would want Holly to come to them at a time like this. Holly wouldn't be with them for long.

She had things to do—someone to find.

There was no way that Holly was going to let her stepfather get away with it. Come hell or high water, she was going to find him. And, by damn, she would make him pay.

She drove down the long dirt lane that led to Jana's log cabin, which sat far back in the woods on the outskirts of Kansas City. When she saw Jana walk out of the cabin to see who was coming to call, tears sprang to Holly's eyes. She had seen Jana only a short while ago, at the cemetery.

They had held hands as the preacher said the last words over Holly's mother's grave.

Just before Jana had left Holly alone to say her final good-bye to her mother, she had given Holly the rose to place on her mother's grave.

"Holly?" Jana said, stepping up to the horse and buggy as Holly drew a tight rein before the cabin.

Jana wore a cotton dress and soiled apron, her brown hair in long pigtails down her back. Her oval face was dotted with freckles and her eyes were deep brown and friendly.

"Holly?" Jana said again, her voice drawn. "Oh, honey, was it too hard to go home and be alone? Do you need to stay here the night? You know you're more than welcome." She laughed softly. "But the kids might drive you crazy. They're in a fretful mood. They've been fightin' since we've been home from the cemetery."

"Jana, my stepfather sold my mother's home, and people moved in while . . . while I was burying Mama," Holly blurted out as she stepped down from the wagon.

Jana's lips parted in a loud gasp and her eyes widened in disbelief. "He did what?" she asked, glad when her husband came to her side and slid an arm around her waist.

Jana leaned into Frank's embrace, so happy to have him. It hurt her to feel Holly's loneliness.

"I knew he was no good the day your mother introduced him to me," Frank growled. He sported a thick black beard, and his hair hung down past his shoulders. He was dressed in bib overalls for working in his garden and tending to the animals.

"You're going to stay with us," Jana said, reaching out a comforting hand to Holly.

"I do need a place to stay," Holly said, wiping tears from her eyes. "But I won't be here for long. I just need a place where I can think and plan. I . . . I need a place to store my things."

"Store your things?" Jana said, her eyebrows raised. "It sounds like you're going someplace. Where, Holly? You have no kin that I know of. Surely you will be better off stayin' here with me and Frank and the kids."

"I just can't impose that much," Holly said, looking from Frank to Jana. "But I do appreciate the offer."

"Well, young lady, you just come into our house and stay as long as you like," Frank said. He placed a comforting arm around Holly's waist and ushered her toward the door. "One of the kids will let you use their room. You can have it for as long as you want it."

"I hate to do that," Holly said, wincing at the thought. Frank had only recently finished the cabin, which had enough bedrooms so that the children could have their own separate rooms.

"I built a spare bedroom overhead," Frank said. "The loft."

"I can take the loft bedroom," Holly said as she was swept on into the cabin, where smells of hot bread and pies wafted from the kitchen. "I'll stay up there."

"I won't have it," Frank said, waving a small four-year-old boy toward him. His three-year-old sister stood aside, clutching a teddy bear and shyly watching. "Sonny, go and get your toys you'll be wantin' to play with while Holly is staying with us and take them to the loft. Holly is going to use your room."

"I get the loft?" Sonny said, smiling widely up at his dad. "Pa, can Kathy stay with me? We'll have such fun."

Frank tousled Sonny's thick blond hair. "You couldn't wait to have a bedroom to yourself and now you want your sister to stay with you?" Frank said, laughing heartily. He gave his son a slight push. "Yeah. Go ahead. Tell Kathy to get her doll. Your ma will make up the bed in the loft pretty soon."

Kathy and Sonny ran off, squealing and laughing, as Jana and Holly embraced.

"I'm so sorry about everything," Jana murmured. "But you'll make it fine, dear friend. I've never met anyone with such a strong constitution as you."

"Yes, I'll make it," Holly said, in her mind already planning her strategy, how to find her stepfather and see that justice was done.

Jana started walking toward the kitchen. "I smell my pies," she said over her shoulder. "Frank, go and get Holly's things while I take the pies out of the oven. Then I'll show her to her room."

"It's good as done," Frank said, as he walked out of the cabin.

Holly followed Jana to the kitchen, the aroma of baking reminding her once again of her mother. She had loved making pies, especially apple, in the autumn when apples were picked from the trees in an orchard at the edge of town.

Filled with loneliness and melancholy, she watched Jana take one pie, then another, from her oven. She couldn't help but smile when Jana raised the kitchen window and set each pie on the sill to cool. How many times had she seen her mother do that? If she closed her eyes now, she would be with her mama in *her* kitchen.

"Holly, come now," Jana said, jarring Holly out of her deep thoughts. "You look worn out. I'll take you to your room. After Frank brings your things, why not get into somethin' more comfortable and stretch out on the bed for a nap before supper? I'll come and fetch you when it's on the table."

Holly nodded, yet she knew that she wanted to do anything but go to sleep. Plans were already swirling through her head—plans that she hoped would, in the end, put her evil stepfather behind bars!

She smiled at the children as they watched her walking toward the hallway that led back to the bedrooms. Then she went inside the small room. She sighed when she saw how sweetly and delicately it had been decorated for Kathy.

"Holly, I think you'll be more comfortable here in Kathy's room than in Sonny's," Jana said. She gently pulled a patchwork quilt down from the pillows. "It's so pretty and feminine in here, don't you think?"

"You've made a perfect room for a perfectly sweet little girl," Holly said.

She walked slowly around the room. She smiled as she saw the dolls, then ran a hand over a lacy dress that hung from a peg on the wall. She remembered seeing Kathy wearing this very dress at church only a week ago when Holly and her mother had gone to the Sunday morning services.

She turned quickly away from the dress and the memory that made her heart ache, knowing she would never sit in a church pew again with her mother.

Was this all real, truly real? Was her mother gone from her life so quickly, and was she now alone without family?

It tore at her very being to realize that, yes, it was true.

It was real.

Except for friends, she was alone.

"Kathy likes her room just fine," Jana said, smiling at Frank as he made several trips in and out until all of Holly's worldly possessions were there.

Holly's gaze lingered on the rifle and then on the bag that held the clothes that she had worn on long bounty-hunting outings with her father. Since she had received word that a renegade had killed him—even though no body had ever surfaced to prove it—she had not once looked at those clothes. She knew that they would evoke painful memories.

But now—would she?

Yes she would. She would not only look at them, she was going to wear them.

Life, everything about her life, was different now. Because of Rudolph Anderson her life's plan had been totally altered.

"Holly?" Jana said. She gently touched Holly's

arm. "Are you all right? Your mind seems to be drifting so often."

When Holly didn't respond, but instead lowered her head and covered her tear-filled eyes with her hands, Frank gently took his wife by an arm.

"Honey, come on and leave Holly to her thoughts," Frank said softly. "She's got a lot of sortin' out to do. It's best done by herself, don't you think?"

Jana nodded, going with Frank to the door.

She stopped to look back at Holly, then rushed to her and hugged her. "Sugar, everything will be all right," she said, her voice breaking. "Frank and me, we'll make it so. We love you as though you are family."

Tears streamed from Holly's eyes. "I love you as much," she said, returning the hug.

Jana stepped away from her, brushed tears from Holly's cheek with the palm of her hand, then left the room with her husband.

Holly walked dispiritedly to the door and closed it, then leaned against it and hung her head. Now alone, where no one could see her, she allowed herself a good cry.

After a few minutes, she wiped her eyes and began thinking in earnest about what she had to do. She must see that justice was done, somehow.

As she slowly paced the room, back and forth,

back and forth, she thought back to her father and the sort of life that she and her mother had shared with him.

Her father had been a bounty hunter. He hadn't meant to teach Holly his profession, but she had silently observed him and now knew many of the skills he had so cleverly used to "get his man."

For a while, before her father purchased the beautiful home in Kansas City, they had led a nomadic life, moving often as her father had followed—had sniffed out—the trail of various outlaws or murdering renegades.

As the years passed, her father became wealthy enough to settle down, but he couldn't stop his life of bounty hunting. He hadn't hunted down criminals for the money or the glory of it. Everyone who knew him knew that he wasn't money-hungry, or bloodthirsty. He was a man who wanted to see justice done when others managed to outwit the law.

But worrying that Holly was becoming too entangled in the bounty-hunting life, her father had purchased a home for his wife and daughter so they could have a more normal life, and he had stopped letting them travel with him.

The last time she had seen him, he was heading out to search for a renegade, alone. It was rumored that he had been killed, but his body had never been found. Because of this, Holly had held out some hope that he might still be alive.

She was sixteen when Sheriff Hawkins brought the terrible news to her and her mother. That was three long years ago, and she had heard nothing of him since.

She had forced herself to believe that he was dead, reasoning that if he wasn't, he would have found a way to contact his wife and daughter. Or better yet, he would have returned home, for never was a man more dedicated to family than Edward Thomas Wintizer.

Nor was any child as dedicated to a mother as Holly had been to hers.

"I'm now nineteen," Holly whispered as she stood before the full-length mirror and looked at herself.

She was old enough to do whatever she felt was necessary to ensure that Rudolph Anderson got his comeuppance.

As a plan developed in her mind, she lifted a hand to her waist-length golden hair and ran her fingers through it.

"Papa, I am old enough now to follow in your footsteps," she whispered, a shiver of excitement riding her spine at what she was actually planning to do.

Yes, I'm old enough to be a bounty hunter, aren't

I? she thought, and smiled mischievously at herself in the mirror.

But she would lay claim to that title only because she needed money to back her journey to Montana. That was where she hoped to find her stepfather. He often had talked of wanting to go back to Montana, where he had learned the love of trapping and buffalo hunting.

He had even mentioned a particular town where he had done his trading.

Three Forks, she remembered. Three Forks, Montana.

The only way she could get enough money to travel clear to Three Forks, Montana, was to go to the sheriff's office in Kansas City and study the Wanted posters in hopes of finding someone whose trail would take her to—would pay her way to—Montana.

And while she was there, she would kill two birds with one stone. She would find the wanted man and she would find her stepfather.

She would get paid in dollars for finding the outlaw, but her payment for tracking down her lying, cheating stepfather would be to see him behind bars and, she hoped, sentenced to death.

She owed it to her mother to see that this was done, for she knew in her heart that Anderson had robbed her mother not only of everything she owned but also of her life.

Holly was almost certain that Anderson was guilty of murdering her precious mother!

That thought spurred her to action. She knelt before her personal possessions and, with trembling fingers, opened a bag and took out a pair of denim breeches, shirt, and her favorite leather boots, which were very worn and scuffed.

She smiled as she pulled on her hat, but her eyes filled with tears again when she picked up her Henry Repeating Rifle. Holly's father had bought the firearm for her for the sole purpose of protecting her and her mother while he was away.

Holly knew well how to use it. Her skill with firearms was as good as any man's.

She just hadn't ever thought she would be using a gun in the way she now planned to use this one.

She laid the rifle aside, draped the clothes across her arm, then stood up and gazed into the mirror again.

To fit the role of a bounty hunter, which would be much safer than traveling alone and allowing men to see that she was a lady, she must take on the appearance of a man.

"Even if that means cutting my hair," she whispered.

She grimaced at the thought, for she had always been proud of her long and wavy golden hair. But sometimes fate forced one to do what the heart ached not to do. Holly had no choice. Cutting her hair was a way to set her plan in motion, to help her to achieve her goal.

"Yes, I'll do it," she decided. "For you, Mama. For you."

She turned and looked slowly around the room, searching. On a table, she saw a pencil, paper, and blunt scissors, probably used by Kathy to cut out paper dolls.

Without hesitation Holly went to the table and picked up the scissors. With a pounding heart, she stood before the mirror again.

Her fingers trembled as she grasped a long lock of hair in one hand and the scissors in the other. She winced when she cut off the first long golden lock. Tears filling her eyes, she snipped off one strand after another, not stopping until her hair was short enough to lay just above her collar.

She replaced the scissors, then bent and gathered up the hair from the floor. Sadly she went to the window, slid it open, and threw the hair out. She watched as it blew away like golden beams of sunlight in the wind.

After slowly closing the window, Holly turned to finish the chore of preparing for the long journey ahead. She put on the men's clothes and her boots, slapped the hat on her head, and looked at herself again in the mirror. This time she smiled, for she doubted that anyone would take her for a woman.

The only thing that might foil her plan was her breasts. Although they were small, their shape could be discerned beneath the shirt if one took the time to look.

Sighing, she placed all of her feminine attire in a trunk for safekeeping until her return from Montana. She stopped long enough to reach inside the trunk and lift one of her mother's dresses to her nose. Its lacy white collar still held the aroma of her mother's French perfume.

She smiled, recalling how her mother was a study in contrasts—she could love French perfume, manicured nails, lacy dresses, and fancy hair arrangements one day, then the very next she might be wearing pants.

Holly's mother had loved life, especially the chance to live on the wild side, at times, alongside her adoring husband.

It had rubbed off on Holly, for she had the same adventurous nature. Holly thought it was fun to wear dresses, as well as breeches. She had learned the arts of cooking and baking from her mother, and the arts of shooting and riding from her father.

Still smiling, she decided to pack a hooded blue broadcloth Red River coat with brass buttons, as well as a shirt of buffalo calfskin with the hair left on, for the cooler evening temperatures of Montana.

She sorted through her other things, took a plain cotton sleeping gown from a trunk, and set it aside with everything else, hoping it would be enough to get by with until she finalized her bounty-hunting venture.

"My harmonica!" she exclaimed, her eyes lighting up when she reached inside the trunk and retrieved the musical instrument that meant so much to her.

It had been a gift from her father a long time ago.

He had his own, and when they were on a family adventure, he often played by the campfire. He had taught Holly the same skills, and they had frequently played together.

No, no journey like the one she was going on would seem right without her harmonica. It would be almost like having her father with her.

After stuffing everything into two leather travel bags, Holly grabbed her rifle.

Carrying the firearm and the two travel bags, her wide-brimmed hat atop her head and her leather boots on her feet, she left the bedroom.

Holly could tell by Jana and Frank's expressions that they were stunned by the way she was dressed. Neither had ever seen this side of her personality. Jana was visibly shaken when she saw that Holly had cut her beautiful hair.

After Holly revealed her plan to them, they were speechless. Then they both tried to talk her out of it.

"I will not rest until my stepfather pays for what he did to me, and especially to my mother," Holly said solemnly. "Can I leave what I'm not taking with me here until I return, along with my buggy?"

"Are you absolutely certain this is what you want to do?" Jana asked, wringing her hands nervously. "Don't you know the chances are you . . . you might not make it back home? That someone might take advantage of you? That you might even die?"

"I'll risk everything to make my stepfather pay for his sins," Holly said evenly.

"Then, honey, go on. We wish you the best of luck," Frank said, his voice drawn. "Just know, though, that we're here for you. Always."

"Thank you," Holly managed. Deeply touched by her friends' sincere love for her, she found it hard not to burst into tears again.

But now was not a time for any more tears.

It was a time for action.

Frank went outside and detached the buggy from Holly's horse, then stood back with Jana and watched Holly saddle her steed and shove her rifle in the gunboot at the right side of the saddle.

Her father had given her this prized horse when she was ten. She had proudly named it "Chocolate" because of the chocolate-colored stripe that ran down its backbone.

Jana hurried back into the house, and Holly worried that she was not strong enough to stay outside and say a final good-bye. But she soon returned, with two rolled-up blankets and a sack of food that she had quickly put together for Holly. Holly smiled.

"Thank you so much," Holly said as she took these offerings and slid them into her saddlebags.

Her pulse racing from a mixture of excitement and fear, Holly swung herself into the saddle. Her eyes widened when Frank suddenly pulled several bills from his wallet and held them out to her.

"Thank you, Frank, but I'll get by," she murmured, too proud to take charity, especially from someone who needed the money for his family. Still, she eyed the money longingly as Frank slowly slid it back inside his wallet.

"God be with you," Jana choked out, stifling a sob behind her hand.

"Godspeed," Frank said. He wrapped an arm around his wife's waist, ignoring their children as they burst out of the house chasing one another, giggling, oblivious to the seriousness of the moment.

Holly slapped her reins, sank the heels of her boots into the flanks of her horse, and rode off. She didn't look back, for fear of changing her mind and returning to the safe haven of her friends.

She rode onward into Kansas City.

Thinking this might be the last time she saw it if things went awry on her journey of the heart, she slowed and took a lingering look around.

It was a lovely town. Tidy, white clapboard storefronts and handsome stone buildings the color of melted butter huddled along the steep, narrow streets. Ivy, healthy and green, crept up some of the more weathered facades, false-fronted buildings that were some of the town's first.

She stopped only when she arrived outside the sheriff's office.

She dismounted, and after tying Chocolate's reins to a hitching rail, she pulled the hat low over her brow so that it shadowed her eyes and a good portion of her face.

With the gait of a man, she sauntered into the sheriff's office and went to the poster area where the likenesses of wanted men were tacked onto the wall.

She carefully studied the Wanted posters,

locked on a painting of an Indian who, she read, was from Montana.

His name was Jake Two Moons. He was wanted for murder and bank robbery!

"Montana!" she whispered to herself, excitement building. She would not let the knowledge that the man was a murderer make her hesitate to hunt him down.

Yes, Montana—it was perfect!

Her search for this man might take her to the very place she thought her stepfather would be.

Smiling, she yanked the Wanted poster off the wall and carried it over to the desk, where the sheriff sat smoking a fat cigar.

His eyes slowly assessed Holly as she slapped the poster down before him.

With the brim of her hat still shadowing her face, Holly could see that the sheriff was momentarily fooled. He didn't recognize her, even though she had been in the office countless times with her father. The sheriff even went to the same church she attended. They saw each other every Sunday morning.

But all of those times she had been wearing a dress and her long golden hair had hung down her back.

Now, she felt that she had succeeded at looking very, very much like a man.

She enjoyed the moment, but knowing that

time was wasting, she lifted the hat and revealed herself to Sheriff Blade Hawkins.

"What on earth?" Blade said, snatching his cigar out of his mouth and resting it on an ashtray.

His pale gray eyes twinkled as he ran long, lean fingers through his thick crop of rusty-red hair. "What in tarnation has got into you, Holly Wintizer? Why are you dressed like that? And, God a'mighty, you've cut your hair!"

He glanced down at the Wanted poster, and then at the rifle she clutched in her right hand.

"I want to go and find this Jake Two Moons," she said firmly. "Blade, may I have half of the reward money now and the other half when I bring the man in? I need pocket money to finance my search for my stepfather."

Stunned speechless, Blade only stared at her.

So she told him everything, ending with how she had returned home from burying her mother to find that her stepfather had sold the house.

"Now do you see?" Holly asked, her voice breaking. "I need money to be able to go and find my weasel of a stepfather who ran out on me and mother, who . . ."

She stopped short of telling him that she suspected her stepfather had murdered her mother, for time would reveal the truth soon enough.

He tried to talk her out of going, warning her

of the dangers and telling her it was foolish to set out alone.

"Must I remind you that you and my father were best friends?" Holly argued softly. "Please, in his memory—in my mother's—help me. I must find that man. I must see that justice is done."

"Neither your father nor your mother would want you to do such a dangerous thing," Blade protested.

"But I *am* going to do it, and if you don't agree to help me, I'll just go to the next town and ask the same favor of the sheriff there," Holly said, her jaw tightening. "How's it to be, Blade? Your help—or a stranger's?"

"Holly, you know from your father's dealings that no one gets paid in advance," he stammered.

"Please?" Holly pleaded. "I have to do this, and in order to do it I need pocket money. You know my word is good. I'm not asking for money. I'm going to earn it."

Blade reached inside a drawer and took out several bills from a strongbox. He held them out toward Holly. "Here," he said softly. "And it's nothing to do with this damn outlaw. It's money from me. From my own pocket to yours. Your father *was* my best friend, and your mother was dear to me as well."

"I can't take money like that," Holly said as

she stared at it. "Like my parents, I will always earn my keep."

"Well, then, take it, and when you bring the man in, I'll give you the other half," Blade said, his voice drawn. "I just wish I could talk you out of this foolishness. I could send out a posse to search for Anderson."

"I don't believe you've ever sent a posse as far as Montana, have you?" she asked, gently taking the money from his outstretched hand.

"No, cain't say that I have," he answered solemnly.

"I didn't think so," she said, shoving the money into her breeches pocket. "Thanks, Blade."

She plopped her hat on her head, grabbed the Wanted poster, and half ran out of the office.

As she was stuffing the poster into her saddlebag, she felt a presence behind her. She turned with a start and found Oliver Braddock, the town coroner, standing there nervously. His face was ashen and his eyes wavered.

"Holly, is that you?" he said, looking her slowly up and down.

"None other," Holly replied, swinging into the saddle.

"Where are you off to?" Oliver asked, idly scratching his brow.

"Montana," she said, eyeing him speculatively. She sensed that he had something to tell her. He was fidgeting with the narrow black tie tucked beneath his stiffly starched white collar, shifting it from side to side. The breeze lifted the tail end of his coal-black jacket away from his black breeches.

"Good God, why Montana?" Oliver asked, dropping his hand to his side

"It's a long story, Mr. Braddock," she said. "But I was going to come and see you before I went. I need to know what the autopsy uncovered."

Oliver hesitated, then said, "You were right, Holly, to suspect someone caused your mother's death." He cleared his throat nervously.

"What do you mean?" Holly asked, her heart skipping a beat.

"There were traces of strychnine in her body," he explained, again fidgeting with his tie. "Holly, your mother, she was . . . murdered."

Holly's eyes filled with rage. She knew without a doubt that her stepfather had poisoned her mother. He once had bragged about using strychnine for buffalo hunting, but he had never elaborated. She knew that he would have ways to obtain it.

She knew that he was a cold-blooded murderer.

Even more determined now to find him and bring him in, to see him hanged for his crime, she asked the coroner not to tell the sheriff about what they both believed to be true. Although

Blade had admitted that he had never sent a posse as far as Montana, he might now, and she wanted the chance, alone, to capture Anderson.

"I don't know," Oliver said, wiping pearls of sweat from his brow with the back of his hand.

"Please, let me do this my way," Holly pleaded.

He hesitantly agreed.

She nodded in thanks, then rode off.

She would board a paddle wheeler that would take her up the Missouri River into Montana. Her adventure had begun.

Holly looked heavenward and prayed that she would succeed.

Rudolph Anderson was going to regret having set foot in Kansas City, and having duped a woman out of her money—and her life!

He *was* going to pay!

Holly would not rest until she saw that he had gotten what he deserved.

2

Father, father, where are you going?
O, do not walk so fast.
Speak, father, speak to your little boy,
Or else I shall be lost.

—WILLIAM BLAKE

One month later—

It was July, "the Moon of Ripening Cherries."

In the far distance, striated canyon walls glowed amber, lilac, and peach in the sunlight. A lone raven rode the cliff currents and swept low over *Minnishushu*, the Missouri River.

The morning light illuminated a large tepee in the Gros Ventres Indian village. The bleached skull of a buffalo bull, bearing red hieroglyphics, faced the entranceway. In the center of the lodge, where coals of a fire smoldered, sweet grass was burning.

Winter Raven, a tall and noble warrior whose life measured twenty-eight winters, sat dressed in only a breechclout and moccasins at his ailing father's bedside at the back of the lodge.

His chieftain father, Yellow Knife, gazed at him

with admiration, and Winter Raven recalled how he often had been embarrassed when his father had openly bragged about him to others. Many women Winter Raven's age, who listened to his father praise him, fantasized of having him as their husband.

Yellow Knife knew his son, with his waist-length black hair, penetrating coal-black eyes, and sculpted facial features was handsome. Yet Winter Raven had not taken another wife after Beautiful One, whose life was taken two winters ago while she tried to give birth to their second child.

His wife and unborn child were now among their Gros Ventres ancestors at the Sand Hills, the place where all Gros Ventres went when they passed on to the other side.

Earlier, though, Winter Raven had been blessed with a daughter whose age was now eight winters. Because of her large and slanted brown eyes, which from the moment of her birth always seemed to be smiling, she had been named Soft Eyes.

Soft Eyes was the center of Winter Raven's universe, even though his mother had taken her in to raise. He felt it was better for Soft Eyes to have the guidance of a woman since soon she would be past her youthful years and would be a woman herself.

Winter Raven had a separate lodge from his mother, but his daughter came often to stay and spend time with him. Their bond could not be closer. His mother now had her own lodge away from her ailing husband.

It was his father who concerned him. Once a noted hunter and warrior, an energetic leader who had worked tirelessly to maintain his supremacy, now Chief Yellow Knife could not shake his illness.

He was hanging on to life, not ready to travel to the Sand Hills just yet. He had not finished his role on earth. His life still had a purpose.

As Winter Raven sat beside his father, Soft Eyes was playing with friends her own age outside on the banks of the mighty Missouri River.

Winter Raven's mother, Prairie Blossom, looked much younger than her husband, with her beautiful face and black hair, which hung down her back in one long, thick braid. Dressed in an exquisitely beaded doeskin dress, she sat beside her husband opposite Winter Raven. Her gaze never left Yellow Knife, who was stretched out on a comfortable, plush bed of pelts and blankets.

"I have summoned you today, Winter Raven, for I have dreamed," Chief Yellow Knife said, his eyes still intently on his son.

"*Ho*, yes, Father, and this time what did your dreams tell you?" Winter Raven asked. He was patient with Yellow Knife's fear of dreams, which had seemed to age him too quickly. His father, now fifty-five winters, had recently summoned Winter Raven to warn of his own upcoming death.

That had unnerved Winter Raven, and today he was reluctant to hear about the new dream that was troubling his father. By the look in his father's eyes, Winter Raven knew that this dream had not been a good one either.

"Son, I am old, my blood has grown lazy," Chief Yellow Knife said, seeming as if he were purposely postponing what he had to say to his son. His wife sat as a silent witness.

"Father, all things grow old," Winter Raven said softly. "Trees, flowers—"

"Son, my dream last night was filled with the spirit bear," the chief said somberly, suddenly anxious to tell the dream, even if he had to interrupt his son.

"But, Father, so many of your dreams have been about the spirit bear," Winter Raven said. He reached over and gently placed a hand on his father's lean, bare shoulder exposed above the blanket.

"Of late the dreams have come more frequently. They all contain the spirit bear of my past," Yellow Knife said. "They have become frightening to me, an old man. In the dreams, Spirit Bear People shame me for having taken the bear's life, and then its teeth and pelt, so many moons ago. Worse yet, it was a mother bear that my arrow downed. A cub escaped, but not before it was harmed. It got in the way of one of my arrows. I saw the arrow lodged in one of its front paws. The cub limped away, the arrow still there."

Yellow Knife looked from Winter Raven to the floor. "Often in my dreams I have seen a three-footed bear—the cub now grown and still snow white," he said, his voice breaking.

Yellow Knife stole a glance at his son. "This time last night, the spirit bear came to me for a different purpose than to shame me for my past deeds against her," Yellow Knife continued, his troubled eyes mirroring his soul.

"For what purpose this time? Why do your eyes reveal a battle within your heart?" Winter Raven asked, placing a hand on his father's brow.

"The three-footed spirit bear is going to be threatened by a more powerful weapon than an arrow," Yellow Knife said. "This time it will be a white man's fire gun."

"You are saying the bear is being tracked?" Winter Raven asked, slowly drawing his hand away.

"*Nah*, no. But soon the white man may discover the bear," Yellow Knife answered, swallowing hard.

"But the white spirit bears are on an island," Winter Raven said reassuringly. "Water separates them from buffalo-hunting land. The white hunters, with their fire guns, would have no need to cross over the water to go to Spirit Bear Island. There are no buffalo there."

"Just as the bears strayed long ago onto land where hunters roamed, so might this bear and others stray now," Yellow Knife said. "Winter Raven, you must ensure that the spirit bears, all of them, are protected from a cruel death."

"Father, I will do what—" Winter Raven began, but was interrupted by Yellow Knife whose torment could not keep his voice still.

"You *must* go, to keep the whites from slaying the spirit bears," the old man said, reaching over and desperately grabbing Winter Raven's arm. "Then take my prayers of forgiveness. Explain to the Spirit Bear People that I, those long moons ago, did not know that the bear I downed was a special holy bear . . . a spirit bear. But I know now. Since I killed the bear, dreams have haunted me. Of late, they come more often."

He reached back and grabbed a snow-white pelt made into a robe and a necklace made of bear's teeth and placed them on his bed before Winter Raven. "Son, you must return what I took from the mother bear to Spirit Bear Island. Only by doing so can your father die peacefully and walk a contented road with our ancestors in the Sand Hills.

"Do this for me?" Yellow Knife asked. He shuddered visibly.

"Father, I do not want to leave you," Winter Raven said. "Each day you go farther away from me, not only in spirit but in body as well."

"I will not take my last breath until you have returned with the Spirit Bear People's forgiveness," Yellow Knife said, his chest rumbling ominously as he coughed. "The white hunters that you must watch for? They are like a plague across all lands. Some call themselves buffalo hunters, while others are called skin hunters or wolfers. To me they are all demons whose hearts are black and cold."

"Skin hunters—wolfers—really might be near?" Winter Raven gasped, thinking about the death that such men left behind them once their hunting sprees were over.

"My dream tells me so," Chief Yellow Knife said somberly. "It also reveals a massive slaughter of buffalo. I fear they will be slain until they are no longer a part of our land."

He grasped Winter Raven's hand tightly. "Son, make things right with the Spirit Bear People. Hopefully, in turn, they will help us by bringing luck our way instead of taking it from us. If not, the future for all red men is bleak. And for the buffalo. I fear for them."

"But, Father, there are so many buffalo."

"Never enough, especially when white men kill in such great numbers, and only for skins, not for food," Yellow Knife said, easing his hand away.

This omen made Winter Raven's insides grow cold, for his father had foretold many things that had come to pass.

"Son, I must ask even more of you today before I die," Yellow Knife said, pleading with his eyes. "I ask you to return the bear teeth that I have worn as a necklace for many years, and the white pelt that I made into a robe, and to keep a watch out for hunters that are a threat to the bears and buffalo. But there is something more."

"And that is . . . ?" Winter Raven asked, raising an eyebrow. This was the longest conversation that he had had with his father since he had taken to his bed with this strange, debilitating illness.

He glanced over at his mother, who had stayed silent during this council. It hurt him to see how she struggled not to cry. Prairie Blossom was a woman of much strength. Her face usually revealed a quiet radiance and her smile melted one's heart.

She turned toward Winter Raven and slowly nodded, in her quiet way telling him to continue to listen well to his father and to try to understand his needs. Winter Raven returned the nod and gazed back at his father. Yellow Knife continued to talk, yet this time in a rambling manner. He reached over and clutched Winter Raven's hand again.

"It was because of the spirit bears that you have your name," Yellow Knife told him. "Even then, on the day of your mother's labor, before you took your first breath of life, I was troubled over having killed the white bear and having wounded its cub."

He closed his eyes, swallowed hard, then went on. "Long ago, at the time when the land was white and covered with ice and snow," he said softly, "the Mystical Raven set an island aside for the Spirit Bear People. On the shores of this island, the Spirit Bear People were meant to live in peace."

Winter Raven watched as his mother dutifully and lovingly reached over and dabbed tears from his father's cheeks with a soft piece of doeskin. His father smiled a silent thank-you at her.

Then his father continued.

"It was shortly after I killed the bear that a harsh winter came to the land of the Gros Ventres," he said. "A raven came and perched on a limb of a tree close to my tepee where your mother lay in hard labor. The raven stayed and stayed. It was then that I knew the raven was sent to give a sign. That was why my firstborn son was named Winter Raven. I hoped that by giving you this powerful name, the name of the Mystical Raven, my nightmares about killing the white spirit bear would cease."

"Then moments later another son was born," Prairie Blossom said in a voice as soft as a spring wind. "He was named Two Moons, because as the blizzard ceased and the moon came out in its full glory, it cast its light down onto the *Minnishushu*, the Missouri River, which ran beside our lodge. The reflection made it look as though two moons were there, instead of one, and your father took this as another sign. He named our second son for what the sign had shown him."

"*Ho*, yes, and through the years I came to know that the raven had arrived beside our lodge not only to help give a name to our firstborn," Yellow Knife said. "The raven stayed with me in my nightmares. Although you, my son, respectfully and dutifully carry the name of the raven, the dreams still torment me. Only recently, when I learned that I was going to die, did I see that you had a purpose other than to succeed me as chief. You are to do for me what I should have done many moons ago. You will make things right with the Spirit Bear People. This is what the raven means in my dreams."

"My father, I promise to do what you have asked of me, but what is this other thing that you want me to do?" Winter Raven asked, watching his father's fingers shake as he eased his hand from Winter Raven's arm.

Winter Raven saw that this council was tiring his father, yet he knew that once everything was said, his father could have a long rest and he himself could begin the quest.

"My son, search for your brother and bring him home so that this old, ailing father can make peace. I lost him to his demons long ago," Yellow Knife said, his voice breaking. "It has been so long . . ."

Winter Raven went dead inside at this request. He and his twin brother no longer saw eye to eye on anything. Winter Raven was a man of good heart. His brother was bad, through and through. His brother was a known criminal who allied himself with outlaws and even rode with them. He had added a white man's name to his Indian name and was now called "Jake" Two Moons.

Winter Raven's emotions were terribly conflicted over his brother. He deplored what Two Moons had become, and knew that his twin had broken the law and should be punished, yet a part of him would always love his brother, as only can twins love and feel protective of each other. Winter Raven could not help but feel that bond. They had shared the same womb. They had absorbed the same nourishment from their mother's body before they emerged from it.

A slow ache circled Winter Raven's heart as he thought of his brother's possible outcome in life. Any day he could be struck by a bullet while out on his criminal sprees! If that did happen, Winter Raven knew almost certainly that he would feel his brother's pain at the moment Two Moons felt it. He might even feel his brother's life draining away as though it were his own spirit being taken to the Sand Hills.

"My son, where has your mind drifted to?" Yellow Knife asked, interrupting Winter Raven's troubled thoughts.

"To my brother," Winter Raven replied, finding it difficult to push such thoughts back into the deeper recesses of his mind. He knew that his fears that Two Moons would probably die young were justified. Each moment of his brother's life was one of danger and deceit.

"And what memories were you having of Two Moons?" Yellow Knife asked softly, his eyes searching Winter Raven's.

Winter Raven was not about to tell his fragile father the truth. It would not only cause the old man intense pain, but it also would devastate his mother, who still sat quietly by, listening.

So he reached deep inside himself for good

memories, those that he treasured . . . memories of his brother before he became a stranger to his family—to his entire tribe of Gros Ventres.

"As young children, Father, Two Moons and I did everything together," Winter Raven said, glad that he could still fondly recall the good side of his brother. "We took our first steps at the same moment. We chased butterflies together. We practiced skills with a bow and arrow that you taught us. We even rode our first horse together, both on the same horse."

"I often relive those moments myself," Yellow Knife said, his voice breaking. "And there were many more times when you two were as one. Back then, it was a time of joy and laughter."

"Father," Winter Raven said quietly, "I will do what I can to find Two Moons, but I must keep in mind that he is Jake Two Moons now."

"*Ho*, yes, Winter Raven, please do what you can to bring our son home to us," Prairie Blossom said, suddenly flinging herself into Winter Raven's arms. "It has been too long since our family sat as one heartbeat beside the lodge fire, talking and laughing . . . loving."

Winter Raven stroked his mother's back gently. "I will bring your son home to you," he found himself saying, even though he knew the chances were slim.

But he would try.

"The Great Spirit will guide you every step of the way," Yellow Knife said.

Winter Raven eased away from his mother and stood up to leave. He gazed from one to the other, then left the lodge for his own tepee, where he would prepare his travel bags for the long journey ahead.

As he packed, Winter Raven became lost in thought, but his mind was on something other than the quest for his brother.

One day soon he must find a wife.

His father's failing health had been a reminder that his mother herself soon would no longer be as strong or as young. In recent months, it had become obvious to Winter Raven that it was getting harder and more tiresome for Prairie Blossom to care for Soft Eyes.

It was time to put his mourning for his beloved wife behind him and choose another wife, who would mother his child—and who would warm his blankets as well.

Ah, but his life had been so lonely since his wife's passing. He ached to have someone to share laughter with by an evening fire. He wanted his lodge to be filled with the hearty fragrance of food cooking over the flames of a fire.

A wife.

Ho, yes.

It was time to take a wife.

He was entering into his twenty-ninth winter.

If he was to have many sons, as he wished, he must end his celibacy and focus on finding a woman.

He went to the entranceway and held back the buckskin flap to watch his daughter, Soft Eyes, as she played with the other children out in the middle of the village, near a central fire where food cooked over hot coals.

He filled his eyes and his heart with the image of his precious daughter, so that he would be able to tolerate the days without her that lay ahead.

He was concerned about being away from her for too long, and about waiting too long to bring a mother into her life for guidance.

He had been worried about how Soft Eyes often chose to mingle with young braves her age instead of maidens. She wanted desperately to go on the hunt with the braves. She loved to shoot guns and was very skilled with the bow and arrow. She often chose to wear breeches instead of dresses.

His mother hadn't succeeded at discouraging this behavior. Perhaps a younger woman, a woman he chose for his wife, could.

Sighing, he returned to the task of packing. Soon he would be pushing off in his canoe, his heart set to fulfill his father's requests.

For now, that was his priority.

Later he would set out to find a woman whom he could bring home as his wife, a woman who would, in turn, be a mother for his daughter.

He sighed deeply as he tried to picture such a woman, discouraged that no one special came to his mind's eye. It would be hard to find someone who compared with his Beautiful One!

3

O, how thy worth with manners may I sing,
When thou art all the better part of me?
What can mine own praise to mine own self bring?
—WILLIAM SHAKESPEARE

The long journey by steamboat behind her, Holly rode Chocolate into the town of Three Forks, Montana.

She was relieved when only a few men on horseback turned to get a look at the newcomer in town. With her hat pulled low over her brow, shadowing her face, she seemed to be fooling the men. Some rode past without even a nod, while others gave her a lazy "Howdy" and then went on their way down the rut-filled dirt street.

She grimaced at the sight of piles of dung on the street, flies buzzing around them. Empty whiskey bottles lay here and there, as did spent bullet shells.

As she rode onward, she saw on each side of the street buildings with high false fronts of un-painted boards and dark, narrow passages be-tween the buildings.

Horses were tied up at long hitching posts, nodding and stamping at flies.

Only a few women, in fancy hats and even fancier dresses, passed along the warped, mud-covered boardwalks in front of the buildings. It was obvious that they were uncomfortable as men whistled and jeered at them from the open doors of saloons, from which spilled out the clink of coins and raucous laughter.

Wanting to get her own business behind her in this little one-street town, Holly checked the signs on each building. She smiled when she finally saw the one she was looking for.

The sheriff's office.

She had gotten plenty of rest on the boat trip to Montana, so as soon as she had made contact with the sheriff she would head out to search for her stepfather and Jake Two Moons.

She wouldn't establish herself in a hotel room. She saw no reason to waste money on it. She wouldn't need a place to store her things while on her manhunt, because she had brought only the essentials to get her by until she achieved her goal.

Afterward, she would return to Kansas City and try to begin a new life, alone. She hoped to be able to find a fine, upstanding man like her father one day and settle down and have a family.

Children.

Oh, how she would love to have children!

But, first things first, she thought to herself, her eyes narrowing angrily at the idea of her step-father running around free and spending money that he had gained by murdering his wife, a woman he had married only for what he could get from her.

Holly could hardly wait to show the murdering cheat that he had not gotten away with it for long!

She rode up to the hitching rail in front of the sheriff's office and swung herself out of her saddle. After tying her reins to the rail, she stopped long enough to catch her breath, then walked tall and straight into the office.

As soon as she was inside, she grimaced and covered her nose with a hand. Someone had tracked in dung from the street, and cigar smoke was so thick that she could barely see her way to the sheriff's desk.

Suddenly realizing that she had forgotten the Wanted poster, she turned and rushed out of the office, getting a reprieve from the stench for as long as it took her to grab the poster from her travel bag. She stopped, inhaled a deep breath of clean air, then headed back inside—and ran straight into a tall, thick-waisted man, who blocked her entrance, his badge picking up the shine of the sun.

"Who the hell are you and what do you want?" Sheriff Chance Stone demanded as he placed his fists on his hips.

The man towered over Holly. She looked up at him and saw a thick black mustache on an otherwise clean-shaven face. His eyes glinted dark through round, gold-framed glasses. His shoulder-length hair was as golden as Kansas wheat.

Not wanting to reveal that she was a woman, and afraid he would guess if she allowed him to keep on looking down at her, Holly averted her eyes and moved past him into the office. She went to his desk and found a space clean enough of debris for her to spread out the poster. She unrolled it and glanced over her shoulder as the sheriff came and stood beside her.

"I'm a bounty hunter," Holly said in as masculine a voice as she could conjure up. "I'm lookin' for this man. Do you know if he's in these parts? Here on the poster it says he's from Montana."

She was afraid that she had said too much, for the more she talked, the more chance that she might give away her true identity. She certainly didn't want this man, or anyone else in this town, to know who she was.

She already felt somewhat uncomfortable to be

in such a place, yet from her earlier experiences of the area with her father, she had known how it would be.

Yes, Montana was a far cry from Kansas City. Even though outlaws could come into town and shoot it up in the blink of an eye, Kansas City did have its more civil side these days.

But Three Forks? It was a place to pass through, not to live in.

"And so you're another bounty hunter to get in my way, are you?" Sheriff Stone grumbled, coming to stand beside Holly. "Oh, hell. Let me see that thing. If you can find a wanted man, it'll just give me one less criminal to worry about."

After he studied the poster, he nodded slowly. "Yup, he's from around here, but no one has seen hide nor hair of him for some time now," he said, sauntering around behind his desk.

The chair creaked as he sat down on its split cushion, the fluff of its insides hanging out. "This Jake Two Moons? He's a Gros Ventres renegade," the sheriff rumbled. He relaxed against the back of his chair and steepled his fingertips in front of him. "Let me tell you, I don't have any love for *any* savage. If I had run across Jake Two Moons, no doubt I'd have had him locked up." He chuckled. "That is, before I hung the stinkin', polecat savage."

Trying to ignore this man's obvious prejudice

against Indians, Holly slowly rolled up the poster again.

She decided against telling the sheriff that she had received an advance on finding the renegade. She didn't trust him any more than she trusted the outlaw that she was after.

"Where do the Gros Ventres make their camp?" she asked. "I'd like to go and question them about this Jake Two Moons."

"You'd be wastin' your time goin' there," Sheriff Stone said, lighting up a fat cigar. The smoke spiraled up into Holly's eyes and nose, and she fought back the urge to cough as she stepped away from the desk.

Sheriff Stone continued. "You see, Jake Two Moons has been gone from his village for a long time. His people regard him as an outcast. I'm certain his chieftain father wouldn't claim him as his son now, even if he came face-to-face with him."

He rose slowly from the chair, leaned over the desk, and put his face close to Holly's. "No man has been able to find the renegade," he said. He yanked the cigar out of his mouth. A slow smile quivered across his lips and his eyes danced. "Most certainly no lady dressed up like a man can find the savage and get the best of him."

Holly took a quick step away from him, but not soon enough. He reached out and grabbed her hat off her head. She stiffened at his mocking laughter as he looked at her short hair.

Her jaw tight, her heart pounding, Holly snatched the hat from him, glared at him as she plopped it back on her head, and ran out of the office with the poster.

Threatened that he had seen through her disguise, she wondered if every man might do the same if he took time enough to study her. Somehow, she must guard her identity more cleverly. She knew it would be best to get out of town as quickly as possible. Once out on the trail, alone, she could relax with her plan again.

She had learned more than one thing from the meeting with the insulting sheriff. It would not be easy to find Jake Two Moons. Although his tribe was established in the area, that evidently meant he would keep away because of his people's feelings toward him.

But she smiled and reminded herself that finding Jake Two Moons was not her true purpose for coming to Montana.

Her stepfather was.

Finding *him* and seeing that he paid for his crimes were of prime importance to her.

When she caught up with him, she would also reclaim her family wealth, at least, what he had not already spent. From that money she would repay Sheriff Hawkins the advance that he had been generous enough to hand over to her.

Still, she would not give up on looking for Jake Two Moons as well, for she knew the importance of stopping his renegade ways. If she succeeded with her bounty-hunting efforts, wouldn't her father look down at her from the heavens and smile with pride?

Once she had the two men rounded up and taken care of, though, she wanted no more of this sort of life.

She hungered for the tight bond of family again.

She did want a husband.

She did want children.

Most of all, she wanted roots!

Glad to put the town behind her, she rode onward until she came to a bluff. Beyond, more craggy bluffs rose at improbable angles. Below her there was a low divide of grassland with scrub timber in the hollows and ravines. Drifts of daisies covered the meadows like a summer snowfall. Lupines, poppies, and coreopsis pierced its blanket of white. Past there she could also see the country far into the distance, its rough hills and ridges covered with dark timber.

She looked farther still and saw the banks of the great Missouri River, broad and shimmering silver-blue. It rolled along between narrow bluffs with no valley or timber on either side. The bends of the river were heavily wooded, the inlets banked by thick forest and occasional limestone bluffs. Ospreys circled above the water's glasslike surface. Cormorants and herons sunbathed in the shallows and shoals.

Something attracted her attention, and she turned her horse to look in a different direction. She could see an Indian village in the far distance. Lazy spirals drifted out the smoke holes of the tepees, and she could just barely see people coming and going from their lodges. She also saw many horses in corrals behind the village.

"This must be the Gros Ventres the sheriff was talking about," she whispered to herself.

Holly was tempted to go to the village and bring up Jake Two Moon's name, yet she thought better of it. She decided it was not in her best interest to let the Indians know that she was a bounty hunter searching for one of their own to take to jail, possibly to be hanged.

No. She knew it was best not to come face-to-face with any Indian, unless it was the renegade himself.

And she truly doubted that that would ever happen. The sheriff seemed too eager to see the Indian dead not to have done everything within his power to find him already.

She wheeled her horse around and gazed at

the river again. She realized that it curved toward the village, which sat on its banks. She would go to the water and follow its trail, but make sure she started her journey after she was far past the Indian village.

"Come on, Chocolate," Holly said, patting her horse fondly on the neck. "Let's cover some more ground before we have to search for a safe place to make camp for the night."

Chocolate neighed back to her, as though he understood what she said. They made their way down the side of the bluff toward the shine of the river.

It gave her cold shivers to realize that she would soon spend the first night of her trip beneath the stars, alone, for the very first time in her life. The last time she had been beside a campfire under the stars and moon, she had been with her parents.

Had it truly been so long ago? she wondered, aching for those times again, yet knowing they were gone forever.

She bent low next to Chocolate's ear. "At least I still have you," she whispered, smiling.

4

O time, cease thou thy course, and last no longer,
If they surcease to be that should survive!
—WILLIAM SHAKESPEARE

Winter Raven's canoe created frothy plumes as he guided the vessel down the long avenue of the Missouri River, the route he had chosen to take instead of traveling on land.

This was the time of the midsummer buffalo hunt for many redskins. If he hadn't been on a mission for his father, Winter Raven would have been among the warriors of his village, hunting in groups.

But he was entirely alone, and he felt that aloneness like a heavy burden on his heart. He must achieve his goal, for his father was depending on him.

And it was hard to think of his father lying in bed anxiously awaiting his return, when Winter Raven knew that what he must do would take time.

It would take several days just to arrive at Spirit Bear Island.

He must travel steadily, stopping only long

enough to eat and sleep a few short hours before moving on again. At the same time, he must keep his eyes open for skin hunters who might threaten the existence of the spirit bears.

He would also watch for the one bear that had been injured by his father's arrow when it was a cub. Although the bear would be quite ancient by now, it was a known fact that spirit bears lived longer than other species of bears.

If this bear had lived—Winter Raven felt almost certain that it had, because it had been a part of his father's recent dreams—Winter Raven would be able to tell it from the others because it had only three paws.

As he rhythmically drew his paddle through the water, he began to notice a bounty of bear food along the banks. He saw the rotting, headless carcasses of dog salmon and he spotted bear tracks on the muddy shore.

He could also tell that the meadows reaching out from the river were full of grizzly bear digs. In midsummer, bears typically appeared for tasty meals of corms and roots.

Winter Raven became excited when he spied the grizzlies. There were three of them. A mother and cubs.

From this distance, the bears appeared as little more than brown dots against the blue Montana sky, but he could see how the larger bear lumbered along, while the cubs, all fat and fur, tumbled playfully behind her.

Winter Raven frowned as he recalled his father's sense that white hunters might be in the area. They killed not only buffalo but also bears.

Even cubs.

He wished there was a way he could communicate to these three innocent travelers that danger might be near.

But as always, he knew that he must let nature have its way. He hoped that the bears were more cunning than the white men and their powerful guns.

Focusing again on his own travel, his quest, Winter Raven propelled himself down the river in his sturdy birchbark canoe.

To his left side, like tentacles, inlets and coves snaked into the miles of shore, and marshes exploded with waterfowl.

Fish breathed bubbles in the ripples.

Raven and eagle feathers were on the tide line.

Winter Raven enjoyed the sight of a bulbous-headed harbor seal as it appeared momentarily in the wake of his canoe, on the skin of foam where the mottled white backs of spawned-out salmon twisted listlessly in the current.

Then he was alone again on his journey of the heart. Loneliness was not all that new to him, not since the day of the death of his wife and unborn child.

He needed something to fill that emptiness ... someone. More and more he hungered to have a woman in his arms, to have her lie with him in his blankets at night.

He wondered if it would ever happen again, if he could love another woman as deeply as he had loved his precious wife?

If not, it would mean that he would live the rest of his life alone, which seemed unbearable at the moment. His father was lying on his deathbed and would soon be gone from Winter Raven's life, too. Winter Raven thought it unlikely that he could be happy again anytime soon.

He forced his thoughts on to other things. Miniature buttercup flowers grew along the riverbank. Their blossoms were so tiny that they clung to the soil like sparks. Pillows of moss campion, covered by dozens of pink flowers, provided bright patches of color. He also spotted small, star-shaped flowers and buds, as well as vigorous delphinium and wild geranium that bore lavender flowers.

He caught sight of a wolf as it loped along the shoreline, its eyes finding his own. They stared at one another, soul mates for the moment, it seemed. Then the wolf was gone, and Winter Raven was alone again.

He thought hard about his reasons to be on the river, rowing away from the direction of his village, where his heart was truly centered. He slowly scanned the land for any sign of skin hunters, or of a three-footed white spirit bear. His father's dreams were not to be ignored, for he was a man of mystery and magic, a powerful, beloved chief.

5

Overhead—look overhead,
'Mong the blossoms white and red—
Look up, look up—I flutter now
On this flush pomegranate bough.
—JOHN KEATS

Riding at a steady lope on her lovely roan beside the Missouri River, where everything was serene and beautiful, Holly was remembering how her stepfather had bragged about buffaloing in Montana. He had said more than once that after buffaloing got in your blood, you never forgot it.

She truly expected to find him. She believed that he had returned to Montana to enjoy the slaughter again, even though she had not seen any buffalo or buffalo hunters yet.

So far, her journey had been without confrontation. But she reminded herself that this was her first true day on the search.

She glanced up at the sky, at the angle of the sun, and saw that she still had some time left before she would be forced to stop and make camp for the night. She doubted that today would bring her any success in the manhunt.

But there was always tomorrow.

She was determined not to give up until her mother's death was avenged.

Having been in this area with her father on a bounty hunt a few years ago, Holly thought she might know Montana almost as well as her stepfather did.

What a surprise he would get when she managed to find him. And after she turned him in, she would reveal the results of her mother's autopsy to the sheriff. Any sheriff would then gladly slam her stepfather into a jail cell. She hoped Rudolph Anderson would get the hanging he deserved!

Still lost in thought, she slowly stroked her horse's thick mane. She couldn't help but wonder if she would experience the same feeling of triumph that her father had always felt when he had succeeded, when he had rid the world of another bad man.

Only a few nights before she had seen her father for the last time, before he had gone on a deadly manhunt for a renegade, Holly had talked with him about his work. He had told her that he had felt that God had put him on this earth to help rid it of those who were guided by Satan.

He had explained that it made him feel good

and clean inside when he made sure that an outlaw could never take another life or rob anyone else of their life's savings.

She would never forget the look in his eyes when he had received the final payment for a job well done. It was not that he was money-hungry. It was just that he had worked hard and had sacrificed to deserve it.

He would spend a good portion of the money on his daughter and wife, never using it to gamble or drink. When he was not out on a hunt, he was a quiet man who loved his home and family.

She thought again of how she hungered to be a part of a family once more. As her father had said so many times, "Family is the true reward of life."

Familiar with the Missouri River, she stayed close by it to keep herself from getting lost. On one of those manhunts with her father years ago, she remembered seeing an Indian village on the banks of the river. In her mind's eye, she saw that village again and realized that it was the Gros Ventres, for she had seen that very same village today.

She thought about the poster and the likeness of the Gros Ventres warrior-turned-renegade painted on it. When she could look past the fact that the Indian was a murderer, she was able to see the handsomeness about him. In a strong, noble way, he was a handsome man.

It was too bad that such a man had been ruined by a criminal life, she thought with a toss of her head.

6

What may count itself as blest,
The heart that never plighted troth.
But stagnates in the weeds of sloth;
Nor any want-begotten rest.
—ALFRED, LORD TENNYSON

Winter Raven guided his canoe closer to shore. His hair, unbraided and loose, ruffled in the gentle breeze. The cottonwood trees rustled their long, bent limbs hanging over the river and giving off the sound of softly falling rain.

He tried to stay out of view, using the tall weeds along the shore as a barrier between him and whatever—or whoever—might be lurking close by.

If his father's dreams were right, white skin hunters might be around any bend in the river, ready to kill not only buffalo and bears but also a lone red man.

The rocky shore came into sight, and the view made his heart suddenly leap with warning. A fresh trail of blood led away from the river and past a thick stand of brush.

Wondering what or who might be injured, and

if the injured party needed his help, Winter Raven beached his canoe.

With his rifle clutched in his hand, he stealthily followed the blood.

When he saw that it led into a cave, he was hesitant about going inside. If there was a wounded white man, he might still be able to fire a gun, and Winter Raven might be stepping into a trap.

But if the blood was from a red man, a friend, Winter Raven must do whatever he could to help him.

Being a man of much heart and kindness, always ready to help someone in need, Winter Raven's choice was clear. He brushed aside some tall weeds and carefully moved into the cave.

After he got inside, where there was just light enough for him to see, he was stunned to discover exactly what was injured.

It was a white bear.

It was stretched out on its left side with its eyes half closed in obvious pain. From where Winter Raven stood, he could hear the bear's shallow breathing.

"Skin hunters," Winter Raven rumbled.

Ho, yes, his father had been right. Skin hunters *were* near, and they were killing bears!

It suddenly came to him that this must be one

of the spirit bears. They were the only white bears within miles of the area.

His heart pounding, not only because the bear was wounded but also because it was a beloved spirit bear, he inched closer and knelt down beside the animal.

Winter Raven checked the bear's front paws, to see if one of them might be missing. He soon saw that the bear had four healthy paws, but it became obvious that it had been mortally wounded. There were two severe bullet wounds on its right side, and blood continued to pour from them. The white fur had turned crimson, and the ground beneath the bear pooled with its lifeblood.

Winter Raven sensed that the bear probably was taking its last breaths of life as it lay there, panting hard and too weak to fight him off. Under normal circumstances, no man would have been able to get this close to such a massive wild beast.

Even though Winter Raven knew that the bear was sure to die, he had to do what he could to help it. If not to make it well, at least to help lessen its pain.

"I shall return soon," Winter Raven said, suddenly trembling when the bear looked at him and held his gaze.

It was not a trembling caused by fear, but by being in the presence of such a majestic thing.

Everything about the bear made a man seem trivial in comparison. Even a man who would one day be chief!

And since this was a spirit bear, Winter Raven's reaction was even more intense, for his father had taught him long ago of their value and goodness.

He now understood why his father had placed so much importance on making things right with the Spirit Bear People.

Ho, yes, Winter Raven felt their presence now, as though they were there with him, and he felt humble and proud to share this moment with them.

When the bear let out a low moan of pain and its eyes slowly closed, Winter Raven was shaken back to reality, reminded of what must be done.

He must do what he could for the bear before returning to his canoe and resuming his journey. He didn't want to think about how if one spirit bear was this far from its island, more would be as well. Skin hunters would think nothing of maiming a bear, so many bears could die.

Torn over what to do—whether to search out the other bears and try to protect them from the deadly white man's firearms or to go on his way to Spirit Bear Island with his father's plea of forgiveness—Winter Raven felt the burden of his new responsibilities keenly.

He left the cave and went to his canoe, where

he removed an empty buckskin parfleche bag from his belongings. Hurrying into dense forest, he found the necessary herbs, plants that were known to lessen the pain caused by flesh wounds. He took these to the cave.

At the river he filled a parfleche bag with water, and quickly brought it to the cave. There he sat down beside the bear.

In a low chant he repeated things that he had heard his people's shaman say while medicating wounds. Winter Raven began gently cleansing the injury of blood.

He winced when the bear flinched. It tried to growl, but instead the noise came out as a moan.

Winter Raven paused for a moment to stroke the bear's thick white fur just beneath its chin. He tried to be as gentle as possible until the wound was exposed. Thankfully blood no longer gushed from it.

As he sprinkled the herbs over the raw wounds, a keen sadness overwhelmed him. Upon closer observation, he realized that the bear was female, with milk-filled breasts. There must be cubs out there somewhere close by that might die without nourishment from their mother, he thought sadly to himself.

Winter Raven figured the cubs were not with their mother now because the gunfire had frightened them off.

He stopped and stared at the cave entrance. The person who shot the bear might be hunting for it, to claim the body, and the blood trail would lead right to this spot.

He reached over and brought his rifle closer to his side, then continued medicating the animal's wounds with herbs while talking softly to it.

When the bear slipped into unconsciousness, Winter Raven bowed his head and began praying over it. It was not the prayer sent from his father, as this was not the bear of his father's past.

This prayer was Winter Raven's own, coming from the depths of his heart, for a creature that did not deserve to die so soon, especially in such a way.

He also prayed for the bear's cubs, for their safety in a world gone mad.

7

Over all is the sky,
The clear and crystalline heaven,
Like the protecting hand
Of God inverted above them.
—HENRY WADSWORTH LONGFELLOW

As Holly continued to make her way alongside
the Missouri River, she remained vigilant for any
signs of buffalo hunters off in the distance. Her
ears were keen to all sounds as she listened for
gunfire or the bellowing of buffalo on this beautiful day in July.

She had heard her stepfather talking about how
midsummer was a good time to hunt the large
animals. They would have shed their heavy winter coats, and they would be well fed and fat from
the fresh grass sprouts of the season. It had sickened her when he had explained how he enjoyed
watching the mighty beasts fall under his gunfire, the slamming of their heavy bodies against
the earth sounding like claps of thunder.

But then again, there was the strychnine. He
had not told her how he had used that on his
buffalo hunts. It was enough for her to know that

he had, to make the connection with another one of his victims.

He had slowly fed her mother small amounts of the lethal poison—small enough to prevent anyone from becoming suspicious, yet large enough to get the job done—so that he could flee back to the life he had said that he "hungered for more than a juicy steak in a loud Kansas City saloon."

"I'll get you," Holly whispered, gritting her teeth angrily at the thought of the goal she had set for herself.

Nothing would stand in her way.

Nothing!

She looked back at the river hoping to feel a moment of peace instead of the anger that was so new to her.

She had been angry when she learned the news about her father's fate, but that anger was different from what she felt now. No one knew the true details of her father's death, or even if he really was dead. She only knew that a redskin renegade had bragged about being the one to finally get the best of Edward Thomas Wintizer.

The anger that she felt now was so deep and intense because she knew the man responsible for her mother's death. And she knew it would not go away until he was found and punished.

She smiled as she saw a fish leap out of the

water and then splash into it again, leaving a pattern of ripples in its wake.

Her gaze shifted upward. She watched a redtailed hawk fly in a slow circle over a sandbar, its majestic wings wide, its eyes on something that was trying to hide in the brush that grew out of the sand.

When the hawk suddenly dipped out of the sky and flew like a streak of lightning down to its target, she was taken aback by how rapidly it had clasped a tiny chipmunk in its sharp talons. The bird was quickly high in the sky again, its mighty wings flapping. It must be headed for a safe haven to enjoy its prime catch of the day.

An involuntary shudder raced across Holly's flesh at the speed with which life could be snuffed out by a predator that killed so easily.

She knew the danger she herself was in, and she realized she had to be alert at all times so that no one could catch her off guard.

A beautiful patch of wildflowers in a myriad of colors took Holly's gaze away from the river.

A short distance ahead she noticed something else, but it was nothing so trivial as flowers. Her throat went dry and her fingers tightened on the reins when she spied a canoe beached on the rocky shore.

She looked sharply to her left, away from the river, for she knew that wherever there was an

Indian canoe, an Indian couldn't be that far from it. She slowly scanned the land for any signs of the Indian, but saw none.

She rode up closer to the canoe to inspect it and to look for footprints. Holly gasped and grew cold inside at the sight of a spattering of blood on the riverbank not that far from the canoe.

Scarcely breathing, eyes wide, she drew a tight rein and stopped Chocolate. She slid from the saddle, her heart pounding.

When she studied the blood more closely, she saw a string of drops that ran away from the canoe toward a thickening of bushes and towering cottonwood trees.

"The Indian must be injured," Holly whispered, tethering her steed on a low limb where it could nibble the short buffalo grass that grew beneath.

She was uncertain of what to do. If she went and found the injured Indian, would he see her as an enemy and shoot her before she had the chance to prove that she wasn't?

But if he was badly injured and she didn't offer him help, would she be able to live with knowing that she could be so coldhearted?

She didn't have ill feelings toward all Indians because one renegade had bragged of having killed her father. In fact, she sympathized with

Indians over how they had been taken advantage of by white people.

But their known dislike of whites might be exactly why she should get back on her horse and ride away and forget she had ever seen the blood. If this Indian hated so intensely, he would not even want her help. He would resent her mere presence.

"Then again, what if it's Jake Two Moons?" Holly wondered aloud, knowing it was a long shot.

Still, the thought caused her to yank her rifle from its gunboot. She set her jaw firmly, for she knew that she must not be cowardly now, not after having come this far.

Perhaps it was Jake Two Moons, injured after finally having been caught by one of his victims and shot. If it *was*, she would find a way to get him back to Three Forks and send a wire to Sheriff Hawkins, that she had captured one of the two men she was after.

As she crept along, following the path of blood, she knew that it was unlikely that she would find Jake Two Moons this quickly. What were the odds that it could happen? She doubted that it was him, yet she had to see.

And she could not ignore the fact that *someone* was injured and needed her help.

Realizing her vulnerability, Holly held the rifle tightly. She stopped with a start when she discovered that the trail of blood led into the mouth of a cave.

She was so afraid, her knees were weak and her stomach felt strangely tight, but she had known when she set out for Montana that there would be times like this, times when she would be faced with danger.

That was the life of a bounty hunter—danger and excitement, and the fulfillment that came after a job well done.

But this was different, she reminded herself. She was not the bounty hunter that her father had been, with the same cunning, the same courage and stamina.

She was a woman.

And she was facing danger alone for the first time in her life.

"Get hold of yourself," she told herself as she inhaled a deep, trembling breath.

She was her father's daughter, and that meant that she was not a coward, never would be.

I'm brave, she chanted to herself over and over again as she took a step past the thick brush into the cave.

That first step was enough for her to see what was there.

No, not *what*.

Who.

Only a few feet from her, an Indian was kneeling over an injured bear.

The blood! Lord, she had never seen as much blood as she saw on the cave floor beneath and beside the bear. And its white coat was turned crimson.

With a thudding heart, she quickly leveled her rifle at the Indian. His thick, black hair hung down his bare, muscled back to the waistband of his breechclout.

From this vantage point, looking at him somewhat sideways, she could see how strong his copper legs were. She could see the corded muscles of his arms as he sprinkled something over the bear's open wound.

Her eyes swept over the Indian again and she saw his beaded buckskin moccasins and—

Her thoughts were stilled and her heart felt as though it had leapt into her throat when she heard a low growl that could not have come from the wounded bear. It came from behind her!

She grew cold inside with fear at the realization that where there was one bear, there well might be others.

She remained quiet, although her whole body tensed with the horror of the situation—here she was, with an Indian, who saw all whites as enemies, in front of her and a bear, who saw all humans as enemies, behind her.

Too afraid to turn and look at the bear, she stiffened and waited for it to pounce.

Having heard the growl, Winter Raven jerked his head around and jumped to his feet with a start. Outlined by the light of the bright sun, a man stood in the cave entrance his rifle aimed at Winter Raven.

Winter Raven was stunned speechless that someone had been able to sneak up on him in such a way. Normally his senses, especially his hearing, were acute.

He stood his ground and slowly held his hands out away from his body so that the stranger would not think that the knife sheathed at his right was a threat.

He tightened his jaw at his carelessness. He should have rested his rifle on his lap while he saw to the bear, so that it would have been ready for use.

He *never* allowed himself to be caught off guard like this.

He tried to see the face of his ambusher, but the sun was shining too intensely in his eyes for him to see very clearly.

But the sunlight hitting his face made Holly recognize exactly who the Indian was!

The stunning discovery made her temporarily forget the bear behind her.

She couldn't believe that she could be this lucky.

She had found Jake Two Moons!

And she had him cornered!

She held her rifle steady, keeping him at bay. "Don't make a move toward me," she said, hating the tremble in her voice and knowing that Jake Two Moons also heard it. It made her sound afraid—and she was!

No matter how proud she was to have found Jake Two Moons already, she was fighting off trembling knees and a pounding heart as he stood his ground, his midnight eyes gazing intensely at her.

She knew, though, that he was blinded by the sun, and that gave her an advantage. He wasn't able to see that she was a scared-to-death woman pretending to be a man.

Yes, she was scared, and she was no longer ashamed of it. What woman wouldn't be frightened at a time like this, when an Indian was so close and a . . . .

She went pale as she suddenly remembered the bear behind her. How could she ignore it when it let out another growl, this time much closer?

Should she swing around and shoot it?

No, that would give Jake Two Moons the opportunity he needed to pounce on her and disarm her.

She had managed to become trapped and didn't know what to do.

When she felt something brushing up against the back of her leg, she had no choice but to turn.

Winter Raven took advantage of Holly's distraction. Seeing that it was only a bear cub that must have sniffed out its wounded mother in the cave, he lunged for her.

He grabbed her legs and brought her down underneath him as he tackled her.

Stunned by the fall, she had dropped her rifle when she hit the hard rock floor of the cave. Holly lay there for a moment to overcome her disorientation.

She felt foolish that the Indian had gotten the best of her, especially now that she saw the growling bear was only a cub. It had not been a threat at all.

Shaking away the stars that had been flashing off and on inside her skull from having hit her head, Holly turned over onto her back. She grimaced when she found the Indian holding her at gunpoint, standing over her with his muscled legs slightly spread.

Winter Raven had stepped into the shadows of the cave so that he could see the man whom he had tackled more clearly. Yet now the man's face was too far in the gloom for him to get a good look.

It was enough that he had the advantage now, instead of the man.

"White man, what are you doing here threatening me with your rifle?" Winter Raven growled. "Are you the one who shot the mother bear?"

He only glanced at the tiny cub as it bounced past him into the cave, but he heard it crying, proving that the downed bear was its mother.

He centered his attention on the man, awaiting his answer.

Holly realized that the Indian believed she was a man. She smiled cunningly and slowly moved to her feet. "Jake Two Moons," she said in her best masculine voice, "had it not been for the cub, you would not have been able to get the best of me."

She tried to sound braver than she felt, guessing it would be the best way to survive. Bravery was admired by most Indians. She hoped that it was the same for renegades.

"Jake Two Moons, unless you kill me, you'd better watch your back," she said. "I won't allow you to slip through the cracks so easily. The law owes me some more money for bringing you in."

Her heart ached when she heard the whimpering noises coming from the small bear. She knew that the cub had just found the other bear and that it must be able to sense that its mother was mortally wounded.

The realization brought her back to the question Jake Two Moons had asked. "No, I didn't shoot the bear," she said, swallowing hard. "I . . . I love animals."

She went pale knowing that she had just ruined her bluff. She had forgotten who she was pretending to be and had spoken in her normal way.

She had revealed that she was a woman.

Winter Raven was taken aback by the voice, by its pitch. He gestured with his rifle toward Holly. "Move out of the shadows so I can see your face," he said.

Holly stiffened, then did as he directed. He was the one handing out orders now, and she had no choice but to obey.

At least for now.

She hoped to catch him off guard again so that she could capture him and hand him over to the law.

Otherwise, what was to become of her?

Would he kill her?

Or would he rape . . . ?

She brushed that last thought from her mind and boldly held her chin high as the Indian gazed at her, slowly, up and down.

Her hat lay somewhere behind her, having fallen the moment he tackled her. She knew that her short hair was not enough to protect her true identity, nor were the clothes that were supposed to hide her feminine traits beneath them. As she stood proudly tall, she knew that her breasts could be discerned beneath the shirt.

She held her breath and waited for him to announce that he had discovered the truth.

Now that Winter Raven could see her fully, he studied her face. He saw its pretty, gentle features, his gaze lingering on her slightly tilted nose and her perfectly shaped lips.

Her face was oval and lightly browned from her time in the sun, lovely despite the stubborn glower she wore.

Although she dressed as a man, he could see her shapely body, her breasts small yet perfectly rounded. She was taller than most women he knew, but that made his interest in her, which was climbing by the minute, even stronger.

And then there was the way she had denied having shot the bear. Something about her made him believe that what she said was true.

Once he got past the discovery that she was a woman, and a beautiful one, he concentrated on what she had said, what she had called him. She had called him by his twin brother's name.

And she had said something about the law paying her for finding his brother.

His pulse raced to learn that his brother was a wanted man, yet he knew that he should not be surprised. His brother rode with outlaws and committed wrongs against all people, even those whose skin was red like his own.

But to find out that his brother's crimes were so terrible that he would be hunted like an animal? It made Winter Raven's heart ache to think of his twin being at the mercy of those who hunted him.

Winter Raven could understand how he could be mistaken for his brother, though. Born only moments apart, they were almost an exact image of one another.

"Why are you hunting Jake Two Moons?" he asked warily. "What has he done this time that the law would send someone out for him?"

It was at this instant that Winter Raven realized this woman must be a bounty hunter.

His intrigue was building every moment.

Holly put her hands on her hips and glared angrily at him. "Don't act so innocent," she spat out. "You know there are Wanted posters of you from one end of the country to the other. I've come to collect on you."

Although having expected the worst, Winter Raven's spirits sank to hear the truth. He had always known that his twin was troubled. He just hadn't known how out of control he had become.

Still, how could Winter Raven ever want to see his brother captured by whites and put in a white man's prison? No red man should suffer in such a place, where whites could be free to torment him.

If this woman imprisoned Two Moons, how could Winter Raven fulfill his father's request? Maybe Yellow Knife could even persuade him to give up his life of crime. He must at least be given the chance!

Winter Raven had to find a way to keep this woman away from his brother, and hope that no one else was after him, too. He wanted to make sure that he would be the one to locate Two Moons.

"White woman, you are wrong," Winter Raven said, speaking to her in the perfect English that he had learned from a trader when he was a child. The man had taken time to teach Winter Raven many things about whites. When he had been killed by renegades, Winter Raven had seen to it that he was buried in the Gros Ventres tradition, since he had no family.

"How am I wrong?" Holly asked, her voice filled with hatred. "You are who you are. Faces do not lie. And your face matches the face on the Wanted poster."

"My name is Winter Raven," he said, hoping he could lower the firearm and talk things out with her calmly. "Two Moons is my twin. He took on the white man's name 'Jake' because he associates himself with whites now, instead of with his own people. He has abandoned his life as a Gros Ventres. I, on the other hand, live my life for my people."

He paused, then added, "I have not seen my brother for many moons. If his likeness is on posters, I could see how you might confuse my face with his."

"Sure you have a twin," Holly said sarcastically. "And I am the president of the United States."

To prove his point, that he was who he said he was—a man of peace, a man of good heart and honor—Winter Raven handed the gun back to Holly.

"No guilty man would do that, would he?" he asked.

"A *stupid* man would," Holly said, aiming the rifle at Winter Raven again.

The cub started making much louder noises, crying as it rubbed up against the larger bear. It tried to suckle but couldn't get any milk from its mother. Both Holly and Winter Raven watched, speechless.

They saw that the mother bear had died.

The cub licked its mother's face for a moment. Then, as though it finally understood, it darted past Holly and Winter Raven and left the cave.

"Blood is on the cub's fur," Holly exclaimed,

almost at the same moment that Winter Raven said the same thing.

They looked at one another, their eyes wide.

"The blood might attract animals to it," Holly added. "It might be killed!"

"Or the man who shot its mother might still be nearby," Winter Raven said.

He stepped toward Holly, put a hand on the rifle barrel, and lowered it. "I must go after the cub," he said, his voice determined. "I cannot allow it to be killed. It is as innocent as a human child."

He looked deeply into her eyes, putting into motion his plan to distract her from thinking about Jake Two Moons. "We can search for the cub together," he said smoothly.

Holly saw the warrior's compassion and knew that Jake Two Moons, a man who had committed many atrocities, had no such compassion. He probably couldn't care less if a cub lived or died. Jake Two Moons certainly would not have taken time to kneel over a downed bear and apply medicinal herbs to its wound.

Holly could not help but believe that this man was who he said he was.

If it had been Jake Two Moons, he would not have handed her firearm back to her. He would have used it on her.

And she herself would be lying dead beside the downed bear.

In a hurry to find the cub and protect it from harm, Winter Raven started to slip past Holly. Unsure of what her next move might be, he took the chance of being shot.

"Winter Raven?" she said tentatively, speaking his name for the first time. He stopped and turned toward her, convincing her that it really was his name. "I didn't shoot the bear. I'm certain now that you didn't, either. Who do you believe is responsible?"

"It is the work of whites who are called skin hunters," he answered, pleased that she had changed her attitude toward him so quickly. "I have not actually seen any in the area at this time, but I have ways of knowing they are near. As I was paddling down the river in my canoe, I spied the blood on the ground. Like you, I followed the trail of the blood to the cave."

"We've waited too long already," Holly said, holding the rifle at her side. "We must go and find the cub. It's horrible to think that hunters might kill the sweet, innocent thing."

She swallowed hard as she recalled her recent loss and the grave beneath the weeping willow tree back in Kansas. "It's hard to bear the thought of the cub now being without a mother," she murmured.

"Your heart is brave and big," he said to flatter her, picking up his rifle. Inside his own heart was resentment for everything she stood for. He would play this game with her until she abandoned her search for Two Moons. Winter Raven would succeed at finding his brother first.

"Holly," she said as she grabbed her hat and ran out of the cave after him. "My name is Holly."

When he glanced at her, she could not define the look in his eyes, whether he saw her as a friend or foe. Most likely a foe, because he knew that she wanted his brother behind bars.

But she regarded him differently. She was deeply touched by his kindness toward animals, and she was taken by his handsome features.

And not only that. Everything about him suggested greatness. She had to wonder if he might be a chief, or if he was destined to become one.

Then again, there was the slight chance that he was Jake Two Moons after all, and he had cleverly duped another victim.

Without a doubt, she would be on guard at all times while she was with him!

8

Our pace took sudden awe,
Our feet reluctant led.
                    —EMILY DICKINSON

The cub had succeeded in eluding Winter Raven and Holly. They stopped and sat down together beside the river to rest before she returned to her horse and he to his canoe, to continue their separate quests.

"I will not entirely give up searching for the cub," Winter Raven promised as he gazed into the shimmering, sun-splashed water.

He slowly turned to look at Holly. "Nor will I give up searching for the person who shot its mother and left her to a slow death," he said. "Skin hunters visited my father's recent dreams. He took that to mean that they are near. White men who come to heartlessly slay buffalo also kill bears that might get in the way."

"Your father sees things in dreams that come true?" Holly asked, eyes wide. "I have always been fascinated by the ways of Indians, even though . . ."

She stopped short of saying that her father supposedly had been killed by a red man.

She always found it hard to talk about. Speaking of his death made it come back to her as though the news had been brought to her and her mother only yesterday. She wondered if she would ever truly get over losing both her father and mother. When she found a man to fill her empty life, perhaps then she could finally let go of the past.

"You did not finish what you were about to say," Winter Raven said. He searched her eyes with his and saw the sudden pain there.

"No, I didn't," Holly said.

She looked quickly away. When he had gazed so intensely into her eyes, she almost felt overwhelmed by the wondrous, mystical quality of his.

His eyes were the most beautiful she had ever seen in a man, so dark, so alive, as though the entire universe was centered there.

She knew that it was foolish to allow herself to be drawn to this man. He was bound to another man, his twin, whom she was going to find and hand over to the law. When she did so, Winter Raven would be out for blood—hers.

No, she had to make certain that the only emotions she felt for Winter Raven were those appropriate between a white woman and red man. She must remain guarded and reserved.

"After I find the bear cub, I will find the man responsible for the bear kill," Winter Raven said to fill the sudden silence that had fallen between them.

Holly seemed to be a woman of many moods, he thought to himself. As he saw it, she went far beyond anything normal for a woman.

A bounty hunter? Who had ever heard of a female bounty hunter?

He would guard well what he said to her, especially when it came to his brother. He certainly would not tell her that he felt his brother's presence in the area, for twins had a way of knowing things about each other.

"Although I have other things I must do, I, too, will be sure to watch for the cub," Holly said.

She removed her hat to allow the wind to blow through her hair, which had grown damp from perspiration while they searched for the cub. It unnerved her to see how Winter Raven was staring at her hair, but she did understand why he would. She couldn't remember ever having seen any woman anywhere with such short hair.

She shivered at the thought that she had cut it. She did not even like to look at her reflection in the river as she knelt to drink.

She had begun to calculate in her mind just

how long it would take for her hair to grow back to its normal length. It would be many months.

She would never take scissors to her hair again, even if that meant that it grew so long it touched the ground.

She smiled at the thought.

Trying to be at ease with the silence that had once again fallen between them, she reached out and plucked a wildflower. She would rest for a moment or two longer, and then she would be on her way.

She had to wonder, though, if their paths would cross again. If so, would it be after she had jailed his twin?

She didn't want to think about how Winter Raven would feel about her then. Instead of looking at her with a mixture of curiosity and interest, he would surely glare at her with deep hatred.

Knowing that was how it would be, she hoped they would not meet then. She wasn't sure if she could stand having this man hate her. She could not deny how being near him affected her. For the first time in her life she truly felt like a woman.

That made her smile again, for it was strange to feel like a woman when she looked anything but.

Winter Raven knew that Holly was very aware

of him studying her, yet he could not stop himself.

He gazed at her attire again, raising an eyebrow as he examined her men's clothes. He stared in disbelief at her cropped hair while she idly wiped sweat from her brow with the sleeve of her shirt.

He had never seen a grown woman who wanted to take on the appearance of a man. Women, especially women as beautiful as *this* one, enjoyed wearing beaded dresses and proudly showing off their long hair.

Of course, there was Soft Eyes, his daughter, he reminded himself.

But she was a mere child.

She would soon grow up into a woman, though, and if she was allowed to choose, she would not wear a dress ever again.

What truly troubled Winter Raven was that his daughter had more close friends who were young braves than girls. Recently she had even gone on a hunt with a bow and arrows that she had made for herself.

His concern for his daughter had grown of late. He planned to talk with her again soon about this path of life she had chosen, before she grew into a lady like this white woman who wore men's clothes.

He wanted grandchildren.

And for Soft Eyes to attract a man, she would have to look and behave like a woman, one who would make a good wife. She could not seem to enjoy hunting more than kissing and making love.

Holly was taken aback when she caught Winter Raven still staring at her, seemingly lost in deep thought.

She wondered what he was thinking about.

She looked away but in her mind's eye she contemplated how he looked, especially how handsome he was.

He was more handsome than any other man she had ever known. Even her beloved father. Her father had been handsome, but in a more rugged way. This man, this Indian, was handsome in a unique way, and it stole her breath away.

She marveled over how two men, two brothers, could look so much alike yet be so different otherwise. She had always thought that twins were like two peas in a pod with twin personalities too.

Twins shared a powerful connection, that she did know. Surely Winter Raven eventually, unknowingly, would lead her to Jake Two Moons. If he was concerned about his brother's welfare, wouldn't he try to warn him about her search, perhaps to persuade him to change his life?

"Why did you decide to become a bounty hunter?" Winter Raven asked, jarring Holly out of her thoughts.

"Why?" she said, her eyes wide as she gazed at him. "I, well, I . . ."

He saw that she was having trouble responding to his question. "I have never known women who took on men's jobs," he said.

He started to reach out to touch her hair, but reconsidered and drew his hand back again. She had stiffened when she had seen his gesture.

"Does it bother you to look like a man? You could be a beautiful woman if you wore women's clothes and allowed your hair to grow long," he said, curious about this strange side of her nature. "What could drive a woman as beautiful as you to look and behave like a man?"

He was intrigued by her, and he wanted to know these things about her. Yet he also hoped that her answers might help unravel the mystery of his daughter's boyish behavior.

And he needed to know why this woman would spend time searching for a red man gone wrong instead of pursuing a happy family life with a husband.

All of a sudden, he knew how he could take his ploy to distract her from searching for his brother one step further. Winter Raven would do almost anything to be able to find Two Moons first, to persuade him to go home to their father before Yellow Knife began his long journey to the Sand Hills.

He did not hesitate this time when he reached out toward her. He gently touched her cheek with his fingers. "Your skin is as soft as a woman's," he said, glad that she did not slap his hand away, or draw back in revulsion, which many a white woman might.

"Your lips," he continued. "They are as inviting as a woman's."

Winter Raven drew his hand away from her face and almost dared to touch her breast through her shirt yet thought better of it and dropped his hand to his side. His eyes trailed down her body.

"I can tell that your breasts are small beneath your shirt, but they would be enough to fill a man's hands," he said softly.

He was aware of how stunned she was by his words, so much so that she sat and stared at him with her eyes wide and her lips parted.

Yet he continued with his tactic anyway, hoping to draw her away from thoughts of his brother.

"You are taller than most Gros Ventres maidens, but that does not detract from your appearance," he said. "It even is good that you are this height. You would not have to stand on tiptoe to reach a warrior's lips."

He smiled slowly at her. "Although you are slim and willowy, you would fill this warrior's arms wonderfully," he said. He did not attempt to reach for her, knowing that would be going much too far.

But as soon as he said these things to her, he knew it was no longer a ploy. Deep down, he could not help but truly want to pull her into his arms and experience the wonder of kissing her.

Absolutely stunned by Winter Raven's boldness to speak so openly about kissing her and filling his hands with her breasts, Holly felt a little threatened.

The very reason she had dressed like a man was to hide all of her womanly features, and here was a man looking past her disguise to see a woman—a woman he obviously desired.

She suddenly felt very vulnerable.

It came to her then why he was saying all of these personal things. He didn't mean them, after all. He wanted to get her on his side, to get her to change her mind about jailing his brother, should she ever find him.

She slid her rifle back onto her lap and tightened her fingers around it. She even slid her finger toward the trigger.

Should this man decide to try and overpower her, to test his theory about her lips and breasts, he wouldn't live long enough to boast about his conquest to his warrior friends. A bullet to the belly would make him realize that although she was a woman, she had been taught the skills of a man.

Sensing that he might have insulted her by having told her the kinds of things that many Indian maidens had welcomed hearing, Winter Raven started to offer a sincere apology. When he touched Holly's hand a surge of passion swept through him at the contact.

Surprised by this, he drew his hand quickly away. The intensity of his feelings left him speechless.

He could tell that she, too, was shocked by the touch and his sensual reaction to it. Moments ago she had stiffened when he had touched her face, and he had been so distracted by her response that he had felt nothing.

This time she had not drawn away from him.

This time he had felt pure ecstasy in the touch.

Knowing women well, he recognized desire when he saw it. He wondered when the change in her attitude toward him had occurred, and why?

Needing to put space between them, Winter Raven moved quickly to his feet. He knew these feelings were not in his best interest, especially since Holly wanted bad things for his brother.

He watched her stand up, still silent since the

touch that had ignited flames within his very soul, and also seemingly in hers.

He felt awkward with her now, a new feeling for him in the presence of a woman. None had ever rendered him as clumsy as he felt at this moment, nor had he been so much at a loss for words before.

"I must go," he said. "It is time for me to continue my journey down the river. I shall watch for the cub from my canoe."

Relieved to know that he was not going to try and manhandle her, Holly nevertheless strangely desired his arms around her. She even felt herself hungering for his lips, the thought creating a surprising tingling at the juncture of her thighs. She inhaled a quavering breath and started walking with him again.

She was now feeling vulnerable in ways much different than before. She couldn't allow herself to have such feelings about this man!

She didn't even understand how it had happened—or why.

"I have to be on my way also," Holly murmured. "I must find a place to camp."

She didn't say that she was growing more afraid by the minute of her first full night alone in the outdoors. The thought of the person who had downed the bear being in the area gave her goose bumps. If a man could shoot a bear and leave it helplessly wounded, might he have as little regard for a lone woman?

While she was asleep, she would be defenseless if someone came upon her. She certainly couldn't sleep with her hat on, and that was her only effective disguise.

She gave Winter Raven a sideways glance. If he were to stay with her and make camp with her, she wouldn't have anything to fear. She trusted him now to be a gentleman in that respect. She could go to sleep and know that he wouldn't suddenly be on top of her, lust clouding his good judgment.

He had proved to be a man of honor.

Again she found it hard to believe that brothers could be so different! She wondered how it had happened that they had taken opposite roads in life.

"I must go back to the bear," Winter Raven said, turning to gaze into Holly's eyes. "I must cover the bear's body with rocks to keep it safe from hungry animals. The bear that was killed by those heartless hunters is a white spirit bear. She must have wandered from Spirit Bear Island."

"I haven't heard of such bears, or such an island," Holly said. "Why is the bear called a spirit bear? Where is the island?"

They began walking back in the direction of the cave.

Seeing that Holly was truly interested, and feeling that the strain between them had lessened, Winter Raven told her about the island, the bears, and even about his father's dream. But he refrained from telling her about wanting to find his brother for his father.

When his brother's restlessness had led him away from his people, Winter Raven had felt as though half his heart had been ripped out. He had never been able to understand how his brother could leave, and then stay away. Surely Two Moons ached, as well, for his twin brother, Winter Raven!

Yes, he would search for his brother alone, and when he found him, he would look into his eyes and see into his soul. Winter Raven would know then his brother's character.

His jaw tightened as he once again realized that above all else, he must do everything within his power to keep Holly from finding his brother. If she found Two Moons and somehow managed to best him, she would turn him over to the law for the reward money before Two Moons had the chance to say a final good-bye to their ailing father.

As they continued to make their way back to

the cave, Winter Raven asked Holly about herself to steer her thoughts away from Two Moons.

He asked her why she pretended to be hard and uncaring, for he knew, even from the short time that he had been with her, that she was anything but.

Holly found herself opening up to him too easily.

And she knew why.

She must fight her feelings for him. They were of two separate peoples, two separate worlds. Their goals most certainly were not the same.

In a rush of words she told him about her life as the daughter of a bounty hunter. She described how a part of her heart had died when she had received the word that her father had been killed, but she didn't tell him about the renegade who had bragged about downing her father. She explained that her mother had married a shifty drifter who had made his living by buffalo hunting, and who robbed her mother of her life's savings and disappeared. Holly told him how her life had suddenly, drastically, changed.

Winter Raven seemed truly interested as he listened intently to her, and Holly began to feel much of her burden lifted from her shoulders. She told him about her mother's death and burial, and about what the autopsy had proved—

that her mother had been fed small doses of strychnine until it finally killed her.

"I must find my stepfather and see that justice is done for my mother," she said, a sob lodging deep in her throat. "That is my true reason for coming out here. My stepfather had told me of his love of buffalo hunting and casually mentioned the town of Three Forks. That is how I knew to come to Montana, and where in Montana to search for him."

She refrained from telling him that the bounty on Jake Two Moons was the only means she had of paying her way to Montana. That was best left unsaid for now. No matter what, she must make sure Winter Raven didn't get in the way of what she had set out to do.

Winter Raven was glad to know that Holly's purpose for being in Montana was not, after all, to find his twin brother. That gave him hope. He would help her forget Two Moons and think only about the evil white man.

Now that he knew so much about her, and why she was in Montana and dressed as a man, he saw her in a new light. He saw the hurt that had been caused by her stepfather, and he also saw her soft, gentle side when she let down her guard.

He was drawn more and more toward her and wanted to protect her. She had suffered enough.

But no matter how much he felt for her, and understood her need for vengeance, he still had to protect against her ever finding his brother.

Whatever it took, he had to get Two Moons to their father's bedside! His brother had to have the chance to make peace with his father, and then, Winter Raven hoped, with the Great Spirit, so that he could once again become the good person he had been as a boy.

9

The gleam of an heroic act,
Such strange illumination—
The Possible's slow fuse is lit,
By the Imagination!
                    —EMILY DICKINSON

Holly walked silently beside Winter Raven, in awe of the eagles overhead, riding the wind, soaring. She saw droves of black-tailed deer scattered among the cedars that lined the shore. She even spied a male blue grouse establishing courting areas. It was busy showing off and strutting around, displaying its colorful neck glands, eyebrows, and wing muscles, while fanning out its tail feathers.

Although an astute observer, Winter Raven saw none of these. His attention was drawn elsewhere. His alert hearing had picked up the splashing of oars in the river.

Unsure who might be approaching, since they were out of sight around a bend in the river, Winter Raven grabbed Holly around the waist protectively.

Before she could realize what was happening

or do anything about it, Winter Raven had taken her into hiding behind a thick stand of bushes.

He yanked the rifle out of her hand and thrust its barrel through the bushes, stopping before anyone would be able to catch the shine of the barrel in the afternoon sun. Holly gasped and stared at him.

"What's wrong?" she asked, annoyance evident in her voice.

She saw how Winter Raven tightly gripped the rifle, his eyes peering around the bush at the river.

"Why did you feel the need to hide?" she asked heatedly, not seeing or hearing anything that might have caused his sudden strange behavior.

Her eyes took on an angry glint as she reached for her rifle, but she didn't actually attempt to take it from him. "Give me back my firearm," she insisted.

"Quiet, woman," was Winter Raven's only reply, his voice a fraction above a whisper. His eyes never left the bend in the river where he expected to see travelers any moment. He hoped those who rode the waves today were men with red skins. If not, he knew to expect danger.

He had his answer when two huge mackinaw boats suddenly came into view.

Holly also saw them and now understood why Winter Raven had grabbed her and forced her into hiding. With the reflexes of a warrior, he had heard the boats approaching, though she had heard nothing. Grateful that he was so skilled, Holly moved closer to him.

Her eyes widened in horror when she saw that both boats were piled high with dried buffalo tongues and packs of buffalo robes.

Several white men manned the boats. With their whiskered faces and long, greasy hair, they looked like wild creatures.

She felt the color drain out of her face when she looked closer at the men and saw that their clothes were bloody. The unkempt men obviously had been killing and butchering animals for some time.

They were buffalo hunters!

Winter Raven's insides tightened at the thought of the buffalo kill it must have taken to provide so many tongues and pelts. He knew that there had to be more men hunting in the area for the boats to be filled to such capacity.

He could not help but be concerned about the warriors from his village who were on their own hunt, even though he knew they had gone farther south than where these white men must have been. For now, his warriors were safe on their hunt.

After the boat had moved past Holly and Winter Raven, he stood up, silent and brooding. He handed Holly's firearm back to her as they emerged from hiding.

She looked at the rifle, then at him, and realized that trust was growing between them.

"Not to mention other things," she thought to herself, not wanting to say good-bye.

As Winter Raven stared down the river in the direction of the mackinaws, Holly could feel his emotions as though they were hers. She felt the same loathing for the white hunters who had slaughtered the buffalo in such great number.

Then her heart skipped a beat. Caught up in what she had seen, and in what Winter Raven had been feeling, she had forgotten about her stepfather. He too was a buffalo hunter.

She took a quick step toward the river and frowned, straining her neck to get a glimpse of the boats. She wondered if her stepfather might have been one of the whiskered hunters.

Holly inhaled deeply and returned to stand beside Winter Raven. If her stepfather had been among those men, he was now long gone. The hunters had a destination. They would travel the Missouri until they came to their desired trading post, where they would unload the tongues and pelts for a great deal of money.

If only she knew where that would be, then perhaps she could catch up with her murdering stepfather.

There was so much wealth in tongues and pelts in the boats that he would not have the need to hunt again anytime soon. But she had no idea where he would go to spend his ill-gained riches.

The thought reminded her of something else. He probably had not had time to spend all of the money that he had accumulated in Kansas City. He would have had to put it in a bank for safe-keeping. But which bank? And where?

"Three Forks," she thought to herself.

Yes, he must have put the money in the vault at the only bank in Three Forks. Wouldn't he have to go there to claim it before moving on?

But she knew that she was getting ahead of herself. More than likely her stepfather had not been among those hunters on the boat, which meant that he still might be in the area.

Except for the men on the boats, though, she had yet to see any hunters.

Maybe she was on the wrong track.

Maybe she was fooling herself into believing that she would ever achieve the justice she had promised her dead mother as she stood over her grave.

"The white eyes are thinning the buffalo herd so quickly," Winter Raven said sullenly, bringing Holly's attention back to the present. He remembered his father's premonition. "One day there will be no buffalo left for anyone, but there is nothing that can be done about it. There are many more whites now in Montana than red skins, and the red man can no longer win a war against them. Even if many valiant warriors tried to defend what is ours, there would be a slaughter that would outmatch what is being done to the buffalo. Many of my people's women would be widowed. Children would be without fathers. Grandparents would weep until tears would come no more. And then they, too, would die, for dried-up tears would mean dried-up hope. And without hope, the elderly are no more."

Moved heart and soul by the emotion in Winter Raven's voice, and seeing the despair and defeat in his eyes, Holly wanted to fling herself into his arms and comfort him.

But doing so might release the feelings between them that, until now had been under control. If she hugged him, and he returned the hug, that could lead to something even more beautiful. To be kissed by this warrior surely would be the ultimate ecstasy!

Forcing herself to keep her feelings at bay, she walked next to him as they resumed their journey back toward the cave. She had decided to help him cover the bear with rocks, and then she would be on her way, and he would be on his.

When Winter Raven reached out and grasped Holly's hand, stopping her, she looked at him questioningly. "Why are you stopping me this time?" she asked softly.

She glanced over her shoulder at the river, then looked anxiously back at him. "Do you hear another boat approaching?" she asked guardedly. "Do you think more buffalo hunters are on the way?"

"*Nah*, no, that is not my reason for stopping you," Winter Raven said. He released her hand and knelt to study tracks that led out of a pool of water created by a recent rain. The shape of the tracks indicated that they had been made by a bear.

"Do you see the tracks?" he asked, glancing up at Holly.

"Yes, now I do," she said. She knelt down beside him and rested her rifle on the ground next to her as she studied the tracks along with him. "They are so small." She looked at him, hope causing her heart to beat faster. "Do you think it's the cub? The one that fled from us?"

"*Ho*, yes, it could be that cub," Winter Raven answered.

He moved slowly to his feet as his eyes followed the trail of the tracks.

He nodded toward a path worn through the brush straight ahead of them. "The tracks lead toward a deer trail. Come. We will follow them. If the Great Spirit wishes it, we may find the bear cub today after all."

"I hope so," Holly said.

She lost sight of the tracks for a moment, but saw them again up ahead, where flat rocks and rotten logs had been turned over. The cub might have been searching for bugs or mice.

Holly gripped her rifle tightly as Winter Raven broke into a slow lope. She followed his lead. She could not help but notice the way the muscles of his legs flexed with each movement. She also saw how his breechclout flapped away from his body with each step, partially revealing what was encased in the tight buckskin beneath it.

Blushing, and with a nervously pounding heart, Holly looked quickly away. Strange how seeing what a well-endowed man he was made her weak in the knees. She felt stirrings in the pit of her stomach that were new to her. Winter Raven made her aware of a part of herself that had never been awakened before. And she realized the deliciousness of those feelings. Surely this was how a woman felt about a man when she was falling in love with him.

In awe of these new sensations, she realized that she must resist them, yet she truly wished she did not have to. She forced herself to focus on where they were going, and why.

The cub. She must center her attention on the cub, not on her infatuation with an Indian warrior's anatomy!

"Shame, shame," she could hear her mother

say, if she had been able to know her daughter's thoughts.

Yet, in her mind's eye, Holly could also imagine how her mother's eyes might have danced. Perhaps she would pretend to be scolding Holly, while actually enjoying seeing her daughter behave like a woman entranced by a handsome man.

Holly frowned as Rudolph Anderson once again came into her mind. Until that scoundrel had ruined everything, Holly and her mother had had fun watching the various men walk by as they had shopped in Kansas City.

It had all been in good, clean fun, but Holly had understood that one day she would be serious about such feelings about men.

"Except not when I'm wearing these damnable breeches, and sporting such disgustingly short hair," she thought to herself. Yet her mother had looked beautiful and womanly even when she had worn breeches on manhunts with her husband.

Holly was startled out of her reverie when she and Winter Raven suddenly came upon something far different than an innocent, lost cub. She gasped and felt lightheaded.

They had found a wolf kill.

Several large wolves were stretched out in

grotesque postures, their stomachs ripped open and exposed to the sun.

At once extremely nauseated, Holly rushed behind a bush and bent over. But the shock of what she found there quickly drove away the waves of nausea.

She could hardly believe her eyes when she spotted two empty bottles labeled with the word "strychnine." The very thing that had been used to kill her mother must have killed the wolves!

She rushed back to Winter Raven. "I . . . I . . . found empty bottles," she stammered, her heart beating rapidly. "They had been filled with strychnine."

She inhaled shakily before following Winter Raven's lead. He knelt down to give the carcasses a closer look.

His jaw tightened at the distinct smell of strychnine. Hunters had slashed open the wolves bodies to saturate them with the deadly poison.

He had heard wolfers claim that wolves killed more buffalo than Indians and whites combined. Wolfers poisoned wolves either for their pelts or to lure buffalo to feast upon their poisoned carcasses, which was considered good service in the protection of herds of wild game.

Of course, Winter Raven believed nothing of the sort. Regardless of why they chose to kill the wolves, the wolfers were wrong to do it.

He took Holly's hand and urged her away from the animals. He gazed into her eyes.

"Skin hunters called wolfers are responsible for this kill," he explained. "Wolfers poison the animals and saturate their bodies with strychnine so that hungry buffalo will feed upon them. The hunters save the price of a bullet by gathering up hides and tongues of buffalo killed by the tainted meat."

He turned and looked off into the distance. Earlier he had seen wolves numbering fifty or more following the scent of buffalo borne by the wind. More than likely many of those wolves had also been killed and their bodies tainted with strychnine.

"This is the work of very evil men," he said, his anger fierce. He doubled his hands into tight fists at his sides. "Wolves are revered by the Gros Ventres. It is against everything in nature to kill them!"

A thought quickly crossed Holly's mind. "The cub," she said, bringing Winter Raven's gaze back to her. "Oh, Lord, what if the cub found this tainted meat and ate it?" She swallowed hard. "Is the darling little cub even now somewhere, dying a torturous death?"

"We must hurry and search even more diligently than before," Winter Raven said, taking

Holly by an elbow and ushering her away from
the wolf kill.

It seemed so natural now for Holly to be with
the Indian. She had never met a man besides her
father that she felt so comfortable with.

It was as though they had known each other
forever. Had it been their destiny to meet?

She recalled how Winter Raven had spoken of
how beautiful she was, and her heart soared.

She glanced over at him. The longer she was
with him, the more handsome and special he became in her eyes.

Then her heart sank when she remembered
why he had said such things to her.

A ploy!

He had complimented her only to distract her
from his brother.

Even so, she could not help how she felt about
Winter Raven. It seemed useless to battle her
heart.

Suddenly Holly flinched at the sound of rifle
fire a short distance away.

She and Winter Raven glanced quickly at each
other, then fell to their knees and crawled toward
a rise in the land. Beyond it they expected to see
another buffalo kill.

It was at this moment that Holly realized she
had gotten far more than she had bargained for
when she had made plans to search out her step-

father. Each moment seemed to be some sort of new challenge for her and she wondered what the next moments would bring.

She could not help but be sorely afraid.

10

My heart aches, and a drowsy numbness pains,
My sense, as though of hemlock I had drunk,
Or emptied some dull opiate to the drains.
—JOHN KEATS

Holly winced when she got her first look at what was over the hill.

Lying on her stomach beside Winter Raven, she peeked over the slight elevation of land and saw a great herd of buffalo and several whiskered white men.

It seemed that the strychnine had not downed as many buffalo as the hunters had thought it would. They were now using a quicker method of killing the shaggy-haired beasts. The men loaded, fired, and reloaded their heavy Sharps rifles from well-filled cartridge belts.

Holly slowly shifted her eyes to the right to look at two wagons, each attached to a team of four horses. Then she returned her gaze to the massacre at hand.

Spurts of white smoke filled the air as the men sent shot after shot crashing into the dazed buffalo herd.

Winter Raven was horrified. He watched the helpless buffalo, bewildered by the noise of gunfire and its effects. The bulls and cows that had not yet been shot stopped to smell the blood that covered the ground all around them. One after another buffalo sank to their knees before falling over dead.

The men continued their vicious attack. Although each shot stirred the whole herd, none of the buffalo seemed to have the sense to flee from the slaughter.

Winter Raven flinched at every rifle report, as if he felt the impact of the bullets himself. He could not believe this wanton slaughter, but then recalled how he had seen the spoils of such a kill in the white man's boats.

That slaughter had taken place far from his home, though. This kill was way too close to his village!

Sickened by what she had witnessed, and knowing that Winter Raven would feel the same way, Holly looked over at him. In his eyes, she saw the shock and hate and noticed one of his hands doubled into a fist at his side.

She saw the tight set of his jaw, his teeth clenched angrily. His body jerked with the repeated gunfire.

Winter Raven felt Holly's eyes on him and turned to gaze at her. The sorrow in her eyes revealed that she was a woman of heart. She too saw the senselessness of what was happening.

"Is this your first time?" he asked, his voice its normal pitch, for there was no need to keep it low. The rapid firing of the guns was like claps of thunder echoing across the land. The hunt was being acted out before Winter Raven and Holly as if it were on a large stage.

But it was real.

Deadly real.

"To see a buffalo hunt?" Holly managed. "Is that what you're asking? Is this my first time to witness such a . . . a slaughter?"

Her eyes wavered and she felt the urge to cry. Only a little while ago, the animals had been pleasantly feasting on thick green grass, the welcome sun hot on their bodies. The hunters were vicious, their greed blinding them to the harm in what they were doing. It was obvious to Holly that if many more kills like this took place, there would be no more buffalo.

That was a shame, for everything created by God deserved to have a lasting place on this earth.

"I can see in your eyes that you feel the same pain that I feel," Winter Raven said, realizing that she was too emotional to speak her mind.

He reached over and tenderly touched her cheek.

He was glad when she did not flinch, but instead leaned into his palm, as though seeking comfort from his touch.

"I am disgusted by what we saw," Holly said, swallowing hard. "It is so senseless."

She felt her heart pounding inside her chest, but that had nothing to do with how she felt about the buffalo. Winter Raven's touch on her face, in a gesture of caring, made Holly realize just how much she was beginning to feel for him. She had never imagined an Indian warrior possessing such gentleness and compassion. Although she had always sympathized with Indians because of the way white people treated them, she had never really thought about what they were like.

She had never been close to a warrior before.

Not only was Winter Raven handsome and noble in appearance, but his behavior set him apart from most white men she had ever known. Somehow, though, she could not help but compare this man's gentle, caring nature with her father's.

Yes, in many ways, they were alike, the differences being only in the color of their skin and how and where they lived.

After her father's death at the hand of a renegade, Holly had always doubted that she could ever trust an Indian warrior. Her hatred for her father's killer had colored her thoughts. Since then, when she had any reason to think of Indian warriors, she always envisioned them with hatred in their eyes and steel in their hearts.

How wrong she had been, she realized as she listened to Winter Raven talking about the buffalo and his people's feelings for them.

"Buffalo, which also are called bison, are honored by my people as a life-giver," Winter Raven said, slowly removing his hand from Holly's face.

He became silent when he again looked over the hillside. He hated that he had no control over what was happening only a few yards away. He kept reminding himself that he was only one man and that should he step into view, he would be equally as unlucky as the buffalo.

One shot could down him.

And then Holly would be next. The hunters would not tolerate interference by anyone.

"Buffalo never should be killed so savagely," Winter Raven said, his voice tight, his eyes filled with angry fire. "When my people go on a buffalo hunt and buffalo are downed by our arrows, we kneel beside the animals and say, 'You have given your life so that our people will gain strength.' We apologize to them and then purify them with sage and cedar burned in an abalone shell."

"That is a beautiful custom," Holly said, in awe of the respect the Gros Ventres paid the animals they had to kill for survival. "But I am sure most of your customs are."

"We live as we have been taught to live by our forefathers," Winter Raven said, glancing over at her. "We pass on, generation to generation, our respect for all things given to us by the Great Spirit. We are as one with nature." He slowly turned his gaze back to the buffalo. "We are as one with all living things, especially those animals that give their lives to help sustain life for my people."

He paused before adding, "Not so long ago, buffalo were so plentiful they were dark, rich clouds moving upon the rolling hills and plains. Soon those clouds will be gone. The buffalo will be gone."

"It's so sad that it's happening," Holly said, looking into his eyes. "But, Winter Raven, it's like when gold is discovered somewhere. Men rush to the fields and do not leave until there is no more shine in the rocks and riverbeds. It's the same with the buffalo. White men have discovered their wealth. And once a run on something is started, there is hardly any way to stop it."

"That is so," Winter Raven said, sighing.

He again looked at the buffalo kill, the white men still firing rapidly into the herd.

"As I said before," he said sadly. "There are far more white men than red. There is no stopping the greed of white men, no matter the cost to others."

"My father worked hard to stop white criminals by hunting them down and removing them from society," Holly said. When Winter Raven gave her a harsh look, she wished that she could take back those words. He must have been reminded all over again why she was in Montana, and who she sought to remove from society. Not a white man this time, but also his brother!

She couldn't see why he would hold that against her, though. If he knew the havoc his brother wreaked across the land, wouldn't a man of goodness like Winter Raven want to stop him, a man whose heart was black?

Or was it the fact that he was a twin that made the difference? Did he think that if he could find his brother, he might be able to make him good again?

Surely Winter Raven was not fooling himself by thinking such things. Once a man had spread blankets of blood across the countryside, she thought, he was too far gone ever to be rehabilitated.

"Are those men killing the buffalo the same ones who tainted the wolves' carcasses with strychnine?" Holly asked, hoping to change the subject from bounty hunting.

She was glad when it seemed to work, for Winter Raven's glower faded. He inhaled a deep breath, nodded, and looked toward the field of dead animals, blood, and white smoke.

"The men in front of us are wolfers, the ones who poisoned the wolves," he said. "Wolfers are even more irresponsible and ruthless than skin hunters. Traveling in carts, they follow the skin hunters, continually moving from place to place. Never before have they come this close to my people's homes."

"Should you do something about it?" Holly asked. "What *can* you do?"

"I am being pulled in many directions today," he said, his voice drawn. "I have promised my father that I will go to Spirit Bear Island, I have the cub to save, and I want to stop the wolfers."

He inhaled deeply again, then added, "I also have my people to warn."

Winter Raven shook his fists toward the sky. "I am only one man!" he raged, keeping his voice low now that the gunfire was coming only in sporadic blasts. "What would my father have me do?"

Holly was amazed at how quickly he seemed to have gotten an answer from an unseen force.

With eyes wide, she listened as he spoke determinedly. "I must go and warn my people about the nearness of these white men," he announced. "I must see that our hunters are warned so that they do not suddenly come upon the wolfers. The blood spilled then would not only be of the buffalo, and too many of my beloved warriors could die."

"While you go and warn your people, I can try to find the cub," Holly offered, in an effort to help ease Winter Raven's burden. She *did* worry about the tiny cub, afraid that it might already have eaten tainted meat.

Winter Raven took Holly's hand. She grabbed her rifle and crawled with him into a thick stand of trees, far enough from the slaughter field that they could not be seen or heard.

"I cannot leave you alone," he said, still holding her hand, his eyes filled with concern. "These wolfers are the lowest form of man. Should they discover you, it is not pleasant to think about what they would do to you ... before they kill you."

Holly shuddered, but she would not *allow* the men a chance to do anything to her. She knew how to elude criminals; she had learned it from her father.

The only way a renegade could have gotten the best of her father was by cowardly means, by coming upon him from behind. Anyhow, that was the way she imagined it had happened. Since there was no eyewitness, no one truly knew. She didn't even know if whoever took his life would have had the decency to bury him.

"I can take care of myself," Holly said firmly. "Please go and do what your heart guides you to do. I'll be perfectly fine on my own."

That was what truly concerned Winter Raven. She seemed too skilled at being a bounty hunter, a woman who knew how to face danger head-on. If he didn't keep her in sight, what if she happened upon his brother?

Winter Raven knew that Two Moons was near. He felt his presence deep within his soul.

Yet maybe he was wrong about this, Winter Raven argued to himself. No one had seen his brother for many moons now. He still could be far away from his homeland.

If he was honest with himself, he'd admit that it was not his concern about leaving her alone with the wolfers or about her finding his brother that troubled him the most.

The truth was, he cared for this woman. No matter why she was in Montana, Winter Raven cared for Holly in ways he knew that he shouldn't.

He felt protective of her. He wanted to wrap his arms around her and keep her safe from all harm. He wanted to teach her the wonders of being a woman.

"Please go on," Holly urged, slipping her hand from his. "Time is wasting. Go, see to the safety of your people, especially those warriors who are out on the hunt. I can fend for myself." She smiled softly. "As your father taught you how to survive, my father taught me."

Believing that was so, and realizing that he must be on his way if his warnings were to be received in time, Winter Raven nodded.

"I do see that you are strong and capable," he said quietly. "I will leave. I will go to my canoe and hurry to my people."

Unexpectedly, Winter Raven pulled her into his arms and gave her a long and passionate kiss. Holly dropped the rifle and her knees grew instantly weak.

When he rushed away, she watched, her pulse racing, her fingers reaching up to touch her lips where his had been.

Her lips still throbbed from the heat of the kiss. She could taste him still. She couldn't believe that he had kissed her, and, even more than that, she couldn't believe how the kiss had affected her!

She had been kissed before, by suitors in Kansas City, but never like this, so passionate, yet so sweet!

Her jaw tightened. She couldn't allow herself to be fooled by this man! He was still playing with her feelings. Would he stop at nothing to get her to change her mind about his brother?

Well, she'd see just how far he would go. She

could play the same game, but she could play it better.

Yet, when she did kiss him again—if they were ever together again—how could she actually pretend?

Oh, Lord, she did care for him. She hungered for his kiss. She had to be careful here or she would lose sight of everything that she wanted.

Nothing other than avenging her mother's death should be on her mind.

But she couldn't help it. Aware that she was trembling, and realizing that it was from awakened passion, Holly reached down and picked up her rifle. She couldn't shake the feeling of floating in the clouds. It was there, inside her, the ecstasy of Winter Raven's kiss, of his arms, of the way he looked at her!

She turned to walk away, to resume her search for the cub, but suddenly she stopped and spun around with a start at the sound of gunfire close behind her.

Afraid of being seen, she hurried behind some bushes and knelt just as the lone gunman stepped into view and moved beneath the towering cottonwood trees to light up a cigar.

As he turned somewhat to the side, and she got a good look at the man's face, Holly's heart thudded to a halt. She recognized this man, even though he wore a thick black beard.

"Lord," she whispered, lifting a hand to her throat in shock. "It's Rudolph Anderson."

Her fingers tightened around her rifle. She had just found her stepfather!

11

God fulfills himself in many ways,
Lest one good custom should corrupt the world!
—ALFRED LORD TENNYSON

Stunned at having found him so quickly, Holly watched him and awaited an opportunity to follow through on her plan.

She gasped at his brutal, unbelievable actions. As the remaining buffalo took off in a thundering of hoofbeats, the other men chased them at a mad run. Her stepfather stayed behind.

He began to remove the hides of the fallen buffalo. The way he did it was sickening to Holly, yet she was somehow transfixed by it.

With his deadly sharp skinning knife, he ripped the skin of the buffalo down the belly and legs, severing the hide around the neck and the back of the head.

Her stomach churned as she saw her stepfather becoming increasingly bloodied by what he was doing, and she almost turned and ran away.

How could she stand being close enough to this man to hold him at bay with her rifle? How could she even think of taking him in this condition, all bloody and reeking of the kill? How would she bring him to Three Forks to hand him over to the sheriff? The stench would be so horrible, she was afraid that she would become violently ill!

But knowing that the other men might return at any time to help strip the animals of their hides, Holly felt that she must act at once. She must go to her stepfather and force him to leave with her.

Now that she was almost face-to-face with the man that she hated so much, she began to have doubts about what she had planned to do.

Could she truly capture him, alone?

Thinking about her mother with strychnine in her veins, she knew that she must. She must take him to the authorities so that justice could finally be done.

If the sheriff questioned her stepfather's guilt, Holly would instruct him to wire Kansas City and get the details of her mother's death from the coroner.

She checked the chamber of her rifle to make sure a bullet was in place, in case she needed to protect herself from this vile man.

When she had verified that the firearm was loaded, she looked carefully around to make sure that none of the other men were near enough to see what transpired. She had to take her stepfather away from this place without being caught.

The other men were no longer in pursuit of the buffalo. Instead they were involved with their own cruel method of skinning the dead animals at quite a distance from her stepfather, yet not so far that Holly couldn't make out what they were doing.

As the men intently went about their task, they didn't look to see how their friend Anderson was doing. Holly knew that this was the time to make her move, and quickly. At any moment someone might choose to join her stepfather.

She realized that she was trembling and worried that her knees might not hold her up for long, so she started to step out into the open. But her breath caught in her throat and she immediately stepped back again into hiding, when she saw an Indian ride into view around a bend. He was headed toward her stepfather.

Frustrated over the delay for she badly wanted to get this over with while she had the chance, Holly kept her rifle aimed at her stepfather through the bushes. In disbelief, she watched the man on horseback drawing closer. She yanked her rifle down to her side when she saw the Indian's face. She had found not only the first man that she was hunting but also the second.

She still could hardly believe her eyes as she stared at Jake Two Moons. He drew his horse to a halt and dismounted next to her stepfather.

Scarcely breathing, Holly watched through the bushes as the Indian took something from one of his saddlebags. When she recognized the same sort of bottle that she had found near the wolf kill, she realized that the Indian was supplying her stepfather with strychnine.

In her mind's eye she recalled the coroner telling her about the results of her mother's autopsy, and she saw the dead, ripped-open bodies of the wolves. Her stepfather and this renegade were responsible for it all.

She knew that it would not be hard now to pull the trigger, if she was forced to, to stop both of these terrible men. She might even make them swallow their own strychnine.

But as she watched the Indian, she was not seeing his likeness on the Wanted poster. She was seeing Winter Raven's!

Could it be? Were her eyes playing tricks on her?

Had Winter Raven only pretended to return home to warn his people of the buffalo slaughter, when in fact he was a part of it?

And Winter Raven thought that she had gone off to look for the cub. He never would suspect that she would be here spying!

She stared at the Indian's horse. Winter Raven had not been traveling on a horse. He had been in a canoe.

But perhaps he had hidden the horse and his supply of strychnine in the cave where the bear had died. Perhaps the bear had threatened him, and he had shot it in order to retrieve his horse and the poison.

Had everything he had said to her been a lie? Had his show of compassion been all pretense?

When he had kissed her, had he done it to fool her into believing all of the nonsense that he had told her?

Her head spun with all of these doubts, troubling her to the very core of her being. Holly shook her head in an effort to clear her thoughts.

Yes, she must get a grip on herself. She must think straight. She could not afford to make a mistake now, especially about Winter Raven!

"I'm wrong to think these things about him," she whispered to herself.

She was never a bad judge of character. She just couldn't have been wrong about Winter Raven.

The man that she had been with had been kind. His outrage at the slaughter had been genuine, and the way he had reacted to the wolf kill could not have been anything but real. He had abhorred it. She had heard it in his voice. She had seen it in his eyes.

Hadn't he explained to her the importance of the buffalo and the wolves to his people?

A man who took part in such brutality could never pretend to be as gentle and caring as Winter Raven had been.

No man could be that skillful an actor.

This Indian was not Winter Raven but his twin. She had to believe this.

In the short time they had been together, she had found herself falling hopelessly in love with Winter Raven. Recalling the wonders of his kiss now, she reached up and gently touched her lips with her free hand. By the way he had kissed her, she knew that he had feelings for her as well. There had been true emotion! Oh, Lord, there had been such passion!

If Winter Raven had lied to her about who he was, she was not sure she could bear it. So much of her heart had already been ripped away by sadness. If Winter Raven was, in truth, Jake Two Moons, there would be hardly anything left of Holly's heart. She would be devastated over losing it to a lying, heartless murderer.

And in her heart, she knew that this never could have happened. Winter Raven was exactly who he had said he was, and the Indian ahead of her was the outlaw.

Holly again focused on the two men. They were still talking and laughing together, but suddenly Jake Two Moons—dressed in a brief breechclout and moccasins, his hair in one long black braid down his back—swung himself into his saddle and rode off.

Holly's heart pounded as she watched him flee. Then she gazed at her stepfather. She was torn. She wanted both men!

But she had to make a choice.

Should she run to her horse and go after Jake Two Moons? Or should she surprise her stepfather by stepping out into the open with her firearm aimed at his gut?

Of course, there was no real question. Her true reason for being in Montana was to find her stepfather and turn him in to the authorities. Finding Jake Two Moons was second on her list of priorities.

While she had the chance, she would capture her stepfather.

Later she would try to round up Jake Two Moons.

Just as she started to step out into the open and order her stepfather to put his hands in the air, two wolfers came riding up on their horses. After they dismounted, they started helping Anderson with the skinning. Holly could tell they were there to stay, at least long enough to foil her plan.

She uttered a few choice curse words under her breath, realizing that she would have to wait until later.

She tried to convince herself that there would be another time when he was alone, when she could capture him at last.

Maybe this was meant to be, a signal to go after Jake Two Moons now. It might be her best chance. Hadn't he successfully eluded the law even though Wanted posters were plastered all over the country?

She sighed. Apprehending her stepfather would have to wait. She had no choice now but to try and find the red skin while he was still close by.

After all, she would hate to have to give back the advance that Sheriff Hawkins had handed over to her. So much of it had been spent already.

Running quietly and low to the ground, she circled around so her stepfather and the men with him wouldn't see her. When she knew that there was enough distance between herself and the men, she straightened up and ran hard until she reached her tethered horse. Her chest heaving, she slid her rifle into the gunboot, swung herself into the saddle, and rode off.

Her eyes searched the landscape for the lone Indian rider.

After a while, she spotted Jake Two Moons up ahead, riding at a hard gallop across the land.

She fell back and stopped abruptly when two other Indians came out of the forest at Jake Two Moon's right and joined him. Suddenly afraid, feeling threatened by the presence of three Indians, Holly managed to hide behind an outcropping of rock. She waited to see what the Indians' next move would be.

When they rode away together, Holly eased out from her position and followed them, far enough behind them, not to be noticed.

Holly saw that they were headed to a small camp where a lone tepee had been set up. She decided to continue following them to see how permanent their camp was.

She didn't want to give up her quest easily. She would hide and study the red men's actions, and when the opportunity arose—if it did—she would capture the murdering renegade.

When she thought about what she had promised Winter Raven that she would do—search for the cub—she felt somewhat guilty. As soon as she met up with Winter Raven again, they could resume the search together. For now she could only pray that the cub was safe.

The three Indians rode into their camp, dismounted, tethered their horses, and went inside the tepee. Holly drew a tight rein and stopped. Dismounting, she led Chocolate into hiding. After he was tethered and contentedly feasting on buffalo grass, Holly went onward, on foot.

Running as quietly as possible, she sneaked up behind the tepee, stopped, and leaned as close as she dared. She heard one of the Indians address Jake Two Moons by name. They talked about going into town for a fresh supply of strychnine. They spoke of a white man there who illegally supplied them with the poison. They paid him with the hides that her stepfather provided them.

Holly scarcely breathed when Jake Two Moons began talking about Winter Raven and their father, saying that he was too close to his people's village not to stop and see his loved ones. Jake Two Moons said that he must first see his father. He sensed that he was not well.

But then he must meet and embrace his brother. He had gone too long without his twin! He must be with him again, at least for a while, before he would leave and say a final good-bye.

Holly's eyes widened when the two other Indians spoke almost in unison, warning Jake Two Moons not to go to his village. Doing so would only alert his people that trouble was near, for they knew that trouble followed Jake Two Moons everywhere he went. They warned him that the buffalo slaughter must be completed before his tribe got wind of it.

There was a long pause, when no one said anything, after which Jake Two Moons somberly agreed. He knew it was best. He would approach his people only in his memories, especially his brother, whom he ached to be with. Memories of their times together as young braves had sustained him.

Afraid the meeting might be coming to an end and worried about getting caught, Holly retreated. She rode back in the direction of the place where she and Winter Raven had parted. She was lost in thought, mulling over what Jake Two Moons had said. He missed his twin brother.

She wondered if Winter Raven missed his brother as much? Would he do anything to see him? Would he even try to stop Holly from—

She turned with a start when she heard a horse coming up behind her.

She was glad that the horseman wasn't in sight, since that meant he hadn't seen her either.

She turned her horse into thick brush and dismounted waiting for the rider to appear. When she saw that it was Jake Two Moons, her eyes widened and her throat went dry.

She started to mount Chocolate again, ready to chase after the outlaw. But she dropped the reins and stared at the renegade as he rode a short distance past her, then dismounted and took his steed over to a stream to drink.

Holly's heart pounded hard inside her chest. She couldn't believe her luck.

Jake Two Moons was alone!

He was so close, so vulnerable as he lingered by the stream, quenching his thirst.

Could Holly truly be this lucky? She listened to gauge if any more horses were coming her way. All she heard was silence, except for the distant firing of guns, which meant that the wolfers had resumed their hunt.

In a way that was good, for as long as the wolfers were still in the area, she might get another opportunity to capture her stepfather.

But for now, at this moment, she would concentrate on surprising Jake Two Moons.

Her pulse racing, Holly gripped her rifle hard and began moving slowly toward Jake Two Moons' back. She was careful not to step on twigs that would alert him to her presence.

Lord, oh, Lord, she was so close now!

12

As a virtue golden through and through,
Sufficient to vindicate itself,
And prove its worth at a moment's view.
—ROBERT BROWNING

As Holly crept stealthily toward Jake Two Moons, a new thought came to her that made the moment even more important. This redskin must have been the source of the strychnine that killed her mother.

That made taking the renegade in for the reward money even more victorious.

She refused to think about how Winter Raven might feel about her if she did take Jake Two Moons to the authorities. Deep in her heart she knew how important it was for her to rid the world of a man like him.

Sucking in a breath of courage, she stepped up behind Jake Two Moons and leveled the rifle at his back.

"Jake Two Moons, do as you are told and this rifle pointed at you won't send a bullet into your cowardly back," she said in a voice that was unfamiliar to her.

She was glad that he had never heard her speak before, or he would have known that she was scared almost crazy to be this close to a wanted man who was a killer.

She saw him flinch, as though her words were a fist slamming into his gut.

She was relieved that he didn't attempt to move or try to look around to see who was ambushing him.

Of course, he would know the voice belonged to a woman, but he didn't know how pale the woman's face was or how her knees trembled.

Courage, she repeated to herself. It would take much courage to complete this task.

But she had seen her father succeed many times. She knew how it was done. She only wished it was as easy as it had looked. She was feeling very squeamish now, as though she might retch at any moment from the fear that had her in its grip. She wondered if her father ever felt the same fear, the same apprehension? The same weak stomach and trembling knees?

No. Surely not.

She had been with him when he had captured more than one outlaw, and he had stood brave and tall, his chin lifted proudly, his eyes filled with the warmth of success.

Well, she would not insult her father's memory by giving in to her quaking fears. She had come to Montana to do a job, and by hook or crook, she would succeed at doing it.

"Renegade, drop flat on your belly," she ordered, glad to hear her voice sound more like herself.

Surely her father was up there somewhere looking down at her, guiding her.

She glanced at the outlaw's rifle that he had laid next to him while drinking from the stream. "And don't get any ideas to grab for your firearm," she quickly warned. "I wouldn't hesitate at sending a bullet right through you."

Faced with the possibility of actually having to shoot a man, she wondered is she truly could.

That thought upset her stomach even worse than it already was.

She prayed that he would cooperate!

"Now, easy-like, Jake Two Moons," Holly said, slowly stepping away from him to give him room to lie down as instructed.

She watched him move slowly onto his stomach.

"Now spread-eagle," she said tightly. "Raise your arms above your head. And don't try to stop me when I take the knife from the sheath at your waist. My finger is on the trigger. One slip and you are dead."

"As you see, I am doing as you have told me," Jake Two Moons said in perfect English. "Who are you? What do you want of me?" He laughed throatily. "Do you think a mere woman like you can get away with this? Do you not know that you won't see another sunrise?"

It unnerved her that this man's voice sounded so much like Winter Raven's. She was glad that she hadn't yet seen his eyes. If she looked square into his eyes and saw Winter Raven there, this would become even more difficult. It would feel like she was taking Winter Raven to the authorities instead of his evil brother.

She pushed these thoughts aside as she very carefully bent to a knee beside Jake Two Moons and slowly reached for his sheathed knife. She kept the rifle steady on the man's back, her finger ready on the trigger.

"I'm certain you know that more than one bounty hunter is looking for you," she said, her voice guarded. "Well, renegade, like my father before me, I am a bounty hunter. I'm taking you in for the reward money."

"What is your father's name?" Jake Two Moons asked, wincing when he felt her unsnap the sheath to take the knife.

"My father?" Holly said, sad to be reminded all over again of his rumored death. "His name was Edward Thomas Wintizer. It was said that some renegade as heartless as you downed him.

If I ever find out the name of the man who killed my father, he will pay."

She smiled when he winced again, proving that he knew her father's reputation.

"So you knew of him, did you?" she asked. "Well, as I said, I am as skilled as my father was, so you'd better think twice before trying anything. You are worth as much to me dead as alive. I won't hesitate to kill you."

She swallowed hard. "And it will give me a feeling of satisfaction to take you in, for in my heart, it will be the same as taking in the man who wronged my father," she said. "The sheriff told me that he was a renegade, just like you."

She hoped that when he finally got a chance to see her, face-to-face, he wouldn't notice the nervous perspiration that had popped out on her upper lip.

She forced her hand to remain steady as she slipped the knife quickly from its sheath and tossed it aside, far from the renegade's reach.

She kept the barrel of her rifle directly against his back, to remind him that she meant business and would shoot him if he dared move an inch. Using her free hand, she took a strip of rawhide from her rear pocket.

"Now slowly place your wrists together behind you," she said throatily, relieved when he did as he was instructed.

She quickly looped the rawhide around his wrists, then tied it in a tight knot. She had learned this technique from observing her father and she'd often practiced on a tree branch the size of a man's wrist.

Sighing at the completion of that task, Holly stood up and stepped away from him.

"Get to your feet and turn around very, very slowly to face me," Holly said, far enough away that he wouldn't be able to knock or kick the rifle from her hands.

When he did as he was told and was facing her, she couldn't help but gasp. Up this close, looking straight at his face, she saw how identical he was to his brother. If she hadn't known better, she would have believed that this *was* Winter Raven!

But there was one vast difference. It was the eyes. What she saw in this man's eyes sent icy sprays of fear through her. They were cold, ruthless, unfriendly, and angry, and she knew that if he had the chance, he would kill her as fast as he could clasp his long, lean fingers around her throat!

He noticed that his appearance had affected her in an unusual way. She stared at him as though she had seen a ghost.

That thought, that possibility made him feel

strange. An image of his brother flashed vividly in his mind's eye.

When he started thinking about his brother, he always brushed such thoughts from his mind. But never could he get his love for his twin out of his heart. If he lingered on thoughts of Winter Raven for very long, he felt ashamed and also so lonely that he could hardly stand it.

Why was he thinking so intensely about his brother now? Why was he missing him so? It seemed to be caused by this woman. If so, why?

And why was she staring at him so strangely? Did she know Winter Raven perhaps? Was she seeing Winter Raven in Two Moons?

Curious, he started to ask her, but then thought better of it. If she didn't know Winter Raven, and her reason for staring at him had to do with something else, then it was not wise to alert her to the fact that he had an identical twin. Might not she then try and capture both men, for double the reward money?

He pressed his lips tightly together and glared at her. He would wait for the right moment, and then he would be the one to get the best of *her*. His lips curled into a tight smile at the thought of making this woman pay for having made him look foolish. Yes, she would pay, and at the same time he would satisfy his long-dormant lust. It had been far too long now.

"I don't know what you're smiling at when *I* am the one holding the rifle on *you*," Holly said, wary of the expression on his face.

The more she looked at him, the more she noticed the differences between the brothers. Although both were muscled and almost equally handsome, they were as different as night and day in many important ways.

Because of this, she hoped that Winter Raven would not resent her for being the one to stop his brother's bloody escapades.

That thought gave her the courage to continue.

She tightened her jaw and straightened her shoulders. "Now walk away from the stream and your horse," she said determinedly. "I will ride my horse. You will walk ahead of me."

She silently prayed that she could see this through to the end.

13

Is there not eternal fire and eternal chains,
To bind the phantoms of existence from eternal life?
—WILLIAM BLAKE

Just as Holly got to her horse and started to reach for the reins, she saw her captive suddenly glance to one side.

Before she could see what had caught his attention, her stepfather leapt out from behind a thick stand of bushes and knocked the rifle out of her hand.

"First I thought a skinny, long-legged man had gotten the best of Jake Two Moons," Rudolph said, laughing.

He twisted one of Holly's arms behind her back painfully, then turned her to face him. "But look what I have here," he said, his eyes gleaming. "My cunning little stepdaughter. Just missed me so much you had to come and find me, huh?"

He looked at Jake Two Moons, then back at Holly.

"What I don't understand is what you want with Jake Two Moons," he said, arching an eyebrow. "I'm the one who killed your ma. Not the renegade."

That he actually openly admitted what he had done made Holly boil with anger. But her ire quickly turned to dread. The fact that he had made such an admission, which could condemn him in a court of law, meant that he had no intention of allowing her to live and tell the authorities about his confession. She had stupidly let down her guard enough to be caught.

She felt like a trapped polecat facing a certain death. But she wouldn't let her fear show in her behavior. She would not die a coward's death.

She had known danger might find her when she had set out alone on this journey of vengeance.

She lifted her chin boldly and refused to answer her stepfather. He could draw his own conclusions about why she had taken the renegade into custody. It should not take him long to realize the situation.

"So the cat's got your tongue, eh?" Rudolph said, stepping away from Holly. He stooped and picked up her rifle, then walked over to Jake Two Moons.

Training the rifle on Holly with one hand, he took a knife from a sheath at his side with the other and sliced the sharp blade through the rawhide at Two Moons' wrists.

"You know this crazy squaw?" Two Moons asked, glaring at Holly as he rubbed a raw wrist. "Did I hear you call her your stepdaughter?"

"She's nothin' to me," Rudolph grumbled. He glowered at Holly. "Nor was her mother."

Rudolph spat over his left shoulder. "It was the money that attracted me," he said coldly. "Her ma was lonesome as hell. It didn't take nothin' but my charm and a couple of kisses to talk her into marryin' me."

He chuckled as he walked slowly toward Holly. "That strychnine helped release me from a fate worse than death," he said. "Marriage *is* worse than death, you know. It's bein' cooped up like in jail. I couldn't wait until my wife took her last breath. I knew it was comin' soon enough, so's I hightailed it outta Kansas City, but not before I cheated the bitch outta everything she owned."

"Even our home," Holly hissed. "You cheating, lying swindler. You murderer. One day you'll get what you deserve. I had wanted the honor." She frowned at Jake Two Moons. "If I hadn't gotten caught up in capturing this damn renegade, I'd have succeeded in taking you to the authorities. Justice would have been done."

"Well, sweet thing, seems I ruined all of your plans today, didn't I?" Rudolph said, laughing boisterously.

"Kill her and let's get out of here," Jake Two Moons said, his eyes two points of fire as he stared at Holly. "She's nothing but trouble. I have never seen a woman as nervy as this one."

"How do you think we should do it?" Rudolph asked his friend. He stepped right up to Holly, making her take a step back.

"Should we pretend she's a buffalo and down her with a bullet and strip her of her hide?" he taunted, his eyes twinkling as he watched Holly's reaction. "Or, savage, do you think we should give her a taste of strychnine?"

"Come with me," Jake Two Moons said, motioning toward Holly's stepfather. "I know exactly how she should die."

Without questioning Jake Two Moons, Rudolph grabbed Holly by a wrist and forced her to walk next to him as they followed the renegade under the dark umbrella of cottonwood trees.

Holly looked anxiously from side to side, trying to think of a plan of escape, but her hopes sank very quickly. She knew that even if she did manage to get free of her stepfather's grip, there was no way she could run fast enough to get away from him.

She couldn't see a place where she could hide from them, either.

But she did see the shine of the river.

It was only a few feet away. Maybe someone

would come by in a canoe, see movement, and stop. Maybe someone would see her being held captive by two devious, heartless men.

She thought about Winter Raven, and that gave her a small ray of hope. If only she hadn't insisted that he leave her alone, if only he had second thoughts and decided to come back to be with her. Then maybe he'd sense what was happening in this small patch of cottonwood trees and save her.

But knowing that Winter Raven felt honor-bound to warn his people about the wolfers, she doubted he'd be thinking another minute about her. She was supposed to be looking for a cub while Winter Raven was gone, not tracking down two evil men.

She felt guilty for having given up that search, for it had not only gotten her in a heap of trouble, it was probably going to get her killed.

"Over there," Jake Two Moons said, motioning with a nod to a place where the trees began to thin and the land became littered with rocks. "Take her over there. Push her into the pit in the ground."

"Pit?" Rudolph asked, raising an eyebrow. "What sort of pit?"

"Just take her there and let her see the surprise that awaits her at the bottom," the Indian said, his eyes glinting as Holly turned quickly toward him. "Yes, white woman—snakes. Do you like snakes?" He laughed. "I have never known a woman who did. My mother ran when she saw snakes, ever since she was a little squaw and had been bitten by one. But these? Their bite is as lethal as strychnine."

Holly tried to remain courageous in the face of her fate, but nothing could stop the trembling inside her or the ill feeling that had laid claim to her stomach. Her pulse raced as she was shoved toward the pit.

Its opening was not all that large, but it was certainly big enough for her body to fit through. The closer she came to the pit, the harder she tried to be brave. Her throat was dry. Her cheeks burned with fear. Her stepfather gave her one more push, taking her to the very edge of the pit.

Her heart pounding, Holly stared down into the hole in the ground. Many rattlesnakes lay curled up asleep at the bottom.

An intense stab of fear gripped her as she waited for the shove that would send her over the edge. She knew that if she tried to turn and run, she wouldn't get far.

To face certain death the way she knew her father must have, she tightened her jaw, looked straight ahead past the pit, and forced herself to focus on things that might make these last moments of her life more precious.

Songbirds sang various melodies in the distance, so sweet and innocent. She caught sight of the large eyes of a doe as it leapt past into thicker brush. Small animals scampered here and there. From the river she could hear the splash of fish as they occasionally leapt out of the water, reaching for the sun.

In her mind's eye she saw the sweet smile of her mother. She saw her father, and even felt his arms around her as he had embraced her that last time.

A vision of Winter Raven came to her mind also, so handsome as he stood before her, his eyes warm with desire. She closed her eyes and relived his kiss, so beautiful that it had made her senses reel.

"This is home to scores of rattlesnakes," Jake Two Moons said, ending Holly's reverie. "For now the sun pours into the hole, making the snakes lethargic and sleepy. Soon, though, the sun will leave, and the slightest movement will set off the rattlers. When they find you there, among them, they will have their way with you."

"She won't last that long," Rudolph said, smiling crookedly at Holly. "The moment she lands, the rattlers will awaken and send their venom quickly into her veins."

"No!" Holly cried, suddenly yanking free of

her stepfather's grip. She turned and started to run, but her stepfather tackled her.

She tried to wrest herself free, in the process losing a boot. Her hat had flown off her head the minute she was pushed to the ground.

"You little spitfire," Rudolph hissed, giving Holly a kick in the side, which made her roll closer to the pit.

One more kick and she felt herself tumbling over the edge.

Her life seemed to flash before her eyes, yet she was still aware enough of her surroundings to grab a thick root that was growing out of the side of the pit.

She hung on for dear life as her stepfather and the renegade stared down at her, laughing.

"Enjoy your last moments. You won't be able to hang on for long," her stepfather said, almost choking with laughter. "Then you will fall to your death. The fall won't kill you, but the snakes will!"

They walked away, their laughter booming like thunder.

She flinched when she heard them ride away.

She was alone now, except for the snakes below her.

Sweat pearled on Holly's brow as she clung to the root. Her fingers burned more by the minute. She was not sure just how much longer she could last!

She looked heavenward and said a quiet prayer. She thought she heard the splash of a paddle in the river.

Her eyes brimmed with tears as she thought of Winter Raven. Maybe he decided against going to his village. Maybe he had worried about her being alone.

Still clinging to the thick root, Holly began screaming Winter Raven's name. Over and over again she screamed it, hoping that her voice was loud enough to travel from the pit to the river.

She prayed that it was Winter Raven who was near, for he would know her voice. He would know that she was in trouble!

But if a passerby heard her and he turned out to be another buffalo hunter, she did not want to think of what her fate might be. She might be saved from one fate only to face another worse.

Nevertheless, she would chance anything to get free of this pit of rattlers!

Again she called out Winter Raven's name. She scarcely breathed as she waited to see if he had heard, her eyes wide as she watched her sore fingers slipping bit by bit from the root.

She knew that if Winter Raven had not heard her and did not come to save her, she was doomed to die a most unmerciful death. Tears filled her eyes. She took one long, shivering look at the snakes, then sucked in a breath of horror.

Her screams had awakened them! Their rattles were making the most ominous noise she had ever heard.

Holly was too afraid to cry out again, but she no longer heard the splash of paddles in the water and that gave her hope. Surely the person in the canoe had heard her screams and was now coming for her.

She fervently hoped it was Winter Raven!

14

I cry your mercy-pity-love! -aye, love!
Merciful love that tantalizes not.
One-thoughted, never-wandering, guileless love,
Unmasked, and being seen-without a blot!
—JOHN KEATS

Having heard a voice crying for help, Winter Raven quickly recognized it as Holly's. He could not get to shore quickly enough. He had to find her and protect her from whatever harm threatened her.

His heart was pounding as he beached his canoe.

He searched around him, grabbed his rifle, then cautiously stepped away from the rocky riverbank onto higher ground thick with waving green grass.

He started to shout back at Holly, to ask her to tell him where she was, but then thought better of it. What if some person had caused Holly's problem and was still nearby? He did not want to alert anyone that he had arrived to rescue her.

Nah, no. He had to move stealthily forward

and hope that she would cry out again, so that he could tell exactly where to find her.

As his eyes scanned the land around him, watching for any signs of Holly, he was very grateful that he had been able to return so soon. After he had gotten close to his village, on his way to warn his people about the wolfers and the massive buffalo kill, he had come across one of his warriors fishing with a net from his canoe. As luck would have it, the warrior had not joined the other men on the day's hunt.

When Winter Raven had seen Fire Eyes, a trusted friend, he quickly paddled over to him and told him what he had seen and why he was headed back to their village.

Fire Eyes knew about Winter Raven's quest for their chief, and he had offered to go to the village himself with the message. That would give Winter Raven the opportunity to resume his mission, for everyone knew of its importance to his ailing father.

Winter Raven had accepted the offer from his friend, then paddled hard back toward where he had left Holly. He had had time to think while alone in his canoe. He would succeed on his father's behalf, but he would also help Holly find her stepfather. Maybe then she would agree to leave finding Two Moons to him, so that he could take his brother home to their father.

Then it would be up to Winter Raven's father—acting as a chief first, a father second—as to what punishment should be handed down to Two Moons. His brother's fate should be decided by the Gros Ventres, not by white eyes who would have no mercy for a red man.

It had been as though the Great Spirit had led Fire Eyes to the river today so that Winter Raven could seek his help and gain the opportunity to do other things of vital importance.

And not only for his father. As he had traveled further and further away from Holly, he had begun thinking of how unwise it had been to leave her by herself. He had not been able to get her off his mind. Although she tried to be as strong and brave as a man, there was no doubt that she was all woman.

Alone, with the wolfers in the area, she was very vulnerable. Probably they had been without women for a long time while on their hunt, and if they came across Holly they would not hesitate to satisfy their appetites.

If anything happened to her, Winter Raven knew he would always feel responsible. He would not be able to forgive himself should the filthy men harm Holly or defile her body in any way. There was so much about her that made him believe that she was a virgin. Beneath her strong and able front, there was an innocence.

Ho, yes, Winter Raven had seen it.

He had even felt it, especially when he had kissed her. Never in his life had a kiss affected him in such a way. And he believed that it was the innocence of it that had made him fall even more deeply in love with her.

Yes, he *was* in love. Hopelessly, endlessly, in love.

He had heard tales of love happening so quickly, but he had always scoffed at them. Now he knew that it could happen. It had. To him.

When he saw a boot a short distance away on the ground, his heart skipped a beat and his throat went dry.

Then he saw a hat—and not just any hat. He recognized it, as had he recognized the lone boot.

"Holly's," he whispered, chilled with the dread that something had possibly happened to the woman he loved.

His heart sank, and a despair he had known only one other time in his life filled his very soul, a despair that had come when he lost his wife.

One more step and he could see a pit in the ground in close proximity to the boot and hat.

He knew this pit. It was the home of many rattlers. And with Holy's boot and hat so close . . . ?

Nah, no!

He didn't want to believe that she was in the pit, that she had innocently fallen—or that she had been shoved into it by someone who wished her dead.

He was afraid that if he did look into the hole, he would not see someone he recognized. If dozens of rattlers had attacked Holly, she would have died a vicious death. Her body would be swollen and unrecognizable.

That thought tore Winter Raven apart inside. Surely when she had cried out for help earlier, it had been at the moment she had fallen into the pit.

Now there was utter silence.

That could mean only one thing!

His eyes widened with wonder when he heard a sound, a sound like someone whispering his name.

When he heard it again and realized that it was coming from the pit, his heart fluttered with hope. Perhaps the voice was Holly's. If it was . . . she was still alive!

He rushed closer and stretched out on his belly, then leaned over the opening and peered downward.

"Holly!" he cried, his eyes widening when he saw that she was grasping a thick tree root that had grown out of the side of the pit.

Holly's eyes filled with tears as she gazed up at Winter Raven. She had heard him call out her name, but she had been afraid to do any more

than whisper his back to him. She was terrified
to look down, for the last time she had, she saw
that the rattlers had begun to slide slowly up the
sides of the pit toward her.

So far as she knew, they were close enough
to . . .

Winter Raven's relief at having found her alive
quickly became fear as he saw how close the
snakes were to her. The sides of the pit were alive,
it seemed, with so many snakes slithering their
way up.

"Please save me," Holly whispered, her fear
mounting in reaction to the look of horror in Winter Raven's eyes. The snakes must be so close he
had no time to save her.

And how could he? She was too far down for
him to reach out and pull her to freedom.

She was afraid that her heartbeats were now
numbered. Soon venom would course through
her bloodstream and she would be dead.

"Do not move," Winter Raven said, only loudly
enough for Holly to hear. "Say nothing else. I will
save you."

He rose to his feet and looked desperately
around him.

He saw a thick, twisted cord of a trumpet vine
hanging from a tree only a few feet away, upon
which were lovely flowers that resembled orange
orchids. His pulse racing, realizing that he had

no time to waste, he yanked the cord down from the tree, bent to one knee, and lowered the thick vine down for Holly.

He could see her fingers trembling as she reached out for the vine with one hand and managed to grab it.

He did not have to tell her what to do next. She let go of the tree root and with her free hand, she wrapped the vine around her waist. Clinging to it with all of her might, she nodded.

He did not dare look past her to see how close the snakes were now. Instead, he kept his eyes locked on hers and began pulling her up.

The moment she felt herself leave the pit, she knew that she was free of danger. She laughed and cried as Winter Raven swept her up into his arms and carried her quickly away.

When they had reached a slight bluff, far enough away from the pit to be safe, Winter Raven and Holly moved together in a flash.

They kissed.

They clung.

She sobbed.

She thrilled.

And then he bent low and set her on a thick, soft bed of moss on the bluff, kneeling before her and framing her face between his hands. "How did you end up in the pit?" he asked, his eyes searching hers. "Was it on accident, or . . . ?"

She told him exactly what had happened, not leaving out who shared the responsibility for it with her stepfather.

"Your brother is my stepfather's ally in many sorts of crimes," she said, seeing the silent pain in Winter Raven's eyes at the knowledge of the depths of his brother's evil. "I'm sorry you have to know such things about your twin, but it's true. All of it. Your brother supplies the strychnine that is used to kill the wolves. He didn't push me into the pit of snakes, but it was his idea. Afterward, both he and my stepfather rode off laughing. I'm sure they believe that I am dead by now."

Her eyes narrowed. "Those polecats," she said, her jaw tightening. "They must have taken my horse and all of my belongings that were on it."

They remained there in silence until a soft neigh came to them on the breeze.

"Chocolate?" Holly murmured, her eyes wide. She jumped to her feet to look down from the bluff, to where she had left her horse tethered in the thick grass.

Her heart sang when she saw that Chocolate was still there. She had hidden him so well that neither her stepfather nor Jake Two Moons had found him!

Winter Raven could not share her enthusiasm, for his heart and mind were elsewhere—on his brother, whose path had changed from bad to worse.

Winter Raven always found it hard to believe the extent of his brother's wrongdoing. And now he knew that Two Moons was responsible for the deaths of many wolves, animals that the Gros Ventres revered. His brother was responsible for the slaughter of buffalo, for harvesting their pelts, and tongues.

But worst of all, his brother had heartlessly left Holly in the pit of rattlers to die!

Holly's smile faded when she turned to Winter Raven and saw his expression.

"My brother," Winter Raven said, slowly settling beside Holly as she sat back down. "My *twin*. As children, we were inseparable. Then one day, at fourteen winters, we got separated while hunting. I returned home without him, exhausted after searching everywhere. I didn't know where else to look for him. Two Moons was gone for many days. When he returned home he was disoriented. He was changed."

When he paused, Holly reached out and took one of his hands in hers, glad that he allowed it. She knew that he needed someone now, and she was happy to be there for him.

This man, this wonderful Gros Ventres warrior, had saved her life!

She owed him so much. Listening was the least she could do.

"*Ho*, yes, my brother was changed," Winter Raven continued. He twined his fingers through Holly's, absorbing deep inside his heart the gentleness this woman was offering him at this troubled moment. He realized that his brother was now too lost, in body and soul, ever to regain his youthful goodness.

"What changed him?" Holly asked, when once again Winter Raven paused and the haunting in his eyes deepened.

"Many things," Winter Raven answered, nodding slowly. "The day of my brother's return home I found a bottle of firewater in his parfleche bag, and I smelled it on his breath. While he was lost, he came across a gang of white outlaws. At first they had imprisoned him at their cabin. They tied him to a chair and left him for hours at a time. When they returned after their raids on innocent settlers, and Two Moons saw the loot and the power that seemed to go with that way of life, he asked to be set free of his bonds so that he could join their gang and ride with them on their raids against whites."

"And they agreed?" Holly asked, surprised.

"After my brother convinced the outlaws that he could lead them to places they were unaware of, since he knew the land better than they—that he was as one with the land, as are all Indians—the outlaws saw the benefits of allowing a red man to join them, and they agreed," Winter Raven said, his voice drawn. "Also, my brother had watched the white men and had seen how firewater had made them laugh and joke so freely and he asked for a drink. They gladly gave him his very first taste of firewater."

Winter Raven withdrew his hand from Holly's and raked his long fingers through his thick black hair, pushing it back from his brow. "I do not know if you are aware of this, but alcohol works much more harshly on red men than on whites," he explained. "The red man's tolerance is much different from a white man's. Firewater seems to go directly to a red man's brain the minute it hits his gut, making him become someone different— a stranger, even to his own self."

He doubled one hand into a fist and angrily punched the air. "The white men, the hunger for power, and the firewater led my brother astray!" he cried, his voice filled with hate. "And no matter how much his parents and shaman, and especially his twin, asked him not to do these things, by the time he was seventeen winters, he was gone. He has only come into the village a few times since, his need for family calling him home. But he was quickly gone again. It broke my mother's heart. It brought shame into my father's life to know that he could father a son who had renounced everything he had ever been taught as a child."

Winter Raven sighed deeply as he again took Holly's hand and gazed into her eyes. "But Two Moons is never totally gone from me," he said. "Twins sense things. Often I have felt the stirrings of pain deep inside and known my brother was the cause, that something had just happened to him. I have always feared knowing *what*. One day I know I will experience a pain so deep it could only mean my brother is dying, or dead."

He placed his fingers gently on Holly's shoulders. "Woman, today, while I was in my canoe hurrying back to be with you, I had the same instinct, that things were not right with you," he said softly. "Do you not see the meaning of this? It means that you and I are connected somehow, that it is our destiny to meet. That we are soul mates."

"You couldn't have had time to get to your village before returning here," Holly said, almost to herself, her heart hammering inside her chest. She was held in the spell of his eyes, and by what he had just said to her.

Soul mates?

Destiny?

Oh, truly he was right, for she felt the same connection, the same longing, the same adoration!

"That feeling you had about me?" she asked uneasily. "Did it make you turn back before you were able to warn your people about the wolfers?"

"I was not forced to choose between you and my people," Winter Raven said, smiling at her. "The Great Spirit sent me my friend Fire Eyes. He went on to my village for me and took the message to our people. That enabled me to turn back to come to you."

"I'm glad you didn't have to make a choice," Holly said, reaching out a hand to stroke his cheek. "I am just so very glad that you came when you did. The snakes, they . . ."

With his fingers on her lips, he silenced the words that he did not want to hear. "Speak of it no more," he said, lowering his mouth to hers. "You are safe. We are together. Would you not say that is enough?"

"I would say that it is a miracle that you came when you did," Holly whispered against his lips. "*You* are a miracle. You are . . ."

His lips came down upon hers in a powerful, passionate kiss, acknowledging the love they now both knew was shared.

But Holly wasn't totally transported by the rapture of the moment.

She was thinking of Jake Two Moons.

She couldn't ask Winter Raven to help her find

him. He was hurting too much already because of his brother. But how could she realize her goal without parting from Winter Raven?

With every fiber of her being, she hated thinking about ever saying good-bye to him, even for a short while. And now she knew the foolishness of setting out on her own, alone. She had come close to dying today!

For the moment, she brushed the worrisome thoughts away.

She twined her arm around Winter Raven's neck and enjoyed the feelings that came with being a woman. Never had anything felt as delicious as being kissed and held by this man. For now, he was the center of her universe, he was all that mattered. For now, everything else came second to Winter Raven!

She was hopelessly in love.

15

Hedge-crickets sing, and now with treble soft,
The red-breast whistles from a garden-croft;
And gathering swallows twitter in the skies.
                                    —JOHN KEATS

Rudolph Anderson and Jake Two Moons rode away from the river on their way back to Jake Two Moons' campsite, where they originally had planned to meet and stay the night with their two Indian friends.

Rudolph gazed intently at the renegade. "How could you have allowed yourself to be captured by a *woman*?" he asked, his voice more sarcastic than he wished it to be. "She not only succeeded at disarming you but also had your hands tied."

Jake Two Moons laughed. "That was temporary. Had you not arrived when you did, I soon would have gotten the best of her," he said.

Jake Two Moons paused and frowned, then looked slowly over at Rudolph. "That woman?" he said, his voice dry. "She bragged about being a bounty hunter. Sounds like there are more Wanted posters on me than I realized, if a poster brought her clear from Kansas City."

"It's not good, Jake, that there are so many."

"It is something I have accepted as part of a renegade's life," Jake Two Moons said, idly shrugging. "And you? One day you will also have your likeness on the walls of many sheriff's offices. It's only because you are white that it has not been done sooner. Red skins? White eyes are always anxious to rid their land of red skins, so they display Wanted posters for all to see. But I have successfully eluded those who have come looking for me like that woman bounty hunter."

Jake Two Moons' eyes narrowed. "You claim to be her stepfather," he said, his voice serious. "This Indian knew her true father. It was I who took him away from her."

"What do you mean?" Rudolph asked, imperceptibly moving his hand so that it rested on the pistol holstered at his right hip. "How would you know her father?"

"Her father was a bounty hunter, too," Jake Two Moons explained. "One of the best, I'm told. He was hunting *me*, but things quickly changed so that I was hunting him. I put an end to his bounty-hunting days."

"You're the one who killed him?" Rudolph asked, raising an eyebrow.

Jake Two Moons only gave him a wry smile, then looked quickly away and grew silent. Rudolph had his answer.

Jake Two Moons weighed heavily on Rudolph's mind. If this renegade was as infamous as it now appeared, with Wanted posters all over the country, then he had become nothing but a problem, a liability to Rudolph's future plans. As long as people were actively hunting Jake Two Moons, and Rudolph was associated with him, then Rudolph was also in danger.

He became lost in thought, remembering how he and Jake Two Moons had ridden together some years ago, wreaking havoc across the land. They had gotten separated just outside of Kansas City about a year ago. Jake Two Moons had gone ahead to Montana. Rudolph had settled down for a while in Kansas City, womanizing, gambling, and enjoying a good bed in the town's finest hotel. He had even gone out and bought himself some spiffy new duds, so he'd look like a legitimate man of wealth.

It was then that he had happened upon Holly's mother in a general store. Rudolph had stopped in to buy himself a box of fat cigars. When he saw her standing there, reaching high above her for a bolt of cloth, he thought that he was seeing an angel.

He was attracted to her, and then more attracted to her money when he realized just how wealthy she was.

It had been easy enough to look past her gentle beauty and marry her for her money. He had known that he should not press his luck by staying in Kansas City for much longer. He knew that his reputation would soon catch up with him, and the law would be breathing down his neck.

Shortly after marrying Holly's mother, he began putting strychnine in her food and drink. Although he probably did love her in his own twisted way, he grew impatient while waiting for her to die. He fled to Montana, where he planned to meet up with Jake Two Moons again.

There they combined forces once more and used strychnine to leave a trail of dead wolves and buffalo behind them.

But Rudolph now realized that the time had come for him and Two Moons to part again. This time it would be in a more permanent fashion.

Yes, he thought calculatingly, Jake Two Moons had to die. And not later. Now.

Rudolph had left the wolfers for the night to camp with Jake Two Moons and the two other renegades, but he decided to suggest a different idea instead. He was already working out a cunning plan that would lead to Jake Two Moons' death.

"Let's not go on to the campsite," Rudolph quickly said, drawing Jake Two Moons' eyes to him. "Didn't we just get rid of my stepdaughter? Let's set up camp tonight away from the others to celebrate. Let's do it the way we used to after a successful day of raiding back in Kansas and Missouri."

Rudolph patted his saddlebag. "My friend, I've got some mighty fine rotgut whiskey in this bag," he said generously, chuckling at Jake Two Moons' wide-eyed expression. "Why should we share it with the others? Let's get goddamn drunk, Jake, just the two of us."

"And we can talk over old times," Jake Two Moons said, his eyes on the saddlebag as Rudolph reached inside and slid out a long-necked bottle. He smiled at Rudolph. "*Ho*, yes. Let us make camp alone, friend. We do have reason to celebrate. Today we once again made a great team."

"I'm glad you like the suggestion," Holly's stepfather said, handing the bottle to Jake Two Moons. "There. Drink from the bottle now. I don't see a need in waitin' 'til later."

Rudolph's eyes narrowed. He pulled his horse to a stop next to Jake Two Moons and watched the renegade remove the cork, then tip the bottle up and guzzle great gulps.

This was good, for Rudolph needed to get Jake Two Moons drunk before he could play a final trick on him. He watched and waited until Jake Two Moons pulled the bottle away from his lips. "Tastes good, huh?" he said, taking the bottle when Jake handed it to him.

He only drank a few swallows then offered it to Jake Two Moons again.

"Come on, let's find a campsite," Rudolph said, riding on. Out of the corner of his eye, he saw that Jake kept drinking. Soon the bottle would be empty. Conveniently, Rudolph happened to have another one tucked away in his other saddlebag. But it wouldn't be necessary to waste it on the savage.

They rode for a while longer and then made camp beside a stream, beneath cottonwoods.

As they sat beside the fire, Rudolph was pleased to see that Jake's eyes were hazed over, and that he sat sluggishly on the blanket, his shoulders slumped.

"I've got fresh meat in my bag that I'll prepare for our supper," Rudolph said, now anxious to finalize his plan.

"I'm hungry enough to eat an entire buffalo carcass," Jake Two Moons said, his words slurred. He laughed and took another deep drink from the bottle. "Get it cooking. I'll try and save some space in my belly for the roasted meat."

"Yeah, you do that," Rudolph said, putting the slab of meat over the fire on a makeshift spit made from green branches.

He leaned back on his blanket and pretended to drink from the bottle when Jake handed it to him. Then he gave it back to Jake and waited for the right moment to make his next move.

That came when Jake Two Moons staggered to his feet, his hands fumbling inside his breechclout as he walked away from the fire. "Much too much firewater," he mumbled, zigzagging toward a stand of bushes.

Rudolph waited impatiently for him to get out of sight.

Soon Rudolph could hear Jake Two Moons relieving himself. His heart beat furiously as he hurriedly reached inside his saddlebag and removed a small bottle.

Smiling wickedly, his eyes dancing, Rudolph reached over and sprinkled the strychnine onto the cooking meat.

He returned the empty bottle of poison to his bag only moments before Jake Two Moons came back to the fire.

Rudolph stared at the meat intently, glad when it was cooked enough to eat.

He looked over at Jake Two Moons, who was stretched out on his side facing the fire, asleep, the empty whiskey bottle still clutched in his hand.

Sighing heavily, Rudolph removed the meat from the fire, cut a long strip from it, then reached over and gave the renegade a quick shake.

"Food's done," he said, dangling the juicy piece of meat before Jake's nose.

Jake Two Moons opened his eyes and grabbed the meat, gobbling it down without even sitting up. Rudolph's eyes gleamed.

"More," Jake Two Moons said, his voice a drunken slur. "Give me more, friend." He chuckled as Rudolph handed him another strip of meat. "You should have been a woman. This tastes better than what my mother cooks."

"Eat it up," Rudolph said, glad that Jake Two Moons was too far gone to even notice that Rudolph wasn't enjoying his own cooking. He tried not to stare as Two Moons swallowed one mouthful after another.

Rudolph scarcely breathed as he waited for the poison to do its work, to set in for the kill.

The end would be painfully slow, but it was too late for the renegade to do anything about it.

Rudolph flinched when Jake Two Moons suddenly grabbed at his belly, his eyes wild.

"Rudolph, what did you . . ."

Jake Two Moons tried to get up, but stumbled back down onto his back, writhing, gagging, and digging at his burning belly with his fingers.

Holly's stepfather stood up and nonchalantly took what was his from the camp and loaded it on his steed.

He kicked dirt on the fire to kill its flames so

that no one would be drawn to the site, at least not until the renegade was good and dead. Dead, just like the buffalo, wolves, and people they had shared in killing through the years.

Jake Two Moons stared accusingly at Rudolph through glassy, blood-streaked eyes, but he was too close to death to speak.

Rudolph rode off, laughing.

16

'Tis the witching hour of night,
Orbed is the moon and bright,
And the stars they glisten, glisten,
Seeming with bright eyes to listen—
—JOHN KEATS

While Winter Raven had prepared a fire for the rabbit he had silently killed with his bow and arrow, Holly had bathed in the river. Now, smelling sweet and dressed in clean breeches and shirt, she lay on a blanket not that far from where Winter Raven slept.

They had found a secluded place for their night's camp. A bluff stretched out above them, and a rock formation beneath the bluff in the shape of a three-sided wall enclosed them.

With the river on the fourth side, they felt protected enough. Hardly anyone rode the river in the pitch-black of night.

Holly turned over onto her back and drew a blanket up beneath her chin. She gazed into the dark heavens.

Without a moon, it was a very dark night, almost ominous. Holly could not even see the stars—they were hidden behind thick puffs of black clouds—but occasionally she saw lurid streaks of lightning flash from cloud to cloud.

The thunder was what had awakened her from a deep sleep. Earlier she had eaten her fill of baked rabbit and had fallen asleep very quickly.

She was glad that she could now see tinges of orange along the horizon, for that told her a fresh new day was not far behind.

The black clouds were rolling south now, and the lightning and thunder had ceased.

She knew that today would be much better than yesterday, for today she would not be alone. She would be traveling with Winter Raven.

She did realize how much she needed his protection.

She turned on her side and gazed at Winter Raven. The flames had burned down to low embers and cast a sheen of orange light onto his face as he lay on his side facing the fire.

He had been so quiet since he had been forced to confront the truth about his brother.

When they ate, she had noticed that his eyes looked troubled, almost haunted, as he watched the dancing flames.

When she had followed his gaze and looked into the depths of the fire herself, she had flinched. She thought she saw Jake Two Moons' likeness there, his own eyes equally haunted as he looked back at his brother.

Two shakes of the head had brought Holly back to her senses, and she realized that she had only imagined seeing something in the flames.

She would never forget Jake Two Moons' leering face looking down at her when she was clinging to the tree root above the sleeping snakes.

That was probably why she had just imagined seeing him.

It was hard to forget that she had almost died because of that man.

She tried not to see Jake Two Moons when she looked at Winter Raven. Being twins, they did look alike, but, in truth, everything about them was vastly different. All she had to do to see that difference was look into Winter Raven's eyes. When he was not deep in thought about his brother, there was such a gentleness there, such a caring toward Holly. She marveled that she had ever confused him with his twin.

Even tonight, before they stretched out on their separate blankets, he had held her and spoken soft words into her ear of how much he loved her.

She had wanted him so badly at that moment it had somewhat frightened her, for she had never before hungered for a man.

And she had never, ever, thought about the sexual side of a relationship with a man.

Not until now!

The feeling was so strong in her heart that she knew that if he had asked her, she would have slept with him tonight.

But being the gentleman that he was, and also having so much else on his mind, he had seen her to her blankets and covered her, then had gone on to his own.

Holly truly believed that he had wanted her just as much, but he had shown restraint, and Holly loved him even more intensely for it. She knew that in time they would come together. And when they did, it would be the most wonderful moment of her life.

She sighed and stared into the glowing embers. Earlier, she had worried aloud about how, even though the flames were hidden behind the walls of rock, the smoke of a fire might draw attention their way. He had explained to her that he had used a particular wood that did not give off smoke.

Holly sat up when she saw Winter Raven wince in his sleep as though he had been slapped. Suddenly he sat up, his eyes filled with dread.

She jumped in alarm when he clutched his stomach, groaning. Thinking that he was going to be violently ill, Holly scrambled up from her blankets and went to him.

She knelt beside him and took one of his hands in hers. He looked up at her with a great wildness in his eyes.

"What is it?" she asked, her voice breaking. "Winter Raven, are you ill? Why are you looking at me like that?"

She glanced down at their hands, at the way his fingers had tightened on hers. There was a desperation not only in how he looked at her but also in how he held on to her, as though it was for dear life.

"I dreamed," Winter Raven managed, unsettled by what had come to him in the dream.

He gasped when he felt stabbing pains in the pit of his stomach again, making his dream seem all too real.

"You dreamed?" Holly asked, chills riding her spine. He took his hand from hers and held onto his stomach as though he were in terrible pain. "What did you dream?"

"My dream was filled with my brother, Two Moons," Winter Raven said, fighting the pain. "In my dream my brother was suffering. It was his stomach. He was clutching at his stomach."

"But it was only a dream," Holly said, stunned that he would be this upset.

She was glad when he moved his hand away

from his stomach, and she hoped the pain he had apparently suffered had gone away.

"Dreams tell the Gros Ventres many things," Winter Raven said, leaping to his feet. He looked down at Holly, his jaw tight. "Especially when one twin dreams of the other. Twins feel things others do not feel. One twin is the extension of the other twin. Often when one twin suffers pain, the other feels it."

He stepped away from her and hurried to a place where he could see past the wall of rock. "My brother is in trouble," he said, his voice urgent. "I sense his pain—his danger."

Holly ran to Winter Raven's side. "What are you going to do?" she asked, swallowing hard.

"Search for my brother," Winter Raven answered. "Now."

She started to tell him that she would go with him, and to ask if they should go by horse or by canoe, but he was already running away from her.

Holly was unsure of what to think or how to react to this new side of Winter Raven, which seemed to be guided by superstition. She grabbed her rifle, then broke into a mad run after him.

When she reached his side he did not acknowledge her presence. He was too absorbed in his search. It was as if she was not even there.

Not wanting to lose sight of Winter Raven, even

though she doubted that his dream meant anything at all—it was just that, a *dream*—Holly continued to run with him. When she was out of breath and her side ached from running so long and so fast, she still didn't pause. Not even after they had covered quite a distance, first in one direction and then another.

In his frantic state, Winter Raven obviously had forgotten to worry about coming across the wolfers, so Holly kept her eye out for them and her rifle ready at her side.

She listened intently for rifle fire as they searched. The sun was high enough now for the wolfers to resume their buffalo hunt, if they had not yet killed their quota.

She was glad that she heard nothing but the morning sounds of birds and the quiet thump of Winter Raven's moccasined feet.

Nearing total exhaustion and fearing that she could not go any farther, Holly was about to reach out for Winter Raven's hand. Just when she was going to ask him to allow her to stop and rest, he stopped.

Suddenly.

Shakily.

Holly looked past him and saw what he was staring at in disbelief that quickly changed to horror. Jake Two Moons lay stretched out on his back, his arms desperately reaching out for Winter Raven, his eyes bloodshot and glassy.

She shuddered when she saw that he lay in a pool of vomit, his face pale and his lips swollen.

She stepped out of sight, glad that thus far Jake Two Moons had not seen her. If he did, he might die of fright, thinking he had seen a ghost.

No, she would not make herself known to him and brag about escaping the dreaded snake pit. She saw the importance of letting the brothers say their good-byes without her interference, for it was obvious that Two Moons was dying.

Winter Raven went to his brother and knelt beside him, then picked him up and carried him away.

Tears filled Holly's eyes when she saw how gently Winter Raven lay his brother down on a bed of fresh, green grass. He sat down and cradled his brother's head on his lap, his eyes filled with shock from having found his brother in such a state.

Adoration was also obvious in the play of emotions that ran across Winter Raven's face.

"My brother, I dreamed that you were in trouble," Winter Raven said, fighting back the tears burning in his eyes. "In that dream I felt your pain. What has caused it? What has downed you?"

Two Moons knew that he had only a few more

moments on this earth. The Great Spirit had spared him long enough to make amends with his brother, and he did not want these last minutes to involve talk of who had fed him strychnine, because he did not want his brother to be consumed with the idea of revenge. And a dream had also come to Two Moons, as he had lain there writhing on the ground, in which he saw Rudolph dead.

Two Moons knew from his dream that his murderer was traveling his own last days of life.

That certainty was enough for Two Moons, so he decided not to mention anything about Rudolph or the poison.

"A snake," Two Moons answered, finding the lie easy since it would save his brother undue grief. "Your brother was bitten by a snake. I . . . I found herbs that helped keep me alive until you came for our good-byes. The herbs induced vomiting."

He *had* found herbs, but not those used for lethal snakebites. The herbs he had found had helped delay his death.

But now?

He could die in peace.

His brother had seen him in a dream, and they had been reunited just in time. Two Moons could now feel his life finally slipping away.

He knew that he had the chance to say only a

few more words, and then he would be just a memory. He hoped that he would say the right things.

When Two Moons mentioned the snake, Winter Raven glanced over his shoulder and looked for Holly, suddenly recalling how his brother left her to die in the snake pit.

Winter Raven saw her standing far enough away so that Two Moons could not see her, and he understood.

Now he looked down again at his brother, pushing away thoughts of what he had done to Holly, for at this moment that was not important. The fact that his brother was dying was all that he could think about. They had things to say. He prayed that the Great Spirit would allow them the time it would take to bring them together again in their hearts, so that when Winter Raven thought of Two Moons in the future, he would think of good, gentle things.

"Winter Raven, twin to twin, I willed you to come to me, to find me," Two Moons said with difficulty. He began coughing, as a choking feeling was seizing him deep inside his throat.

His eyes wild, he grabbed Winter Raven desperately by an arm. Tears spilled from both men's eyes as Two Moons apologized for all of the wrong he had done.

"I especially wronged you, my brother," Two

Moons cried, gasping for breath with each word. "I beg your forgiveness. Please tell our people how sorry I am for all the wrong I have done them, and the pain that I have caused them." He gripped Winter Raven's arm even harder. "Mother and Father? Tell them I have never stopped loving them . . . that I am sorry for being a son they could not be proud of."

Two Moons coughed again, his entire body shaking. "Brother, see that I am buried among our ancestors," he pleaded, his voice now scarcely audible. "Please, brother? Please take me home?"

Winter Raven held Two Moons close to his heart as he rocked him. Tears fell from his eyes onto his brother's coal-black hair. "I forgive you everything," he said, stifling a sob. "I have never stopped loving you. Never. Nor has the love of Mother and Father ever truly waned. I will speak for them by saying that they forgive you, and, yes, I will take you home. I will bury you where you will be finally at peace. The part of you that took you down the wrong road also will be finally at rest."

"Thank you. Thank you," Two Moons said. He reached a weak and trembling hand up to Winter Raven's face and tried to smile. His body lurched and then fell silent forever.

Tears filled Holly's eyes as Winter Raven reached beneath his brother and swept him fully into his arms. Winter Raven stood and gazed upward, then began wailing and crying out his despair to the heavens.

Realizing that Two Moons had just died, Holly remained still, allowing Winter Raven's mourning to be private. She could see just how much Winter Raven still loved his brother, even after knowing the worst about him.

Holly watched as Winter Raven quietly laid his brother's body back on the ground, then knelt beside him. She wondered about the small bundle that he untied from his waist and tied around his brother's neck.

He chanted another prayer before going to Holly.

"He is no more," Winter Raven said, drawing her into his arms, gaining strength and comfort from her as she wrapped her arms around him. "My brother is gone from me forever."

"I'm so sorry," Holly murmured. "I can see by your sorrow how much you still loved him."

"Even though we took different roads, our lives have always been linked," Winter Raven said, stepping away from her to turn and stare down at Two Moons' body. "Even in death there is still a part of me that is with my brother, and that will never die."

He gestured toward the bundle that he had tied around his brother's neck. "I have given my brother my medicine bundle," he said. "It contains my 'mystery.' I have given it over to him to carry with him to the Sand Hills, the Gros Ventres' resting place of the dead. The bundle contains the stuffed head and a strip of the feathered skin of a war eagle. With it I have invoked the aid of my medicine. Since my brother strayed, it will help make his entry into the Sand Hills more promising."

Then he turned to Holly and placed his hands gently on her shoulders. "I promised my brother that I would take him home and see that he is buried among our ancestors," he said, his voice calm. "Is that something I can do without your interference?"

"My interference?" Holly gasped. "What do you mean?"

His silence and his intense gaze made her understand what he referred to. She was a bounty hunter who had his brother's likeness on a Wanted poster in her saddlebag. Without asking her permission, he was telling her what he was going to do in the hope that she would not go against him.

"Yes, take him home," she said softly, ashamed that he had felt the need to ask something like this of her. She was touched that he would ask, though, since it proved that he cared deeply enough about her to consider her feelings at such a time as this.

Winter Raven searched her eyes. "Are you saying, my woman, that you will never come and claim his body? That once he is among his people, he can rest for eternity there?"

"I could never do anything so horrible as to take him from you or your people," Holly said, choked with emotion. "Especially not from you, his twin. Not after seeing you with him in such a way. As I watched you together I saw past your brother's troubles. I saw the goodness in your reunion."

"Come with me to my village as I take my brother home," Winter Raven said, taking Holly by surprise. She was stunned that he had such trust in her, that he would ask her to come with him and share these moments.

"I'm not sure if I should."

"I want you with me not only because I love you and need you at a time like this, but also because I fear for your safety," he said. "Your stepfather will kill you if he finds that you have escaped the snake pit."

"I am deeply touched by your concern and love for me," Holly said, glowing inside. "But won't your people see me, a white person, as a threat, as an interference?"

"My people's emotions will be focused on the loss of my brother," Winter Raven said, enveloping her in his arms, holding her dear and close. "Their hearts will be bleeding for him. Your presence there will not be judged, for a lost son will have been returned to them."

"Then, yes, I will go with you," she said, her voice full of emotion. He reached up and placed a hand beneath her chin, bringing her eyes to meet his.

"After all of this is behind us, and I have finished the quest for my father to Spirit Bear Island, I will help you find your stepfather," he said.

"Thank you," she murmured, smiling up at him. "I accept your offer to help me."

He stepped away to gaze at his dead brother once again. "How are you going to take him home?" she asked sadly.

"By travois," Winter Raven answered. "I will make one and we will attach it to your horse. We will get my supplies from the canoe and then ride together on your horse to return the fallen one to his rightful place among my people."

Holly stood quietly watching as Winter Raven fell to his knees beside his brother's body, her eyes widening in wonder when he untied a small buckskin pouch from the waist of his breechclout. He sprinkled sweet sage from the pouch into the palm of his right hand.

After offering the fragrant leaves to the north,

east, south, and west, he dusted them on his body and rubbed vigorously, chanting.

Shortly after that he lifted his brother into his arms.

Holly walked silently beside him as they made their way back to the campsite. The thought of what lay ahead of her—accompanying Winter Raven to his village where she might be greeted with malice because of the color of her skin— made her extremely uneasy.

17

As sometimes in a dead man's face,
To those that watch it more and more,
A likeness, hardly seen before,
Comes out—to some one of his race.
—ALFRED, LORD TENNYSON

Holly's apprehension grew as they rode into the outskirts of Winter Raven's village.

Ahead, she could see what looked like more than two hundred lodges, smoke spiraling lazily from many smoke holes.

Her pulse raced from fear of being in a village of Indians for the very first time. Winter Raven seemed to sense her feelings and reached around her waist and drew her back, closer to him.

"You are with the chief's son," he reassured her. "Because of this, no one will question your presence. My people know that I never do anything that is wrong for myself or them. And soon, after I have completed my father's mission and we return, they will know you as I know you."

"They will?" Holly asked, her heart pounding. She guessed what he might be referring to and thrilled at the very thought of it.

Did he love her so much that he would look past her color and ask her to be his wife?

Was she no longer going to be so alone, forcing herself to find ways to fill her lonely hours?

Was he going to be with her always, giving her love and devotion, and beaming when she gave birth to his children?

She could not believe how such good fortune could find her so quickly, unless it was God watching out for someone who had lost too much already in her young life.

"When we have time alone, I plan to speak from my heart of things that I hope you will want to hear," Winter Raven said, his voice husky. "But for now? There is a sadness that is gripping my very soul. Those many years spent without my twin will forever haunt me."

Holly turned her head to look into his eyes. "Everyone has something that haunts them," she said. "I have lost loved ones without having a chance to say a final good-bye. That is what has drawn me to Montana. I so badly need to find the man who—"

"And you will find him," Winter Raven promised, interrupting her, because they were now riding further into the village where people could see them. Several people inside their lodges drew aside the entrance flaps so that they could take a closer look. "I will help you, as you have come today to help me through my troubled moments. I thank you for this. My heart will never forget."

"I love you," Holly said, smiling at his wide-eyed look of wonder.

She, herself, was in awe of having confessed her feelings to him.

Love.

Yes!

For the first time in her life she was in love.

She reached a hand to his cheek. "Oh, but I do love you," she murmured. "And I am glad that being here for you is of some help. Whatever you wish of me, just ask. I am yours, Winter Raven. All yours."

"And I love you. The love we feel for one another came to us at this time for a reason," he said. "Your God and my Great Spirit got together with a plan for us at a time when we both needed this special love in our lives."

"I am amazed at how it has happened, and I am so thrilled that it has," Holly agreed.

She gave him one last smile, then turned and faced forward as they moved into the center of the village.

Holly became aware of the many people standing at their entranceways, their eyes full of quiet wonder at what they were seeing.

She looked from person to person, glad that

their interest focused on the travois, not on her. As Winter Raven had told her, no one would suspect who it was that he was bringing home to them beneath the blankets on the travois. No one had seen or heard from his brother for many, many years now.

To some, Two Moons would be a total stranger; to the older generation, he would be known as their chief's absent son.

Since she was not the center of attention as she had feared, Holly found herself more relaxed than she had anticipated. At this moment, the fact that she was a white woman who wore the clothes of a man and had ridden into the village with Winter Raven seemed of little importance to anyone.

But when the time came for Winter Raven's people to learn about her relationship with their chief's son, she wondered how they would react.

And she wondered how she would react to being around so many Indians in one place. She had never even met a red man until she had come across Winter Raven caring for the downed bear.

The only connection she had had with Indians before then was her hatred for the unknown renegade who had allegedly taken her father's life.

She had worked hard at accepting that truth. Her father's murder was one of life's mysteries that would never be solved.

"Father, Father!" a child cried out, breaking the silence in the village.

Holly's eyes widened when she saw a young girl running toward Winter Raven, her arms outstretched and her dark eyes filled with excitement.

The young girl shouted the word "Father" again, her eyes glued on Winter Raven. Holly was stunned speechless. This had to be Winter Raven's child, yet he had not told her about having children.

So where was his wife? Holly's mind raced, her heart sinking with the knowledge that she was not the first woman in his life.

But she knew that Winter Raven was a man of honor. He would not bring her to his village, nor would he have told her only moments ago that he loved her, if he had a wife who was still alive.

That had to mean that she was dead, and that his daughter was his, alone!

Holly remained seated as Winter Raven leapt down from the horse and filled his arms with the beautiful girl. She hugged him eagerly as she laughed and cried, her one long braid bouncing as Winter Raven picked her up and held her. She slid her legs around his waist and locked her ankles together behind his back.

Holly felt as though she was in a deep tunnel, hearing the father's and daughter's words as if from far away. She gazed at length at the young girl, who appeared to be about eight or nine years old.

She was a beautiful thing with pleasant features, her thick black hair framing her copper face.

Holly raised an eyebrow as she noticed what the child was wearing. She dressed in fringed breeches and a shirt, like a boy, her moccasins lacking any beadwork.

"Holly?"

Holly was drawn out of her trance when Winter Raven spoke her name.

She turned to him and smiled awkwardly when she saw that he was staring at her questioningly, as was his daughter.

"Holly, this is my daughter, Soft Eyes," Winter Raven said, slowly sliding his daughter back to the ground. "Amidst my troubles I failed to tell you."

"Holly?" Soft Eyes said, watching as her father helped Holly down from her horse. "Father, she is white. Why is a white woman with you?" Then she slowly smiled as she examined Holly with a long look. "She is a woman, yet she prefers the clothes of a man over a dress?"

Holly's face flushed with color, and she was suddenly glad that she still wore a hat, which hid her cropped hair beneath it. If the men's clothes were such an oddity to this young lady, how would she react to short hair?

"She is a beautiful child," Holly said, extending a hand toward Soft Eyes. "I am so glad to meet you."

She wasn't a bit surprised when the child ignored her. Soft Eyes must be realizing that Holly would be with her father only if she meant something to him.

Holly withdrew her hand, and Winter Raven drew her close to talk privately while his daughter watched, her eyes filled with resentment.

"Go with my daughter to my lodge while I tend to the unpleasant task of revealing who lies in the blankets on the travois," he said. He took Holly gently by an arm, led her farther away from Soft Eyes, and stopped.

He glanced over at his daughter, then looked at Holly again. "She does not know anything about Two Moons," he whispered. "She was born after his flight from our people. I have never spoken to her of him. I saw no reason to talk about someone who I was not sure she would ever get to know. And because he was not spoken about in my village, as though he was dead, I thought it best not to have to explain why he had chosen to forget about us."

"And your wife . . . ?" Holly had to ask before leaving him.

"My daughter does not remember her mother. She died shortly after Soft Eyes had learned how to take her first steps," he said sadly. "My wife died trying to give birth to Soft Eyes's sister."

"How terrible," Holly said sincerely. She gazed at Soft Eyes as Winter Raven went to the child and explained that she was to take Holly to his lodge and remain there until he arrived.

"But, Father, who lies on the travois?" Soft Eyes asked, her eyes filled with curiosity. She looked slowly around her, at how everyone awaited knowing.

She glanced at her grandmother's lodge and saw that she was not standing in the doorway as she usually might. She was at her husband's bedside, grieving that his health had worsened overnight.

"It is someone I will tell you about later," Winter Raven answered, placing a finger gently over his daughter's lips when she started to ask more questions.

"Say no more," he said firmly. "Go. Take Holly to my lodge. Food will be brought. See that she is offered as much as she needs to fill her empty stomach. And, Soft Eyes, stay in my lodge until I return to it."

He went back over to Holly, who still stood far enough away that Soft Eyes could not hear them talk.

"Remember that my daughter does not know about my brother, Two Moons," he said, his voice low and measured. "So do not speak of him to her."

"I understand," Holly said, nodding.

"There was no need to fill a young child's heart with feelings about an uncle she might never know," he said.

"I will guard my words very carefully, I promise," Holly reassured.

"Be patient with her, as you are very new to her," Winter Raven advised. "And not only that. You are white."

"Yes, I know that could be a problem all in itself," Holly said.

He wanted to hug her, but with everyone watching, he refrained from doing so.

He took Holly gently by an elbow and ushered her back to Soft Eyes. Then he stepped away and motioned to his daughter. "Take her, Soft Eyes," he said softly. "Make her welcome in my lodge."

Soft Eyes hesitated for only a second, then nodded dutifully and turned to Holly.

Soft Eyes momentarily stared at Holly before taking her hand and walking her away from the solemn crowd.

Winter Raven led the horse with the travois toward his father's tepee. His heart thudded wildly in his chest, more from the prospect of what he would find inside than from what he had to tell his parents.

The fact that his mother had not come out of the lodge to see who had entered the village indicated that she was not leaving his father's bedside. It meant that his father's condition had worsened.

Regret at not having been able to complete the quest yet filled Winter Raven's heart.

But who would have expected to be sidetracked by so many things?

There was the injured bear, which eventually died.

There was the lost cub.

There were the dead wolves downed with strychnine.

There were the wolfers who were slaying buffalo.

And then there was Holly, the one ray of sunshine he had found on his journey of the heart.

He hoped that his daughter would become her normal sweet self once she was alone with Holly. He knew that the child might resent having another woman in her father's life. He wasn't really worried, though, because Holly was the kind of person who brought out the best in people.

Pushing all of these thoughts out of his mind, Winter Raven stepped up in front of his father's lodge and turned to his people. "I will speak first with my mother and father, and then I will come and unwrap the blanket so that you can see who has come home for burial, and, hopefully, for your forgiveness," he said.

His people gathered into a tight semicircle close to him and his brother's body. He nodded silently to them, then pushed aside the entrance flap of his father's lodge and went inside.

He found his mother kneeling on one side of his father's bed, as the shaman knelt on the other, chanting. Winter Raven's heart sank, for now he knew without a doubt that his father's health had worsened.

He prayed that Yellow Knife was strong enough to get past these next moments without dying from shock.

And that he would cling to life a little longer while Winter Raven journeyed to Spirit Bear Island. This time Winter Raven would not be alone. Holly would be with him. Together they would return what belonged to the island and request forgiveness for the ailing Gros Ventres chief.

"Mother?" Winter Raven said, gingerly stepping up behind her and resting a hand on her shoulder. "It is I, Winter Raven. Come, Mother. I have something to tell you."

He thought that it was best to tell her first, and then his father.

When she heard his voice and felt his hand,

Prairie Blossom turned to look up at him, her eyes sorrowful. "We both know why you are home before your journey of the heart is completed," she murmured. "Where is he, my son? Where is your brother's body?"

He was not at all surprised that she knew. His father must have had another dream, this time about one son bringing the other home to their people.

Now Winter Raven understood the need for the shaman and why his mother was so distraught. His father was not closer to death's door. He was grieving, with the shaman's comfort, for a son that he knew he had lost forever.

"He is outside," Winter Raven said, gesturing toward the entrance.

"I will wait here with your father as you reveal your brother's remains to our people," Prairie Blossom said, suffering at not being able to speak her fallen son's name. It was a custom of their people that once a person died, their earthly name died with them. It was taboo to openly speak the name of the dead.

"Winter Raven, once our people know who it is they are to mourn, bring your brother inside to be with his family," Prairie Blossom said, her voice breaking. "In your absence, I will ready your father for his fallen son's arrival."

Winter Raven swept his arms around his

mother and gave her a heartfelt hug. "We had time, Mother," he said, swallowing hard. "We made peace."

"Then the peace was brought home to us in your heart," she said, a sob lodging in her throat. She clung to him harder. "My son, my son, thank you for being good, through and through. I wish that . . ."

He stepped away from her and smiled. "Do not live with regret any longer for what you could not achieve with my brother," he said softly. "Mother, he is home. Before he died, he requested to be brought home. That is all that should matter. He will be resting soon among our ancestors. He will be walking amid them where there is no good or evil. He will be as one with them, as loved as you and I when it is our time to go to the Sand Hills."

"You are so wise, just like your father," Prairie Blossom said. She wiped tears from her eyes. "Please go now, Winter Raven. Prepare our people. I shall prepare your father. Then tomorrow your brother will be laid to rest."

"Mother, I will not be there," Winter Raven said solemnly. "I cannot rest that long before resuming my journey to Spirit Bear Island. So much has stood in the way."

"*Ho*, yes, we know of the buffalo slaughter," she said, shaking her head. "But, my son, Fire

Eyes warned our hunters. They went and stopped the carnage. All of the wolfers died without even one of our warriors' lives taken in the fight."

Winter Raven thought quickly of Holly's stepfather. If the wolfers had been slain, was he among them?

He looked toward the door and wondered about her now, about how she was faring with his daughter.

He gave his mother another hug before stepping outside and kneeling beside the travois. He scarcely breathed as he slowly unwrapped the blankets, exposing his brother's face. He heard a collective gasp as his people realized the fate of one of their chief's sons.

Winter Raven was not surprised when only a few villagers began to wail in mourning. Many resented his brother for what he had become and were not able to forgive him after all.

Winter Raven continued to unwrap his brother's body, and when it was finally free of the blankets, he lifted it up into his arms. He stopped before taking his brother inside to those who could not help but still love him.

Tears threatened as he gazed down at his brother's face that was now still and at peace. "My brother," he whispered, then lifted the body higher for all to see.

"My brother!" he cried out so that everyone

could hear. "My brother has come home! I have brought his plea for forgiveness with him!"

Everyone became quiet and stared at Winter Raven and his brother.

"I forgave him all that was needed to be forgiven," he said, his voice breaking. "So should you all, for he is not only my brother, he is your chief's second son!"

Only a few seemed moved by Winter Raven's words. He lifted his chin proudly and carried his brother's body inside and laid it beside his father's bed.

When his father gazed down at his dead son, the pain that entered his eyes wounded Winter Raven like a knife sinking into his own heart.

He had to look away, but he could not block out the mournful wails that his father was now sending to the heavens for his fallen child.

His mother, then, too, began to openly mourn.

Winter Raven could not bear any more. He left the lodge and ran into the forest.

Falling to his knees, he gazed heavenward. He stretched his hands toward the sky as tears streamed from his eyes. "My brother! Why?" he cried, overwhelmed with despair.

18

You spared me this, like the heart you are,
And filled my empty heart at a word.
If two lives join, there is oft a scar,
They are one and one, with a shadowy third;
One near one is too far.

—ROBERT BROWNING

The silence in Winter Raven's tepee was awkward. Holly was glad that a pot of food had been brought by a woman. Eating the delicious buffalo meat stew gave her something to occupy herself with as she found Winter Raven's daughter silently scrutinizing her.

Holly had taken a good look at Soft Eyes, but when she saw that the child realized that she herself was being studied, Holly had turned her eyes away. She had tried to focus on things in Winter Raven's home instead. Perhaps, if things worked out, one day soon it would also be her home.

The air in the lodge was fragrant from the shrubwood used as fuel on the open fire in the fire pit in the center of the space. She gazed around her, warmed through and through by the tasty stew. Daylight filtered down from the smoke hole above, and Soft Eyes had thrown a few sticks of cottonwood onto the fire, so Holly was able to see things more clearly now.

She saw that the tepee was made from a very fine buffalo hide, painted with pictographs of Indian scenes and events. She could remember having seen similar drawings on the outside of the lodge as well.

She was surprised to find such a spacious interior. Along the sides of the lodge there were robes and blankets that formed couches and sleeping places. In the shadows she could make out Winter Raven's cache of weapons, as well as buckskin bundles, in which she imagined were his clothes and other personal belongings.

The lodge was empty of cooking utensils, which she understood. There was no woman to cook over the cookfire. Food was brought to Winter Raven by the women of the village.

Although she was still not looking at Winter Raven's child, Holly could not keep her mind from drifting back to her, especially after learning about Winter Raven's wife and the way she had died.

Holly had seen no signs that Winter Raven's daughter lived with him. She wondered where she did make her residence, and with whom?

"Who are you?" Soft Eyes blurted out, startling Holly into dropping the wooden spoon into the stew and splashing the rich gravy onto her lap.

Soft Eyes saw what she had caused by her abrupt question. She rushed to Holly with a buckskin cloth and began to sop up the gravy from Holly's breeches. "I am so sorry," she softly apologized. "I did not mean to alarm you."

She cleaned up the rest of the liquid, then knelt before Holly. "But I do want to know why you are with my father," she said. "Why is he so protective of you? How do you know him? He has never mentioned anyone like you to me."

"Anyone like me?" Holly asked, raising an eyebrow.

Then she smiled as she set the half-emptied bowl of stew at her side. "Yes, I imagine I am an oddity to you, especially since I am white and since I arrived at your village with your father."

"I do not see you as an oddity because you are white. I have met whites before," Soft Eyes said. "I do not see you as an oddity at all. I just want to know how you know my father and why he looks at you as though you are something important . . . something special."

Soft Eyes' gaze traveled slowly over Holly, and then she again looked directly into Holly's eyes. "You wear the clothes of a man," she said. "Do you not know how that offends my father? He says women should not wear breeches." She giggled. "He especially wishes that I would not wear them."

"Then why do you?" Holly asked. "Don't you want to please your father?"

She immediately wished that she could take those words back, because she saw that they had made the child's eyes fill with a sudden, challenging anger.

"My father does not approve of my breeches, yet he wants me to be happy, so he does not force me into dresses," Soft Eyes said, her tiny, sweet voice defensive. Her eyes softened again. "Does your father approve or disapprove of you wearing the clothes of a man?"

That question caused Holly to wince involuntarily. When anyone asked about her father, it reminded her all over again that she had lost someone very dear to her.

She lowered her eyes. "My father, he . . . I . . ." she stammered, for how could she explain to this child that she wasn't really sure what had happened to her own father? He could be dead or alive, out there somewhere, perhaps being held prisoner, or unable to remember he had a family.

The more Holly thought of her father's uncertain fate, the more she wanted to believe that he might be alive. But she also knew that it was wrong to try and fool herself like that. He had been gone now for far too long. If he was alive, surely he would have found his way back home by this time.

No. She had to continue trying to convince herself that he was dead. That was the only way she could stay sane, because if she truly believed that he was alive, she would not stop until she had searched every inch of the earth to find him.

"He is dead?" Soft Eyes asked, bringing Holly's attention back to her. "I am sorry. I can tell that you do not wish to speak of your father. It causes such a deep pain to talk of those who have passed on before you."

She ducked her head, swallowed hard, then looked up at Holly again. "I miss having a mother to talk and laugh with," she murmured. "I . . . I have my grandmother. I live with her because my father said it was best that way, so that I could have a woman's guidance. But living with a grandmother is not the same as living with a mother. Grandmother is older. She does not understand me or my friends."

"Yes, I imagine it might seem so," Holly said, secretly glad to discover that she could fill a need in Soft Eyes' life when she became a part of it. Since Holly wore clothes that the girl identified with, it seemed like the start of what might grow into a close relationship.

But Holly would not continue wearing these clothes after she put her bounty-hunting days behind her and became a wife. She would wear dresses. She could only imagine how wonderfully soft a doeskin dress would feel against her skin.

So what Holly had momentarily seen as a golden opportunity for friendship might soon become a point of disagreement between them.

"You never answered my questions about who you are or why you were with my father," Soft Eyes prodded.

"Soft Eyes," Holly said softly. "Your father saved my life."

"My father saved you?" the girl asked, her eyes widening. "How?"

"He saved me from a snake pit," Holly said, stopping with only that brief explanation. To mention how they had first met, when Holly had held Winter Raven at gunpoint, would probably not be a good idea.

And Holly understood that Winter Raven wouldn't want his child to know the full details of why she was in that pit. She couldn't explain without revealing the truth about Winter Raven's brother, and he had made it clear that he did not want his daughter to know that, ever.

It wasn't a lie. Winter Raven had saved her from the pit. And she would forever be grateful!

Soft Eyes scooted closer to Holly. "Tell me," she said, her voice and eyes filled with excitement. "Tell me all about it. I enjoy hearing details of my father's heroism." She smiled radiantly at Holly. "Is not he the most wonderful man? He is everyone's hero."

"Yes, he is a wonderful man," Holly murmured. "He is perhaps the most compassionate, gentle man I have ever known."

"Did you just accidentally fall into the snake pit?" Soft Eyes asked. "Were there very many snakes? What kind were they?"

"Rattlesnakes," Holly said, trembling at the thought of having come so close to dying. "There were many of them. I . . . I fell into the pit, but I was lucky enough to grab onto a thick tree root that grew out of the side of it. I was hanging there, screaming for help, when your father came and found me. He lowered a vine down to me and pulled me up."

"How exciting!" Soft Eyes squealed. "My father saved you! Now I see why he is so protective of you. He does not want anything to happen to you after having saved you once."

Then Soft Eyes became concerned. "But why were you so alone?" she asked softly. "Were you not traveling with others? It is not good for a woman to travel alone in a world of wicked men. My father taught me long ago that there was evil in both white and red men, and that I must not easily trust anyone if I am caught alone while riding my horse or canoeing. But I am only alone for a short time, because I was taught it is better to move in numbers of two or more."

"Your father is a good teacher," Holly said. "But sometimes there comes a point in your life when you have no choice but to be alone. If you have no family, then you are forced to fend for yourself, even if you are a lady."

"And that is why you travel dressed like a man?" Soft Eyes asked, her eyes dancing as she felt herself growing fond of this woman who talked so easily and honestly with her. She could hear the loneliness in the woman's voice, and something inside her made her want to help erase it. Her father must have felt the same, or he would not have Holly with him now.

"Yes, I saw dangers in traveling, otherwise," Holly replied. She reached up and ran her fingers through her hair. Strange how her short hair had not brought comments from the child when she had first removed her hat. She could tell that Soft Eyes had noticed, since she had been glancing at Holly's hair for these past few moments. But she had not said anything.

Holly smiled to herself as she felt the barrier between her and the child slowly dissolving. She could tell that Soft Eyes was growing fond of her and even sympathized with the fact that she was so alone in the world. If Holly was careful about what she said and how she said it, perhaps she could win the girl over. That would make Holly's return to the village much more comfortable.

"Where did you travel from?" Soft Eyes asked. She moved from her knees and settled down on a blanket beside Holly.

"Missouri," Holly said. "Kansas City, Missouri. I traveled here on the Missouri River, by riverboat."

"That is exciting," Soft Eyes said, then frowned. "While traveling alone, has your disguise as a man worked? Have any white men approached you wrongly?"

"Well, a couple of times, but I managed to elude them," Holly said, knowing that was not altogether honest.

"I know white men can be bad, but I also know that they can be very good," Soft Eyes said, smiling at Holly. "There is this one man, he is blind . . ."

Soft Eyes' words trailed off, for a deep instinct directed her not to tell this woman about the special friend to her people. She would eventually tell her, but only after she knew for sure that she could trust Holly with the things that were important to the Gros Ventres village.

The white woman had much to prove first.

Holly noticed that Soft Eyes changed her mind about telling her something, and she took that as a lack of trust. "I have something I want to show you," Holly said, reaching inside her breeches pocket. She fished out her harmonica and laid it in the palm of her right hand. She knew that if anything could help the girl to relax and begin to trust her, this could.

"What is that?" Soft Eyes asked, her eyes riveted on the shiny little object in Holly's hand. "I have never seen anything like that before."

"It makes music," Holly said, glad that she had thought of showing it to Soft Eyes. "Do you want to hear it?"

"*Ho,* yes, please make music for me," Soft Eyes said eagerly, moving to her knees in front of Holly again.

Holly brought the harmonica to her lips and began to play some of the songs that her father had taught her. The melodies brought him close to her heart again, as though he were there, ready to join in with his own harmonica.

She found comfort instead of loneliness in the music and smiled as she watched her rapt audience of one. Holly finally lowered the harmonica from her lips.

"It was beautiful," Soft Eyes murmured. "Something like our flute music, yet much more complicated in its sounds."

"I do love it," Holly said, running her hand slowly over the harmonica. "My father was very skilled at playing it. He taught me."

"Is it easy to learn?" Soft Eyes asked.

Before Holly could answer, Winter Raven entered the lodge.

Holly wanted to run to him and embrace him, to give him comfort, especially when she saw the sorrow in his eyes, but she held back and watched as Soft Eyes went to him and gave him a long hug.

As they were embracing, Winter Raven glanced at Holly over his daughter's shoulder. His eyes spoke of feelings that had been awakened between them, of a love that was and would be real and wonderful.

Holly sighed. Winter Raven took his daughter's hand and led her closer to the fire, where she sat between him and Holly.

"Soft Eyes, there is much I have to tell you," Winter Raven said, having decided to explain everything about his brother. Now that his brother was home to stay and soon would be buried, all of the children of the village would be whispering about him—how he was the son of a chief, how he was the twin of Winter Raven, and how he had shamed his own people by his wicked ways.

Ho, yes, Winter Raven knew that he must explain to the best of his ability about his twin, who had taken the wrong road in life and had died young because of it.

"Sweet daughter, listen well to what I have to say, for once it is said, I will not want to speak of it again, nor will I want you to," Winter Raven said. He turned to Soft Eyes and took both of her hands in his. "Even when children whisper about this among themselves, you must be the brave, proud girl that you have always been and ignore bad things that they say of your uncle, your father's twin brother."

Soft Eyes gasped. Her eyes filled with wonder. "Father, you have never spoken before of a brother." In a rush of words, she asked, "Where is he? Who is he? Why has he not been here to know his niece?"

Winter Raven had expected the questions and had prepared himself well for them, even though his heart lay elsewhere at the moment, back in the lodge where his brother's body was being prepared for burial.

It hurt him that he would not be there for the rites, but his absence was necessary. He knew it was important for him to go to Spirit Bear Island for his father as quickly as possible, for the death of Winter Raven's brother had taken its toll on the old chief. Yellow Knife might not even live long enough for Winter Raven's return.

Winter Raven would leave soon, immediately after he told his daughter not only about her uncle but also about Holly, the woman he wanted for his wife.

"The man I brought today on the travois?" Winter Raven began. "That man was your father's twin."

He found it even harder than he had expected to tell her about the red man who had chosen to live among white outlaws and who had been labeled a renegade, a man who had turned his back on his culture and his people.

"My brother made this choice many moons ago, before you were even born," Winter Raven said softly. "When he left, he did not turn back. The only way I saw him, then, was in my heart. I felt him, also, at times. I seemed to know when he was suffering, one way or another, for I suffered, also. That is the way with twins, especially twins who are brothers."

"How could he do this? How could he leave and never return, except . . . except when he was dead?" Soft Eyes blurted out. "I have known only happiness and goodness among our people. How could he turn his back on that?"

"It was mainly firewater that caused your uncle's behavior," Winter Raven said solemnly. "When a red man becomes hypnotized by firewater's demons, he turns into someone that even he himself no longer knows. In time, my brother ceased to exist as the person he was, as the person who was loved by so many Gros Ventres. Today? When I brought him home? Only a few began mourning for him. It is sad, but it is true."

He said more that he felt was important about his brother and stopped only when he sensed that he had said enough to help his daughter accept the situation.

"I am so sorry, Father," Soft Eyes said, flinging herself into his arms. "I am sorry for you and for Grandmother and Grandfather. And I am so sorry for your brother. His life was a wasted one. Think of the joy he could have felt while sitting around our family's lodge fire, the joy he could have passed on to others if he had clung to the part of him that was good."

"Yes, he was good before he became bad," Winter Raven said, sometimes amazed at how adult his daughter was at her young age of eight. "That he missed knowing you, his niece, is his greatest loss, Soft Eyes. Had he known you, just being in your presence would have made his heart good again."

Soft Eyes sobbed as she clung to her father.

Holly was deeply touched by the sight of the father and child, and by what Winter Raven had said to Soft Eyes about how she could have affected Two Moons' life. It was the kind of thing that a man like Winter Raven *would* say to a daughter he adored.

Winter Raven had proved time and again that he would be a wonderful father of many children, and Holly hoped to make that a reality one day.

"And now, before I must leave again, to journey to Spirit Bear Island for your grandfather, I have something else—someone else—to discuss with you," Winter Raven said. He noticed that at those words Soft Eyes turned to look at Holly.

Soft Eyes eased out of Winter Raven's arms and sat down again between him and Holly, her eyes now on Winter Raven, waiting.

"When I return from my journey, Holly will return with me," Winter Raven said, glad that his daughter did not look horrified by what he had just said.

He reached out and gently cradled his daughter's soft face. "My little one, my precious," he said. "You have been without a mother long enough. If she is willing, this woman with us now, in my lodge, will soon be my wife. You will then have a mother's guidance."

Holly's eyes shone with joy. She nodded, letting him know how happy she was. She could scarcely breathe as she waited for the child's reaction but she was encouraged to see how quietly Soft Eyes seemed to accept Winter Raven's words.

"Father, I . . ." Soft Eyes began, but before she could say any more, Winter Raven placed his fingers over her lips.

"Daughter, sometimes life has its surprises," he said. "Circumstances bring people together as they brought Holly and me together. I want to protect her forever, Soft Eyes. Not just yesterday, when I brought her up from a pit of snakes. Not just now. But forever. And the only way I can do that is to have her with me."

Soft Eyes reached up and slowly took his fingers away from her mouth. "As a wife?" she asked softly.

"*Ho*, yes, as a wife," Winter Raven said, nodding slowly.

Soft Eyes nodded back in understanding.

Taken, heart and soul, by Winter Raven's daughter, Holly could not possibly hold any resentment toward him for having not shared the news that he had a child. She knew that there had been far more important things on his mind since they had met. Holly reached out a hand to Soft Eyes.

"Child, I will need someone to teach me the ways of your people," she said, warming through and through when Soft Eyes slipped a hand in hers. "When your father is away on his duties, will you teach me everything about the Gros Ventres that I do not know?"

"You wish that I would be your teacher?" Soft Eyes asked, her voice filled with excitement.

"Yes, I would like that," Holly said, smiling.

"I would feel all grown-up teaching you," Soft Eyes said, lifting her chin proudly.

"Then you won't mind?" Holly asked, glad that she had thought of this as a way to make Soft Eyes more receptive to her return.

"I will be waiting with an eager heart for you to come back," Soft Eyes said. She smiled. "Will you also be my teacher?"

"Yes, I will, in any way that I can," Holly said, returning Soft Eyes' smile.

"Will you teach me the harmonica?" she asked, with wide eyes.

"I would love to," Holly said, laughing softly as Soft Eyes quickly hugged her.

Then Soft Eyes jumped to her feet. "Can I go and tell my friends everything?" she asked, her eyes pleading with Winter Raven. "Can I, Father?"

Winter Raven reached for Soft Eyes and drew her down onto his lap. "Now is not the time to go and be with your friends," he said. "Curly Hair is coming to stay with you here at my lodge until I return. Your grandmother is too filled with mourning for you to stay at her lodge, and she will not want to discuss anything for a while. Her grief runs deep, even more so because she grieves for a son that she has not seen for many moons."

"Then I cannot talk to Grandmother about you

and Holly?" Soft Eyes asked, glancing over at Holly and timidly smiling.

"Tell no one," Winter Raven instructed. "When I return, we will have council with the whole village, and I will tell everyone at once that I have found a woman who will be my wife and a mother to you, my precious daughter."

"Mother," Soft Eyes said, as though testing the word across her lips.

Holly's breath caught in her throat. It was clear that Soft Eyes had not considered exactly how things were going to be, that she soon would have a mother.

Even Holly was not sure how to accept that, especially since she had not contemplated having an instant family when she had fantasized about marrying Winter Raven.

Yes, they both would have adjustments to make, but she could tell by Soft Eyes' sweet smile that the adjustments would not be too hard. It was a miracle, but Soft Eyes did not seem to resent Holly at all.

"Soft Eyes, go to your grandmother's lodge and get clothes enough for several days," Winter Raven said. "Your grandmother is in the lodge of the old medicine man, the one with mysterious paintings on it, where my brother is being prepared for burial."

He stood up and walked with her to the entrance flap. "I will stay until both you and Curly Hair arrive here, and then Holly and I must be on our way," he said. He reached down and pulled Soft Eyes into his arms again for a big hug.

Holly watched the intense display of love between Winter Raven and his child, then thrilled at how he came to her and drew her to her feet and into his arms after Soft Eyes was gone.

"Holly, when we return from our journey, I will introduce you to my parents as my future wife," he promised. He stepped away to gaze down at her with a keen seriousness in his eyes. "The warriors of my village found the wolfers. The wolfers are now dead."

Holly's heart skipped a beat. "Dead?" she gasped. "Oh, Winter Raven, does that mean that my stepfather is also dead?"

"There is no way to know," he said. "I hope that in time we will have the answer to that question for you."

Suddenly they both grew quiet. A drum began beating, the sound coming from the far side of the village, followed by the high-pitched voice of the shaman singing his medicine song.

"The true mourning for my brother has begun," Winter Raven said. Holly turned and stared at the entrance flap that was slowly swaying back and forth as the wind whistled outside.

A chill ran up and down Holly's spine. She

seemed to feel a presence suddenly all around them, and then it was gone.

She looked quickly at Winter Raven and questioned him with her eyes.

"I, too, felt it," Winter Raven said, swallowing hard. "We were just visited by my brother. He came for a final farewell."

19

O! Let me have thee whole,-all-all-be mine!
That shape, that fairness, that sweet minor zest.
—JOHN KEATS

Winter Raven had chosen to travel by canoe again, so Holly had left her horse in the corral at his village. The two of them traveled on the Missouri until day deepened to sunset and shadows, then stopped and made camp where stately weeping willows stood beside the river, their beautiful swaying branches dancing in the soft breeze.

Winter Raven's canoe, a much larger vessel than the one that he used while traveling alone, was beached close by on a spit of sand.

Winter Raven cooked the wild turkey that he had caught before it grew too dark to hunt, while Holly readied their camp, spreading blankets and taking essentials for their night's lodging from Winter Raven's pack of supplies.

Then before they ate, Holly had a chance to observe another special custom of the Gros Ventres. She watched Winter Raven fill and light his red-stone pipe, offering its stem to the Mysterious Ones after taking three deep draughts from it himself. Once that was done and the pipe was put away, they had eaten.

Holly smiled now as she sat with Winter Raven beside the fire, his arm around her, holding her near. Both were lost in their own thoughts.

Holly was thinking about the way the many women of Winter Raven's village had taken bundles from their lodges and placed them in Winter Raven's canoe for the journey to Spirit Bear Island.

Inside these bundles were supplies taken from the women's own homes, enough staples to get Winter Raven to Spirit Bear Island and back again.

There had even been dried meat among the supplies, but Winter Raven had wanted to prepare something fresh for Holly their first night. He had gone on a brief hunt and soon brought back the gobbler.

Tomorrow, before they resumed their trip, they would have parched corn and dried meat for breakfast.

As for now, Holly's belly was full and warm. And were it not for Winter Raven mourning his brother, Holly would have been content.

She had to believe that her stepfather had died along with the other wolfers. She could take satisfaction in that thought, even though she had not had the opportunity to take him in to the authorities herself, or to be present when the judge handed down a sentence of death. It was enough to believe that Rudolph Anderson would be unable to hurt any more innocent women.

Today, as she and Winter Raven had made their way down the wide avenue of the river, they had not heard any gunfire or bellowing of dying buffalo. And no more wolves would be killed needlessly by those heartless men!

But Holly knew that she and Winter Raven could not totally let down their guard, for danger might lie just around the riverbend. Even though a few evil men had been stopped, there were always more, stalking, killing, taking.

And just in case her father was still alive, Holly would always be on the lookout for him, or for someone who might have news of him.

"A new moon hangs in the western sky," Winter Raven said, drawing Holly away from her deep thoughts. He gestured toward the sky. "And do you see the 'wolf's trail'?"

"I see many beautiful things in the sky tonight," Holly sighed, feeling entranced by the mystical moon and the beautiful twinkling stars. "But I know not of—what did you call it? The 'wolf's trail'?"

"The Milky Way, which stretches so far across the heavens," Winter Raven said, smiling over at Holly. "And do you smell the wonders of the air tonight? Do you smell the mixture of sage and cedar?"

He leaned close to her and brushed a kiss across her cheek. "And you?" he said huskily. "You have the scent of roses on your flesh."

She laughed softly. "I must have the smell of sweat," she said, giving him a quick look through her lashes. "We have yet to bathe tonight."

"*Ho*, yes, a swim in the river with the woman I love is what I need," he said. "And not only to erase the smell of travel. It is something that can help erase the mournful thoughts of my brother that cling to me."

Holly moved onto her knees before him.

Understanding, she framed his face between her hands, drew his lips to hers, and kissed him deeply. She had experienced the same sort of sadness more than once in her life, first from knowing that she would never see her father again, and then from having to bury her sweet, precious mother.

Except for Jana and her husband, Holly hadn't had anyone to help her get through her loss, and she was well aware of the importance of having someone. She was proud that she was the one who would help Winter Raven through the worst of his grief. She was glad that he saw in her a way to get over those first hours of loneliness for a brother he would never see or talk to again.

The fact that he had had no chance to be with his brother through the years should make it easier to get over losing him. Winter Raven must have accepted that loss long ago when he realized that the life Two Moons had chosen to live would make it unlikely that Winter Raven would see him again.

Things were now final. In that, he could have some reprieve from the torture of not knowing where his brother was, with whom, or the sort of activities he was caught up in day by day.

When Winter Raven suddenly swept Holly up into his arms and carried her toward the moon-splashed river, she wrapped an arm around his neck and hung on tight. There had been no time to undress, and though her clothes needed washing anyway, her boots would shrink if they got wet.

"My boots!" she cried, wriggling to reach down and pull them off. "And my harmonica! I don't want to get it wet."

Laughing throatily, Winter Raven stopped and set her on her feet. "*Nah*, no, we cannot get your boots wet," he said teasingly, his eyes twinkling as he watched her sit down to remove them. "But soon you will not have them to worry about when we choose to swim in the river. You will be wearing the moccasins of my people. A little water does not ruin them."

He paused, then said, "You mentioned the harmonica. I listened to you play it before I came into my lodge. It makes beautiful music."

"Thank you," Holly said, smiling up at him. "I believe Soft Eyes enjoyed it also."

Winter Raven knelt beside her. He took her hands from her boot and started to remove it for her, then stopped and stiffened when he heard a movement behind him in the thick brush.

"What is it?" Holly whispered as Winter Raven moved quickly away from her to grab his rifle, which lay beside the fire.

"Did you not hear?" Winter Raven whispered back. Holly jumped to her feet and stood stiffly beside him, her eyes moving slowly from bush to bush. She *did* hear the sound of something stirring.

"Yes, someone is there," Holly said, her heart thumping wildly. She eyed her own rifle, but it was too far away from her to get it.

"Step behind me," Winter Raven said. "Stay there."

"I'm not a coward," Holly whispered back, but she didn't budge. His arm had seemed to turn to steel as he held her behind him.

"Whoever is there, show yourself and come out slow and easy with your hands over your head, or I will begin shooting," Winter Raven warned, now aiming his rifle at the bush.

Holly waited for a shot to ring out, but not from Winter Raven. She was afraid that they had just been cornered and that whoever was hiding behind the bush was simply taking his sweet time to make himself known.

At any moment now a volley of bullets could down Holly and Winter Raven before they even knew who had bested them.

But still no one emerged, nor were any shots fired.

Holly raised an eyebrow. "It must not be human," she said, looking around Winter Raven at the bushes, which still shimmied. "It must be an animal."

Suddenly a white bear cub romped out from behind the bushes and ran over to where the remains of the cooked turkey lay. The cub began feasting as both Holly and Winter Raven watched, their eyes wide, their lips parted in astonishment. They recognized the cub as the one they had been searching for.

"My word!" Holly said. They watched the cub gulp down the last bite, then begin sniffing around in search of more food.

Holly remembered the dried meat in the parfleche bag, which was not that far from her. She crept to the bag, keeping an eye on the cub and hoping not to scare it away. She took out the dried buffalo meat, then walked slowly toward the cub, which turned and stared cautiously at her. Closer to the cub, she knelt and held out the meat toward it.

The cub waddled over to Holly, gazed into her eyes for a long moment, and then ate the meat from her hand until it was gone.

By then, Winter Raven also had a piece to offer the cub. It moved to him, bit off a big chunk, and lay down on its tummy to chew contentedly.

"We've made a friend," Holly said, smiling at Winter Raven. "Isn't it wonderful that he's alive? That he wasn't killed by that dreadful poison?"

"It is a good sign," Winter Raven said, settling down again on the blanket before the fire. His eyes never left the cub, especially when, with much trust, it scrambled onto Holly's lap.

Realizing that the cub had been not only hungry but also tired, Holly cradled it in her arms, stunned speechless that the tiny thing would allow her to actually rock it back and forth.

The cub's eyes closed and its body went limp as it fell into a deep sleep. Holly felt a deep compassion for the animal, which must have been wandering alone until tonight, its mother gone forever.

"It's so sweet," Holly whispered, daring now to stroke the bear's soft white fur. "I so adore him. I wish we could keep him."

"It has its place in life," Winter Raven said. "Its

place is among its own kind. We will take it to Spirit Bear Island. There it can mature into a towering giant of a bear just like its mother and father. This is the least we can do to make up for the wolfers who killed its mother."

"It will be wonderful to see it returned to its own kind," Holly murmured, still stroking the white fur, knowing that she would remember this moment for the rest of her life.

The bear's trust gave her a peaceful feeling, but on the other hand, she was afraid for it if it could trust this easily. If she and Winter Raven didn't manage to take it back where it belonged, where it would be safe from evil white hunters, it might make friends the next time with the wrong person.

"We must get him to the island," Holly said, her smile fading.

Touched by seeing Holly fall so completely under the cub's spell, Winter Raven moved closer to her and kissed her.

Overwhelmed by a sudden passion, Holly gently placed the cub on the blankets beside the fire and moved into Winter Raven's arms. Her head spun with ecstasy as they kissed and held each other. With a questioning look in his dark eyes, Winter Raven stepped away from her and reached out to the buttons of her shirt.

She gazed back at him with wide eyes, knowing that he was hesitating until she gave him her permission to proceed. And wanting him so much that she was dizzy with rapture, she could only nod. Her pulse raced, and she was weak from a building, strange need that she had never felt before.

For a moment, Holly thought about how her relationship with Winter Raven would be considered forbidden. White men deplored the idea of a red man touching a white woman at all, much less making love with her, for through the years there had been many lurid tales of Indians' abducting and raping captive white women.

But Holly knew that those tales were mostly wrong, for she had never met anyone as kind and gentle, as compassionate, as Winter Raven. She had never met a man like him—a man who made her heart sing.

In truth, she could care less what people said about her choice of men. She adored Winter Raven. She would never again love anyone like she loved him.

She did not feel ashamed as she stood before him now, stark naked, while he slid his breechclout down over his hips. It seemed so natural to be here with him like this. And was not this a way for him to forget the traumas of the day? While making love, both of them would be far removed from everything but each other.

Winter Raven tossed his breechclout aside and stood still for a moment as Holly became acquainted with his body. He could tell by the way she looked at him, slowly up and down, that she had never seen a man nude before.

He had to smile when her eyes lingered on his manhood. Little did she know that usually it was not this way. But being so aroused by his love, it was tight and ready for her.

He went to her, lifted her into his arms, and walked slowly into the water. When the water was waist-deep, he turned her so that she was facing him and her legs were around his waist.

First, he only rested his aching manhood against her body, to prepare her for his largeness before he entered her.

Since she was a virgin, he would go slow and easy. He would be gentle and loving, so that when she recalled that first time with him, she would always remember it with love and passion.

"My woman," he whispered against her lips as she twined her arms around his neck.

He kissed her tenderly as he held her close, his hands cradling her buttocks. He was dizzy with desire now that her breasts were snuggled against his chest, the nipples hard and swollen with her building pleasure. He swept his tongue between her lips and rejoiced over how she met his tongue with hers.

He could not help remembering that since his wife's death he had been celibate. But that would soon be a thing of the past, because he had found the one woman who could fill the hollow place in his heart.

Only there was also someone else that he could not help but think about at this moment—his daughter. Could Holly learn to have deep feelings for Soft Eyes? Would his daughter truly accept Holly?

Would his people, as a whole, accept her? After all, she was white!

But the Gros Ventres had learned that not all whites were bad. They had had a kind and gentle blind man living among them now for several moons. That would make it easier for them to accept that their chief's son—the man who would one day soon be chief—had chosen a white woman to be his wife and the mother of his daughter and future children.

"I love you so much," Holly whispered. "My darling, my body aches for you. Please? Please make love with me?"

Forgetting everything else except this moment with the woman who was now all to him, Winter Raven gazed at Holly. The moonlight fell on her face, revealing the intensity of her love for him in her eyes. He was almost certain she had no idea of what to expect next. He wasn't sure if her mother would have prepared her for her first time with a man.

In case she hadn't, he decided to.

"Your body will react in many different ways tonight as we make love," Winter Raven said huskily. "But most of all, you will feel pleasure. After the pain, there is much pleasure. Relax. Let me show you."

Having no idea what he meant about pain being a part of making love, Holly started to ask him more about it, but his mouth came down hard on hers in a deep, passionately hot kiss, causing her head to spin with bliss. She sighed, closed her eyes, and returned the kiss.

Holly almost swooned from the rapture of feeling his heat delving into the folds of her private place, where she ached wonderfully.

As he moved further into her, she gasped with pleasure from the feel of his tightness filling her. Then she was stunned by a sharp pain and drew her lips away from his when he thrust deeper, sending himself completely inside her.

"That was the pain I warned you about," Winter Raven said, his eyes glazed over. "Now feel the pleasure."

He began moving rhythmically inside her, the river water splashing with each of his thrusts, and Holly soon knew what true bliss was.

She closed her eyes and held her head back,

sighing, for she had not been prepared for the intense passion that came with a man joining with a woman in this way. Each stroke seemed to awaken more pleasure within her.

She groaned and felt herself floating as he moved faster, with quicker, surer movements. The euphoria filling her was almost more than she could bear.

Overcome with a feverish heat, Winter Raven was almost beyond coherent thought. He had been without a woman for so long, he had almost forgotten the paradise that came with making love.

Shaken with desire, he found his knees were weak, yet he knew that he must get Holly onto dry land, for he might not be able to hold her up much longer.

A tempest of emotions whirled within him as he pulled himself free and turned her so that he was cradling her in his arms. He carried her, water dripping from their bodies, to the blankets beside the fire.

After he had Holly stretched out on her back, he straddled her and in one deep thrust was inside her again.

A tremor went through Holly's body, and she opened wider to him. Her hips responded in rhythmic accompaniment as he filled her over and over again with his throbbing heat.

She clung to him and rocked with him, his lips now on her breast, his tongue lapping at the nipple.

Then he withdrew from her, and with his tongue, he made a slow, sensuous descent down her body.

She closed her eyes and enjoyed the way her body rippled in response. She slowly tossed her head and moaned softly. When she felt his fingers at the damp valley of her womanhood, then felt the wet, hot tip of his tongue, the awakening sensations were too wonderful to describe.

As he flicked her tender spot with his tongue, then sucked it, the fires within her fanned into a roaring flame.

Then he was stretched out over her again and was thrusting his manhood inside her with deep, quick movements.

His lips came to hers, trembling.

His hands were on her breasts, kneading.

And then their bodies shook and trembled all over.

Their gasps of pleasure filled the night air.

Afterward, they lay in one another's arms, clinging together. "I still feel like I'm floating," Holly whispered to him, as he caressed one of her breasts. "I want to fall asleep like this. Can we? Can I sleep in your arms tonight?"

"I never want to let you go," Winter Raven

said huskily. He turned on his side and faced her, gasping in pleasure when she reached down and slowly massaged him.

Soon her hand fell away, and he saw that she had fallen asleep.

"I must be more careful next time," he whispered, brushing a kiss across her brow. "I have exhausted you."

He reached over and grabbed the end of the blanket and pulled it over them, moving closer to her. He looked at the bear cub as it still lay curled up beneath its own warm blanket, then looked into the fire. If not for his brother's death and his father's failing health, he would be the happiest he had been in many moons. But these concerns were very real, and they held him captive within his heart. He hadn't realized just how tired, how mentally exhausted he was, until he found himself falling quickly into a deep sleep.

Later that night, Holly awakened with a start.

The dream.

She had dreamed about white bears!

There had been many of them and she and Winter Raven had been surrounded by them.

Glad to be awake, her heart still pounding from the scare, Holly gazed over at Winter Raven. He was fast asleep beside her. He looked so peaceful.

She got to her knees, the blanket falling away

from her, then leaned down and kissed Winter Raven on his forehead.

"I love you so much," she whispered. The wind had picked up as she had slept and she became chilled, so she crawled over to her bag and pulled out clean clothes. She slipped into them, then turned to look at the bear cub. Her heart skipped several beats when she saw that it was gone. She swallowed hard and looked desperately around her. Still she did not see it. It must have awakened and wandered off!

She must search for it. She knew that it would not be safe until it was among the other bears on Spirit Bear Island.

She looked at Winter Raven again. He was still asleep, and she knew that he needed to be. He had experienced a very traumatic day. Although making love had seemed to alleviate some of his pain, his despair over losing his brother was still there. He was drained, emotionally as well as physically exhausted, and it would be wrong to awaken him.

"I'll go by myself and find the cub," Holly whispered, stopping only long enough to pull her boots on. Then she grabbed her rifle and left the campsite, her eyes ever searching.

20

What is't but mine own, when I praise thee?
—WILLIAM SHAKESPEARE

As birds chattered overhead and the new morning sun splashed orange along the horizon, Winter Raven stirred in his sleep.

He found himself awakening with a smile on his face, remembering the previous evening, and the way he and Holly had given their hearts and souls to one another.

He could not recall any time with a woman making him feel like Holly did, not even with his beloved wife. Holly's love was special, so sweet, so *ah-pah-nay*, forever!

He hesitated to open his eyes, his mind replaying every nuance of their lovemaking and remembering that his every heartbeat had been quickened by it. He recalled with much adoration how Holly had lifted him from his sorrow, at least for a while.

The image of his brother brought Winter Raven out of his memories of bliss.

He shivered as he thought about how even now his people would be participating in his brother's burial rites. By nightfall his twin would be walking the long road to the Sand Hills. His brother would soon join his ancestors, who always forgave earthly wrongs. He would be embraced and would then forever feel the blessings he apparently never felt while he was alive, even among those who loved him.

"Brother, brother," Winter Raven whispered as he opened his eyes. He forced himself to put Two Moons out of his mind, for he had much traveling to do today in his canoe. And he could hardly wait to fill his arms with his woman before they set out again.

He turned to reach for Holly, who had fallen asleep beside him only a few short hours ago. He would never forget how it had felt to have her snuggled against him, her warm breasts pressed against his chest.

When he saw that she wasn't there, panic washed over him.

Then he smiled, thinking she must have awakened before him, bathed, and then set about preparing their morning meal.

He sat up to watch her, then went cold inside when he saw that she was nowhere in sight. He swept his gaze around the campsite, and he soon realized that her clothes, boots, and even her rifle were gone.

He could not help but think that she must have

had second thoughts about what they did last night, that she even had reconsidered continuing the journey with him. If she had left voluntarily, because she wished to, it could only mean that she no longer wanted to be with him. After having thought about making love with a red man, had she become repulsed by the very idea?

He knew that many white women detested red men and would not even get near them, much less make love with them. Such women had been taught prejudice by their parents, or had heard many lies about the atrocities performed by Indians against white women.

But he knew that white men were just as guilty of such atrocities. He had known of white men who had been hanged for such crimes.

Confused and deeply hurt, Winter Raven couldn't understand how Holly could have turned her back on him so easily after what they had shared, and after she had agreed to be his wife. He rose gloomily from his blankets and went slowly through the ritual of gathering up his belongings so that he could resume his journey.

He had started out alone that first day after he had promised his father that he would go to the island. Being alone now was no different.

He wouldn't allow himself to think about Holly, not ever again. She was someone who did not deserve his thoughts, especially his love. A woman would not get the chance to make a fool of Winter Raven twice!

Then a thought came to him.

He turned on his heel toward the blankets where the cub had been sleeping peacefully when he and Holly had slipped between their own blankets for the night.

The blankets were still there, but the cub was gone.

That made him even more angry, for it was obvious that Holly had grown so attached to the cub she had decided to keep it with her for a pet. She had ignored the importance of returning the cub to Spirit Bear Island.

"I never truly knew her," Winter Raven mumbled as he furiously gathered the blankets and rolled them into a tight ball.

Then he stopped and gazed into the distance, a part of him admitting the possibility that he had jumped to conclusions too soon. What if Holly had left for another reason? What if she hadn't left willingly?

A coldness surged through him at the thought that someone might have come into the camp while Winter Raven slept and taken Holly away.

He bent to his knees and looked for footprints that were not his or Holly's, but he found none.

"No, no one else was here last night," he said aloud, angry once more. He finished gathering up his supplies, took them to his canoe and shoved them into it.

A part of him wanted to go after Holly, to make her tell him why she left, yet the part of him that was filled with pride told him not to. Never again would he trust a woman whose skin was white!

Frowning, he kicked dirt onto the remains of their cook fire, until all color from the embers was gone and no smoke puffed up from the ashes.

He grabbed his rifle, turned to look slowly into the forest one last time, then stomped to the canoe and dropped his rifle inside.

With one shove he had the canoe out into the water.

He pushed it deeper, then boarded it and paddled out to the middle of the river, resuming his travels toward Spirit Bear Island.

"Betrayed," he thought heatedly. "Never have I felt so betrayed."

Well, that was not necessarily true. When his twin had abandoned him for a life of crime, Winter Raven had felt the deep hurt of betrayal. That was, perhaps, even worse. He pulled his paddle through the water with one long stroke, deciding to fill his heart and mind with the chore that lay before him, nothing more.

He would not stop again before he reached Spirit Bear Island, even if that meant that he would have to travel day and night to get there.

He ached now to be home with his father, to sit vigil at his bedside, to be there for him these last days of his life.

He never should have allowed anything but his father to enter his heart, he thought to himself. This was the worst of times to bring a woman into his life. Her leaving had made him realize that, for she had only brought more heartache when he was already far too burdened.

Holly's voice, calling Winter Raven's name from shore, made him stop paddling and look quickly over his shoulder. His eyes widened and his heart pounded like thunder when he saw Holly splash into the water and start toward him, her rifle held high above her head to keep it dry.

"Winter Raven, why are you leaving me?" she cried, stopping when the water reached almost to her chin.

She waved her rifle toward Winter Raven, who was staring strangely at her.

When she had returned to their campsite and found Winter Raven gone, and had seen that his canoe was missing, she had been totally confused.

She couldn't help but think that he had reconsidered wanting her with him.

She was stunned to believe that could be possible. They had come together as though they were one person last night. They had promised each other so many things—a lifetime together.

To have him leave the first moment he saw his chance was too much for her to comprehend.

Had he used her? Did he love women only then to discard them as though they were only worthless trash?

She was not about to let him get away without telling her why he would abandon her in such a way.

And she would not think the worst of him until he had a chance to explain.

Hope sprang forth in Winter Raven's heart. If Holly was there, surely he had misjudged why she had been gone. With his mind and heart already in such turmoil, it had been easy to allow himself to feel betrayed.

The way she was trying to follow him into the water made him realize that, yes, he had been too quick to judge her.

She hadn't intended to stay away. Something had drawn her from their campsite.

Wanting answers, and with Holly in his blood now like a fire that could never be extinguished, Winter Raven knew there was only one thing to do.

Go to her.

Get answers from her.

He turned his canoe in the direction of shore. When he got to Holly, he saw such deep emotion in her eyes that her reasons for leaving his camp did not even matter any longer.

She was there now.

He could see in her eyes that she was still his! He was wrong to have thought that she had left because she did not love him after all.

"Winter Raven, you were leaving me!" Holly cried as tears came to her eyes. "Why would you?"

"I thought you had left for good," he said, resting the paddle in the bottom of the canoe. He put Holly's rifle there also, then brought her out of the water and onto his lap.

"Why would you think that?" Holly asked, wrapping both arms around his neck. Soaking wet, she moved so that she was facing him, her legs straddling his waist. "I love you. How could you doubt that love?"

"I was wrong to," he said, reaching his hands to her face, gently framing it.

"Yes, you were. Very," Holly murmured. Then she lowered her eyes and swallowed hard. "It was because of the cub that I left. When I woke up at daybreak I noticed that it was gone. I started to awaken you, but you were sleeping so soundly I didn't want to disturb you. You have gone through so many trying times of late. I . . . I felt you needed your rest. So I went searching for the cub, alone."

He looked past her toward the shore, his heart sinking when he didn't see the cub. "You did not find it?" he asked.

"Like before, it's as though it has disappeared from the face of the earth," Holly answered. "I'm so afraid for it."

"The Great Spirit has kept the cub safe up to now, and so will He again," Winter Raven said. "And you? Did you not know the dangers of setting out alone? Although the wolfers are gone, there are always white men, and even renegades, journeying through these forests."

"Yes, I know," Holly said. "But I felt safe since I knew you were not that far away. I knew that I could fire my rifle or scream, and you would be there for me."

"And I left in my canoe," Winter Raven said, "blinded by my anger upon finding you gone." He realized that he had almost let Holly down.

"But we are together again," Holly said, leaning into his embrace. She sighed when he wrapped his arms around her. "I feel so safe when I'm with you. I just wish you hadn't doubted me, or my love for you. How could you not know that my love for you is eternal? I could never live without you."

He placed a hand beneath her chin and lifted her eyes to his, then lowered his lips to hers in a long, deep kiss.

"We should go on now, don't you think?" Holly whispered against his lips. "I can take food from the bags for us to eat as we travel."

"Ho, yes, we will go on," he said, smiling as she left his lap and sat on the floor of the canoe behind him to sort through the bags.

She smiled up at him. "Go on," she urged. "Take the canoe out farther and head toward Spirit Bear Island. I know the importance of making good time today. Your father waits with an anxious heart for your return."

He nodded, but before resuming the journey, he wrapped a blanket around Holly's shoulders.

Then he grabbed the paddle and soon had the canoe rushing down the river once more. Since Holly was with him again, he felt his trust in humanity restored, yet a part of him felt sad for the cub. He doubted they would ever see it again, since it was only by chance that they had seen it twice.

Pausing from preparing a breakfast of dried meat and fruits, Holly watched how magnificently Winter Raven's muscles corded with each pull of the paddle through the water. She shivered at the thought of having returned to the campsite any later. She would have missed him. She probably would never have seen him again!

It was hard for her to believe that he could doubt her love so easily, yet she reminded herself that it might be difficult for any red man to trust a white woman that quickly. As a warrior, his instinct was to be wary of others.

Loving him so much, and wanting to prove it again and again to him, she crawled up behind him and snaked her arms around his neck. "I love you so very much," she murmured. "Please never doubt that I do."

He turned to her and rested the paddle long enough to draw her around onto his lap for a kiss.

When the canoe began to drift toward a sand-bar, Holly quickly moved out of his lap. He reached for the paddle and once again guided the craft downriver as she continued preparing their breakfast. She would not allow herself to think of how close she had come to losing him!

21

A birch-bark canoe with paddles,
Rising, sinking on the water,
Dripping, flashing in the sunshine.
—HENRY WADSWORTH LONGFELLOW

Their morning meal of sliced apples and dried buffalo meat was satisfying, and Holly felt comfortably full. Now in dry clothes, she sat with a blanket draped around her shoulders to ward off the chill from the sprays of water created as Winter Raven kept the canoe moving at a steady pace down the river.

Holly had always enjoyed nature while on her outings with her father, and today was a special treat. Always before, she had traveled on horseback. She had been forced to pay more attention to things close by her, to make sure Chocolate didn't trip in a gopher hole or get spooked by some little animal that might run out into his path.

And there was always the tension that went along with traveling on a bounty-hunting expedition, created by never knowing when that outlaw or renegade might be lying in wait to ambush you.

Today, out on the river, Holly realized that she and Winter Raven were targets for any sick person who might enjoy attacking a redskin and his female companion, especially since she was white.

Holly tried to fend off any thoughts about the complications that might come with marrying an Indian. She would stand proudly tall beside Winter Raven and wish shame on anyone who took a prejudicial view of the man she had chosen for a husband.

But she doubted that would happen very often, for after she was married, she would be mingling among white people only when it was necessary to go into a city for supplies. More than likely, her trading could be done at trading posts, and there all sorts of people were known to congregate. She would not look especially unusual in her doeskin dresses and moccasins in that setting.

She glanced down and cringed when she saw her faded denim breeches and shirt and her scuffed boots. More and more, as each day passed with Winter Raven, she craved a more feminine look.

And she would manage it. As soon as their travels were behind them and she could settle down to normal daily activities, after she had become his wife, she might even burn her denims.

Yes, that was what she would do, and she would make sure that Soft Eyes was there to see her do it. She hoped to convince Soft Eyes of just how much prettier she would be if she dressed and behaved like a female.

She wouldn't push her, but would allow the girl to determine when she was ready to be the "lady" that she was expected to be—maybe it would be when she started thinking about a particular boy and how he might feel about seeing her in men's breeches.

"See the buffalo ahead?" Winter Raven said over his shoulder. "It is good to see that the wolfers did not get the chance to harm them."

Holly looked to her left and saw a huge herd of buffalo feasting on bunches of tall green grass. They seemed so docile standing there beneath the sun, so trusting. As their young stayed close beside the females, the males grazed elsewhere.

She was reminded of the terrible buffalo kill she had seen. Surely had it not been for Winter Raven's warriors' stopping any further hunt, Holly would not have had the opportunity to admire the animals before her.

Holly watched as one large bull charged away from the others and ran up the hillside at full gallop. Even from this distance, she could see how his eyes were glittering. His curved black horns were cocked menacingly, and his sharp hoofs hurled divots of dirt into the air.

Holly gasped, for coming from the other side of the hill was another bull, his eyes just as intent, his shaggy fur flying.

"One must have smelled the other," Holly said, dropping her blanket from her shoulders and moving behind Winter Raven for a better look. He rested the paddle and turned sideways to watch the show being acted out before them.

"It will be more a battle of wills than anything else," Winter Raven said, reaching down to take one of Holly's hands gently. "You see, this is their three-month breeding season. The bulls guard their chosen mates very determinedly. Watch. Listen."

Holly winced when the first bull gave a lion-like roar.

"The one bull hopes that his roar is fierce enough to scare off the other," Winter Raven explained, still watching. "But notice how the other bull was not so easily intimidated."

Holly flinched when the first bull, the one that was guarding his mate, suddenly attacked the second bull.

The interloper stood his ground, and when the two bulls hit head-on, their horns made a tremendous clack.

Snorting, they continued horn-wrestling for a

while longer, and then suddenly they broke away from each other. The first bull returned to the herd, as the other one retreated and disappeared over the rise of land.

When Winter Raven rowed a few feet farther ahead, they were able to see the other side of the hill. Even more buffalo grazed there than on the other side.

"There are so many," Holly said, her eyes wide.

"Seeing so many in both places warms my heart," Winter Raven said, gazing proudly at this other herd, which also had not yet come under the gun of the white man. "With so many bulls, there will be many newborn calves. I hope they will be given the chance to grow and become a part of this proud land, to share it with my people, as they have since the beginning of time."

Holly shivered as she thought back to the many buffalo tongues and pelts that she had seen in the boat that day, and then felt ill to her stomach at the memory of her stepfather skinning the hides.

"When the Great Spirit made the buffalo, he put a power in them," Winter Raven said, drawing Holly's thoughts back to the present. "When you eat their meat, that power goes into you. It heals the body and the spirit."

"That is such a beautiful concept," she said, as a small group of bulls caught her eye.

"Look at some of the buffalo and what they

are doing," she said, pointing. "They are hurling themselves flat on one side, then rolling around so strangely."

Winter Raven glanced at the buffalo she was talking about, then smiled at her over his shoulder. He continued to paddle steadily and rhythmically, for he would not stop again until it was time to make camp for the night.

"In the summer, the buffalo shed their winter coats and roll around in shallow prairie depressions," he said. "Those bulls are wallowing and kicking their legs in order to cover their bodies with dust. That will protect their vulnerable hides from biting insects."

He nodded toward a few buffalo that were standing where the grass had been eaten away. "See those?" he said, pointing. "They are purposely stirring up the hard-packed prairie soil with their sharp hoofs, which will allow it to retain moisture and will encourage new grass growth."

"When you look into their faces, you do not see much intelligence, yet in many ways they seem as intelligent as man," Holly murmured.

"It is as all things are," Winter Raven said, smiling as she repositioned herself on the seat and again drew the blanket around her shoulders. "The Great Spirit made each breathing thing with an intelligence all its own, giving each the measure of intelligence it needs to get through its daily life."

"I have marveled at how birds know just when to make their nests in the spring and how they know to feed their hatchlings so devotedly," Holly said. "And I have marveled over how salmon know how to get where they must go to spawn."

"I marvel over how the Great Spirit knows who to bring together to be man and wife, as He has guided you to me," Winter Raven said, his voice full of emotion. "Everything is guided by destiny. Your coming to Montana when you did was written in the stars even before you were a seed planted in your mother's womb."

"You truly believe that all things are planned so far ahead?" Holly asked, stunned to know that his belief was exactly the same as hers. She now understood that the Wanted poster in the sheriff's office with the likeness of Two Moons on it had been placed there for her to find, so that she had a purpose for going to Montana to meet her intended.

"As you live with me, day by day, you will know all of my beliefs, as will I know yours," Winter Raven said. "And these days spent together now were meant to be also, for once we return to my village and my father passes on to the other side, I will be chief, with many duties that will take me from our lodge more often than not. We must cherish these moments alone and have them to think back on when I am in council as chief, meeting with my warriors, and you are in our lodge."

"I will miss you when you are gone, but there always will be the night hours, and what we choose to do with them together," Holly said, envisioning herself sitting beside the night fire, sewing, perhaps, as Winter Raven carved beautiful designs on a new hand-made bow.

And thinking about what came later, when they would be alone in their blankets, caused a sensual thrill to course through her body.

"What were you just thinking that made such a look enter your eyes?" Winter Raven asked lightly, again having glanced at her over his shoulder.

"You and me together in your lodge in our blankets after we have gone to bed for the night," Holly answered, smiling sheepishly. "I thrill even now at the thought of such moments alone with you."

"Soft Eyes will share our lodge with us," Winter Raven said, gauging her reaction. He was glad that she didn't seem resentful about having a ready-made daughter so close at night.

"I want to do everything to make things right for Soft Eyes," Holly said, trying not to worry about how she and Winter Raven could make love with the child sharing the same space.

"You will make a good mother," Winter Raven said, again watching where he was traveling. "And know this, Holly—Soft Eyes will have her own side of the lodge, opposite the fire and our sleeping place. A wall of blankets will separate us."

He smiled at Holly again over his shoulder. "We will be sure Soft Eyes is asleep before we go to our own blankets to make love," he reassured her.

Holly knew that she was blushing, but she didn't care. She sighed contentedly and once again began admiring the landscape and the wonders of God's skills at making it all so beautiful.

The spring moisture had produced a bumper crop of wildflowers. Holly could see a brilliant glow of red and yellow flowers growing along the riverbank. The big white blossoms of beargrass were plentiful too. And then as the canoe continued slicing its way through the water, Holly saw a field of purple asters and a flock of ptarmigan looking like rocks amid the asters.

She gasped at the sight of a rare golden mantle squirrel. Primarily an alpine creature, it had come down from the heights where it usually lived to explore along the river and among the towering white-bark pines that stood majestically away from the other trees.

Holly noticed a beautiful silver-tip grizzly with two small cubs, then laughed softly when the bear became aware of the canoe and its occupants and stood up to challenge them with serious "whoofs."

After a bluff charge, the grizzly bounced out to the river's edge on her stiff front legs and led her cubs quickly into a thick cover of brush.

Seeing the bear reminded Holly of the lost cub. She had not forgotten it, but she had given up on ever finding it again.

She glanced at Winter Raven, who sat quietly as he continued pulling the paddle through the water. She knew that he had to be feeling many things today, many of them sad.

Although their time together was filled with love and laughter, she could tell that he was disguising his deep hurt and still had much to resolve in his mind.

His twin.

His ailing father.

His quest!

She had her own hurts to put behind her, and as each day passed, she felt herself healing.

In time, Winter Raven too would heal. Until then, she would be there for him, to help him.

Now the beginning of a mountain slope came

into view, and on it she saw bighorn sheep and mountain goats grazing. The goats looked solidly muscled, and their kids ran around them, playing innocently as children.

Absorbed by her surroundings, Holly had not realized just how many hours had passed until she observed that the sun was beginning to descend in the sky. Soon they would set up camp and spend another night beneath the moon and the stars.

Here, far away from where the buffalo slaughter had taken place, and with the wolfers no longer a threat, Holly and Winter Raven would not have to be so careful where they made their camp or burned their lodge fire.

But there was a part of her that could not let go of the fear that perhaps her stepfather had eluded the Gros Ventres warriors. Just as with her father, there was no absolute proof that her stepfather had died. A shiver ran down her spine at the possibility that her stepfather was out there, somewhere. Shouldn't she feel safe enough, though, since he thought that *she* was dead?

Unless he had gone back to the pit and found that she wasn't there.

Heaven forbid if he was alive and he had seen that she was also. He would be seeking her this time, instead of her looking for him.

The not knowing created an uneasiness that

she resented with every beat of her heart. This man, this stranger who had duped her mother, might haunt Holly for the rest of her life!

She eyed her rifle contemplatively.

22

Should e'er unhappy love my bosom pain,
O let me think it is not quite in vain
To sigh out sonnets to the midnight air!
                                    —JOHN KEATS

As Winter Raven guided his canoe closer to shore, trying to find the perfect spot for their night's campsite, he was well aware that the wind had suddenly shifted to the north. Nasty weather threatened them like a bad dream.

As the storm rolled in, with looming clouds and bright streaks of lightning, Holly noticed that the forest stretching away from the river was dark and still. The only sound was the drone of the mosquitoes that were circling in a thick patch on the left of the canoe, just above the surface of the water.

She realized that in a matter of moments she and Winter Raven would get drenched unless they found shelter out of the storm.

She squinted into the darkening gloom of early evening and surveyed the land that the canoe was approaching. She had seen occasional log cabins along the river and had noticed that most seemed abandoned. She had assumed they must have been built by hunters who came now and then to hunt in this part of the woods. It was far enough away from the Gros Ventres village for white men to feel safe from Indian surprises.

She prayed that she would spot one of those cabins now. The air was getting cold, and the wind had picked up in speed and ferocity.

When rain began falling in widely spaced drops, tapping her face and shoulders like icy fingers, Holly knew this was just the beginning. Soon torrents of water would be falling from the heavens.

She was glad when Winter Raven jumped out of the canoe and dragged it onto the rocky shore, beaching it just as the river's waves began to lash its sides, threatening to capsize it.

"Come," Winter Raven shouted through the howling wind. He reached for Holly, but she shrugged him away.

"No, I can make it by myself," she cried. "Help me get the supplies instead. If we don't take them with us, we might lose everything. The river might rise enough to wash the canoe away!"

Winter Raven nodded, then took the time to tie one end of the canoe to a low tree limb. After fastening his quiver of arrows to his back and heaving his bow across his shoulder, he joined Holly and filled his arms with blankets and bundles.

Despite their heavy burdens, each of them still managed to carry a rifle in one hand. They struggled on, leaning against the wind that threatened to shove them back into the river. Just as they reached the trees, where the thick canopy of leaves towered above them like huge umbrellas, the rain began in earnest.

"I wish we could find a cave," Holly shouted through the increasing fury of the wind. "Or a ca—"

Just as she started to say "cabin," she actually saw one through a break in the trees a short distance away. She could not believe her eyes.

She also spotted a narrow path leading to the cabin, somewhat overgrown with weeds. Perhaps the cabin had not been used for some time.

"I see it also!" Winter Raven shouted. He, too, suspected that it might be abandoned.

He glanced at Holly and winced when he saw that she was shivering and her lips were turning purple from the cold.

"We will seek shelter in the cabin for the night," he said, nodding toward it. "Follow me. I will go first to make absolutely certain no one is there. There might be another path coming from the opposite direction that someone could use."

Holly nodded eagerly. "Go on," she urged, her teeth chattering. "I will be very close behind you."

She ducked her head to the stinging rain and

stayed right behind Winter Raven. When they approached the cabin and saw no lamplight in the windows or smoke coming from the chimney, they hurried toward the door.

Vines crisscrossed the rain-bleached door. Cobwebs hung from one corner, the raindrops on them sparkling like crystal in the fading evening light.

Winter Raven used the end of his rifle to knock the vines and cobwebs off the door, then lifted the latch and carefully went inside.

Holly soon stood with him in the center of the one-room dwelling, relieved that they were out of the weather. Although it was summer, in Montana a summer rain could feel almost as cold as a winter snowfall.

Holly dropped her supplies and hugged herself, trembling from head to toe. She was glad, though, to see dust and cobwebs everywhere, proving that the cabin was abandoned.

Yes, she felt safe staying the night here.

"I've never been so cold," she said, shivering uncontrollably. "And I've been many places, both winter and summer, while traveling with my father on bounty-hunting expeditions."

As he emptied his own arms of supplies, Winter Raven frowned at her, and she immediately realized why. Mentioning bounty hunting brought his brother to mind.

She remembered that she still had the Wanted poster rolled up in one of her bags. She would soon destroy it, feed it into the fire once one was built in the stone fireplace that covered an entire wall of the cabin.

Winter Raven seemed to check his reaction to what she said, sorry for causing her to feel uncomfortable. He smiled at her, then knelt before the fireplace and began moving the logs that were stacked beside the hearth onto the grate.

"We're so lucky to find this cabin," Holly said, slowly walking around, surveying its contents. "If we had been forced to sleep out in the cold and rain, we'd have probably both ended up with pneumonia."

"The Great Spirit understands the mission I am on and guided us to this shelter," Winter Raven said confidently, reaching for matches that also lay close at hand. "We will be guided on safely to Spirit Bear Island as well."

"How much longer do you think it will take before we get there?" Holly asked. Her eyes wandered around the room, stopping on a painted elk-skin sack that hung from a peg in a corner. She was familiar with such a sack. It was what white trappers called a "possibles an' fixin's bag," in which they carried outdoor cooking supplies and food that could be warmed quickly over a fire.

Suddenly hungry, Holly ran to the bag and took it from the peg. She only half heard Winter Raven when he told her that it would take one more day's travel and they would be at the island. After eagerly untying the fastening thong on the sack, she emptied its contents onto the rickety old kitchen table.

She wasn't all that surprised at what she found, even though it had nothing to do with food. Scattered across the table from the bag was a small brass telescope, a steel for striking fire, gun flints wrapped in buckskin, a small trade mirror, and many buckskin needles stuck in rows in a greased buckskin, as well as sinew thread.

"What have you found?" Winter Raven asked, stepping beside Holly. His fingers went to the various objects, carefully touching one after another.

"I thought it might be food," Holly said, hating it when her stomach growled. "I envisioned peaches, sweet and juicy. But there wasn't any food in the bag, just assorted supplies."

"We still have food enough left over, but what is more important than food right now is getting you out of those wet clothes," he said, already unbuttoning her denim shirt as he urged her closer to the fire.

He removed the shirt and hung it over the back of a chair as she hurried out of her other things.

After they were both wrapped in blankets, holding them together at the throat, and they had eaten from their supply of food, Holly again took the time to look all around the cabin.

The glow from the warm fire cast a soft light on their surroundings. Rusted traps hung from pegs on the wall, and a battered axe leaned against the wall beneath them. Snowshoes hung on another wall, and rolled-up blankets lay under a small bed, the cotton stuffing of its mattress hanging out from several ripped openings. On a shelf on a far wall, she saw various old dishes, cracked and chipped, and a rusted frying pan.

"I wonder who built the cabin and why they abandoned it without taking their supplies," Holly thought aloud. "You can tell that no one has lived here for some time."

"It is a trapper's cabin, that is for certain," Winter Raven said. He frowned as he gazed up at the rusty traps. "And sometimes a trapper's fate is no better than that of the creatures he hunts. The trapper becomes the hunted."

Holly trembled at the thought. Hoping to soften the mood in the cozy cabin again, she reached over to where she had stretched her breeches to warm near the fire, and fished out her harmonica from a pocket.

As she played softly, the magic of the music

filled the small space like some delicious elixir. Winter Raven listened and smiled.

Recalling nights when she had played her harmonica with her father, Holly became filled with melancholia. She could not stop the tears that began spilling from her eyes.

When Winter Raven saw her crying, he reached over and drew her against him. He removed her blanket and covered them both with his own.

Holly played for a while longer, then set the musical instrument aside and turned to Winter Raven.

Their lips met.

Their blanket fell away.

Holly moved onto Winter Raven's lap, facing him. Their kiss deepened and their hearts raced.

His hands moved over her, touching, arousing, stroking, caressing, lifting her on a wave of desire.

With one sweep of his arms, Winter Raven stretched Holly out onto the blanket, then moved over her.

He began touching her again, but this time his movements were slow and deliberate as he sought her sensitive places.

Again his mouth covered hers with passion.

Clinging to him as he surrounded her with his hard, strong arms and pulled her closer to his heat, Holly gave him back his kiss. Bright threads of excitement wove through her heart as she felt one of his knees part her legs. She shuddered when she felt his manhood, thick and ready, against her.

He crushed her to him so hard that she gasped, but the sweet pain of his entrance turned quickly to pleasure. An intense, sensuous joy swept through Holly as she felt the urgency building within her. This time, she knew exactly what lay ahead—a private place of ecstasy where only lovers went together.

Her body was yearning. Her head was beginning to reel as she became further alive. Her blood surged in a wild thrill as she felt his body trembling. She heard his moans of pleasure as his thrusts within her grew more insistent, more demanding.

Winter Raven brushed his lips against the smooth, soft skin of Holly's breasts, then moved his tongue around her nipples, flicking. When he sucked one, he felt Holly draw in her breath sharply and give off a little cry of sweet agony. Then he kissed her lips again, his hands beneath her buttocks, lifting her closer as he glided endlessly deeper into her.

He gave himself over to the sheer rapture, the pleasure spreading through him like heat. Winter Raven held Holly tightly in his arms as he sculpted himself to her moist body.

He groaned against her lips as their bodies jolted and quivered and they became one in their hearts, minds, and souls.

When finally they moved apart, Winter Raven leaned on an elbow to look at Holly. "You—your face, your eyes, your lips—are all a beautiful dream to this warrior who was so alone until you came into his life," he said huskily.

He gently slid fallen locks of her hair back from her brow and then kissed her there. "I love you forever and ever, my woman, my desire," he said.

Holly flung herself into Winter Raven's arms and gave him a thrilling kiss. Their bodies came together once again. Their hearts thundered as once again they became lost to everything but their own private universe.

Outside, the storm was gone. Raindrops fell from the trees like tears. An owl hooted. A loon echoed its quivering song across the river.

And like a huge, winking eye, the moon waxed and waned.

23

The long and level sunbeams
Shot their spears into the forest,
Breaking through its shield of shadows.
    —HENRY WADSWORTH LONGFELLOW

Finally approaching Spirit Bear Island, Holly was awestruck by the beauty of the land. Winter Raven sat quietly as he guided his canoe through the water.

To Holly, everything seemed carved out of another time, so untouched was it by man. The high cliff above her appeared to be lightning-struck, with extensive veins of quartz and feldspar. As the sun peeked out between the clouds, crystal facets on the white veins of the cliff reflected beams of sunlight.

She saw groves of huge spruce growing in the shelter of the towering granite cliffs. A chalk-white beach beckoned ahead, and Holly envisioned herself there with Winter Raven, gathering clams for a chowder.

Then suddenly everything seemed shrouded in mist as Winter Raven turned the canoe sharply to the right and angled through a small inlet that was half hidden from view.

They traveled for some time, slowly, carefully, through the water, and then Holly saw it. The mist cleared, and the island emerged, beautifully green. She gasped at the sight of a grizzly and a white spirit bear fishing for salmon along the sandy white beach. Several black wolves also fished with the bears, side by side.

"This is Spirit Bear Island," Winter Raven said proudly. He rested his paddle on his lap as he, too, watched the bears and wolves feasting together as though they knew not the meaning of the word "enemy."

"As you see, this island also supports a population of wolves," he said.

"But don't wolves usually attack bears?" Holly asked, still amazed at the sight.

"Sometimes creatures learn to live among one another peacefully, sharing the abundance of the land," Winter Raven said.

He turned and gave Holly a serious look. "Too often two-legged animals are far less intelligent in that way than those that walk on four," he said, his voice tight. "When white men came to land of the red man, we welcomed them with peace in our hearts. It was the white man who made enemies first. Their greed for land and animals blinded them to everything else."

"My father was the sort who could have lived among your people with much love in his heart," Holly said, tears filling her eyes at the memory of her father explaining how Indians had been wronged by whites.

Her father *had* sympathized with the plight of the red man. When his bounty hunting had taken him into Indian territory to capture a white man who had been known to heartlessly kill Indians, her father had taken greater satisfaction in bringing in that outlaw than any of the others.

He had told her that in a sense he had helped the red man by ridding them of one more white scoundrel.

"If he was anything like you, I am sure he was a man of good heart," Winter Raven said.

He thought about his own father and why he had come so far from home. He sank his paddle back into the water and quietly sent his canoe in a wide circle around the end of the island. The bears and wolves were too involved in feasting on salmon to be disturbed by humans.

They traveled through mist again as Winter Raven looked for a place to beach the vessel so he could finally achieve his quest. Holly could tell that he was concentrating only on finding the perfect place to go ashore. When they moved out of the mist, shore was just a short distance away, yet Winter Raven still did not beach the canoe.

He was paddling slowly now, his eyes searching, his jaw tight.

Here the river was stained a chestnut color from rich organic matter. Holly could see salmon swimming just beneath the surface. When she looked toward the island and she once again saw bears, she noticed that they were feeding on berries instead of fish.

She jumped with alarm when the bears caught sight of them and quickly stood on their hind legs. A loud roar filled the quiet air, and Winter Raven chose to move on, to find a safer place to stop and leave his offerings to the spirit bears.

Slowly the canoe inched farther away from shore, and Winter Raven began paddling around to another side of the island.

A little farther out, harbor seals were dipping and playing in the clear blue water.

Along the slate-colored shoreline, Holly saw a lone bear. It was a scene of simple elegance. The white bear repeatedly waited, then darted out into the water, but caught no fish.

The bear appeared to be young, possibly female, with a relatively small head on a body seemingly too large. She was fat in this river's season of sea-run fish. There was a slight reddish-brown tinge along the back of the neck, expanding into a partial yoke that ran halfway down the bear's spine. Her mouth was open, and she seemed too relaxed and preoccupied with searching for food to realize that she was being observed.

Winter Raven stopped the canoe and enjoyed the sight of the beautiful she-bear. The lovely animal picked her way across the shore, then dove suddenly into the river and came out chewing a clump of blue mussels. She looked up at Holly and Winter Raven, seaweed hanging from her mouth.

Seemingly unafraid, she ambled slowly away and was soon out of sight in the dark forest.

"That was a spirit bear," Winter Raven said, breaking the silence. He still rested his paddle as he watched where the bear had gone. "The white bears are not albinos, for their eyes are dark. Not all spirit bears are white. A white mother may have three black cubs, or a black mother could have cubs born white, black, and cinnamon. For food they depend on salmon, which thrives only in cool, clean water such as this pristine river valley."

His gaze followed the line of trees. "The island is yet untouched by man," he said. "But I fear that one day timber companies will look north, to the realm of the spirit bear, and realize the riches of the giant spruce, towering red cedar, and ancient western hemlock. I have heard that the undisturbed lowland forests and thickly forested slopes of ancient trees are sought after by timber interests."

"But no timber companies are anywhere near here," Holly said softly. "And this is an island. Certainly no one would go to the trouble of coming this far to take the trees, not while there are others much easier to harvest."

"I see a time when trees will be like the buffalo, soon to be no more," Winter Raven said, then resumed his paddling. "It will not be in our lifetime. But what of our children's? White men are driven by money. They let nothing and no one get in the way of what they call 'progress.'"

"But surely not Spirit Bear Island," Holly said, horrified by the thought that something as beautiful as this island, and what she had witnessed there, might be destroyed for only a few trees. "The bears. This is their haven. Surely no one will come and needlessly kill them."

"What about the spirit bear that we found and tried to keep alive?" Winter Raven said, glancing at her over his shoulder. "Wasn't it downed by a hunter for no reason, leaving its cub without a mother?"

"The cub," Holly said, wincing when she remembered that they had not been able to find it and make sure it was safely brought home to its own kind. "We didn't find the cub. I wonder . . ."

"The cub is still alive," Winter Raven said,

heading toward shore after spotting a place where he saw no animals. "I feel it in my heart. In time it will find its way back home and be catching salmon with its brothers, sisters, and cousins."

Holly said nothing else as Winter Raven ran the canoe onto the rocky shore, beaching it in the shadow of many spruces. After laying his paddle down, he jumped into the water and dragged the canoe more securely onto shore, then reached out a hand to Holly.

"Come with me," he said. "Be with me as I return to the bears what is theirs."

"I feel like I . . . I might be intruding on a time that should be yours, alone," Holly murmured, hesitating.

"What is mine is now yours," Winter Raven said, still extending his hand toward her. "Even times like this that are sacred to my father and me. I will achieve today what my father cannot."

Holly nodded, smiled softly, and took his hand. When she stepped out onto the rocky shore beside him, he drew her into his arms and hugged her for a moment, then backed away from her and reached inside the canoe to remove a parfleche bag.

After pulling open the top, he paused and looked slowly around him, his eyes lingering on the shadows of the forest, where bears might be lurking and watching.

He withdrew a snow-white robe made from a spirit bear pelt and a necklace of bear teeth, both taken from the same animal many moons ago.

After dropping the empty bag back into the canoe, Winter Raven draped the robe over his left arm and carried the necklace in his right hand. He nodded to Holly as he walked slowly up the beach, toward the tree line.

His heart pounded, for he felt a presence and sensed that it was not the bears, themselves, but the Spirit Bear People, who also made their homes on the island.

He could not help but feel that they understood his reason for being there, and that since he and Holly were there to return what belonged there, they would be safe from bear and wolf interference.

Holly's pulse raced as she guardedly watched the dark shadows of the forest for movement. She felt a presence, but still could not see anything. She feared that at any moment wolves or bears would come out of hiding and attack, unless they could somehow sense Winter Raven's reason for coming.

She hoped they understood *her* reason for being there—that she wanted to share her loved one's moment of prayer and plea of forgiveness for his dying father.

It was a mystical moment, one that would stay with her forever.

When Winter Raven stopped and knelt at the fringe of the forest, it was so quiet that Holly felt as though she could hear her own heart beating. She knelt beside him and watched as he gently spread out the robe on thick green grass and placed the necklace atop it.

She shivered at the sudden breeze that swept out of the woods, as though something had heaved a big sigh.

Winter Raven lifted his eyes to the heavens and began a soft prayer of forgiveness, chanting in his own language words that Holly could not understand.

But the peace that came with the prayer touched Holly's inner self, and somehow she knew that Winter Raven's father had just been forgiven of his wrongdoings of so long ago.

She could tell that Winter Raven felt the same. When she looked at him as he reached for her hand and urged her to her feet beside him, she saw a man whose face was almost holy, so at ease and at peace.

"It is done," he said softly. "My father has been forgiven." He swallowed hard and looked into the shadows of the forest. "I do not even have to take the news of this forgiveness home to my father, for I sense that he felt the blessing today the moment that I felt it."

He smiled sadly. "Now, should he die before I return home, I know that he will die in peace," he said. "So shall I accept his death, with the same peace inside my heart. It was written in the stars, this forgiveness, and his death waited for it."

Suddenly he pulled Holly into his arms. His embrace was not a desperate one, yet she sensed something different about it. She was with a man who had just experienced a heavy weight being lifted from his soul.

She was so glad, so grateful, that she had been given the opportunity to be there with him as he found peace and gave it back to his father, who had not known such serenity since the day he had wronged the spirit bear.

"We can go home now," Winter Raven whispered into Holly's ear, as his hand gently stroked her back. "We are free now to become man and wife."

At a rustling sound on the right, where the beach reached out into the forest, Winter Raven and Holly stepped slowly away from one another.

What they saw made them both gasp, for standing tall and proud was what appeared to be a white bear, larger than what could be real. It was not clearly defined, as though it was a part of a cloudy mist.

Holly and Winter Raven knew that, for the moment, they were being visited by the very spirit bear that had died by Yellow Knife's arrow.

They stood quietly as the bear fell down on all fours and sauntered over to the robe and necklace, its huge body swaying with each step.

Holly felt faint as she watched something so unbelievable it could not be happening. As though becoming one with the objects, the bear and the robe and necklace suddenly vanished into the mist.

"Did we truly see that?" Holly wondered in disbelief, still staring at the place where Winter Raven had left the robe and necklace and where he had prayed. She saw nothing now but the imprint of the objects in the sand.

Winter Raven, somewhat shaken by the experience, stared for a moment longer, then smiled.

"Now it is truly finished," he said, easing Holly fully into his arms and carrying her toward the canoe. "My woman, now we can truly return home."

Holly wrapped an arm around his neck and leaned her cheek against his chest. "My darling," she murmured. "Thank you so much for allowing me to share these moments with you. I shall never forget them."

"When we are old and have grandchildren to tell stories to, we shall share with them the mystery of today," he said. "As we tell it, we shall make it so real to them, they will feel as though they were with us, touched by the miracle of the moment."

"Grandchildren?" Holly said, leaning away from him to smile up at him. "That's so far into the future."

"Time passes quickly," Winter Raven said as they reached the canoe. "The future is always a part of now."

"I want now to last forever," Holly said, sighing. Their eyes met and held.

"If it did, there would be no children for us to gloat over." Winter Raven brushed a kiss across her lips. "Let us go now and find a place to camp. Perhaps the seed of our first child will be planted tonight."

Holly smiled, then melted when he kissed her again. He set her down in the canoe, and they were soon paddling away from Spirit Bear Island.

When Holly turned to take a last look, she found that the island was gone. All that she could see was the same low-hanging mist that had shrouded the land when they arrived. She had to wonder if the mist was not mist at all, but ghosts of past bears keeping guard on the home of their ancestors instead. She shivered as she only now realized the true honor of having been allowed to go to the island, to even set foot on its shore.

Smiling, she moved to her knees and made her way to where Winter Raven sat drawing the paddle rhythmically through the water.

She twined her arms around his waist, yet said nothing, enjoying the knowledge that with him, all things were surely possible!

24

The look of love alarms
Because 'tis fill'd with fire,
But the look of soft deceit
Shall win the lover's hire.
—WILLIAM BLAKE

One more night and day of travel and Winter Raven would be home, to report the success of his quest to his father.

Tonight he had found a special place to camp, where a waterfall cascaded into a cathedral of a valley.

He was sitting beside the campfire, the waterfall's music echoing all around him as he watched Holly making something that she said was a special surprise.

Holly glanced over at Winter Raven while she worked. Until now, on this journey of the heart, too many things had demanded their attention and she had not been able to take the time to make bread. They would eat it with the rabbit meat that was cooking slowly over the campfire. Soon the wondrous aroma of the bread would fill the night air with its sweetness, making it hard to wait until it would finally be ready to eat.

"You are very intent on what you are doing," Winter Raven said, breaking the silence.

"This is the first time I've made this, so I must concentrate on each step," Holly said, giving Winter Raven another quick glance. "I brought the supplies needed for the bread, because I hoped that I would have time to prepare it. It was my mother's specialty while we were with my father on his expeditions. Nothing can compare with the smell of bread cooking over an open fire."

Winter Raven chuckled. "Nothing?" he said, noting how that made Holly blush. Although she had made love with him more than once, it seemed that any reference to it brought out the shy side of her nature.

That was one more reason why he loved her—the innocence that he saw in her. When he had first seen her, she had stood aiming a rifle at him, and he had thought she must be a person with a hard heart who saw the world in a far different light than he did.

It had been good to discover just how wrong he was about that. Once he saw the genuineness about her, he realized that she was not only beautiful but also innocent and vulnerable. He had vowed that nothing would ever harm her again, mentally or physically, not so long as he had breath in his lungs.

"Well, as far as food goes, nothing can compare with bread cooked over an open fire," Holly said, laughing softly.

She gazed at him for a moment longer, now wondering why she had taken the time to make this bread, when she could have been spending it doing other wonderful things, like . . . making love.

She and Winter Raven both smelled clean and fresh from their bath in the river. She had changed into a clean pair of breeches and shirt and was barefoot as she sat close to the fire. Her hair framed her face in tight wet ringlets, and she could see that it was finally beginning to grow out, somewhat. She knew that until her hair was its usual length, everyone would have cause to stare and wonder about it.

"Let's see now," she murmured, forcing herself to concentrate once again on what she was preparing.

From one of her travel bags, she had fished out a little sack of flour and a small frying pan. She had put some flour in the pan, poured water in it, and added baking powder and salt. Now she raked out a lot of coals from the campfire, on which she placed the frying pan at an angle, propping it up with a stick so the heat would strike the bread from both sides.

When the bread was done, they would eat it with the prepared meat, dried corn, and apple slices.

"Bread baked in this way is sweet and satisfying," she said, again glancing over at Winter Raven. "If I didn't have a frying pan, the dough could be twisted around a green stick and baked by pushing the end of the stick in the ground near the fire."

As the bread cooked, Holly wiped flour from her hands on the thick green grass at her side. Then she went and sat down on the blanket beside Winter Raven. She sighed contentedly as he put an arm around her waist and drew her close.

She gazed into the fire, watching the flames lapping around a log, then looked out toward the river. The moon was high and reflected into the swirling pools that splashed down from the waterfall.

She saw a different sort of movement in the water, her eyes widening as she recognized beavers at play not that far from the shoreline.

"Just look at those cute things," Holly said, pointing at the animals.

In the moonlight she could see their dark noses pointing swiftly up and down the river, leaving a V-shaped wake behind them.

It was almost as exhilarating as earlier today, when she had seen the dark bodies of buffalo moving in clusters along the land.

A shiver of dread rode Holly's spine, and the moment of wondrous peace was disturbed. Thinking of having seen the buffalo brought something else to mind—someone.

Her stepfather!

If only she knew his true fate.

Until she knew, she couldn't completely relax, especially when she was out in the open, sitting beside a campfire. Although Winter Raven was with her and had vowed to keep her safe, she knew that her stepfather could sneak up on them and kill them at any time. It unnerved her greatly.

She looked quickly toward the darkness of the forest behind her when she thought she heard something in the brush. She laughed to see that it was only a beaver that had ambled out of the water.

"You suddenly seem tense," Winter Raven said, having noticed Holly's reaction.

"I was just thinking about my stepfather when I heard a noise," she explained. She turned and looked into Winter Raven's dark, magnetic eyes. "But it was only a beaver that got separated from the others."

"I have something to show you that might take your mind off things that trouble you," Winter

Raven said, reaching for one of his parfleche bags. "Watch now. I will bring out special rocks that I carry with me."

Holly turned to face him as he began taking beautiful colored rocks the size of marbles out of his bag. There were seven of them, and each was of a different color—white, red, yellow, black, blue, green, and brown. He placed these rocks in a row between them, so that they both were facing them.

"Do the rocks represent something?" Holly asked, raising an eyebrow curiously. "Are they important somehow?"

"*Ho*, yes, they are important, and I shall explain why," Winter Raven said, slowly sliding them until they were equally apart from each other.

"Each of these stones represents the Rock People," he said. "To the red man, rocks used to be living things. They gave their lives so that Indians could live. Watch now what I do to them."

Holly's eyes widened as he took more things from his bag.

"I will *smudge* them, which means to bless every one of with sage, sweet grass, and tobacco," he said, doing so as he spoke. "Then one by one, I will hold the rocks in my hand. When I was a young boy learning the traditions of my people, the rocks spoke to me in a vision and told me the meanings of their particular colors.

"Hold out your hand," Winter Raven said. When she did so, he placed the white rock in it. "The White Rock People are courageous and have great endurance."

He replaced the white rock with the red one. "The Red Rock People are peaceful and soft-spoken," he patiently explained.

He continued exchanging one rock for another in Holly's hand, relating the meaning of each. The Yellow Rock People had a gift for physical healing, while the Black Rock People had great strength. The protectors who watched over everyone were the Blue Rock People. The Green Rock People enjoyed life and the beauty that surrounded them, and the Brown Rock People believed in the truth and saw the truth in all things.

"We all have these powers, even you, because you are my chosen woman," Winter Raven said, returning the rocks to the bag.

"All of my life I have been drawn to rocks, admiring them and their different shapes and colors," Holly said, surprised to know that they had such meaning. "Do you think that way back then, when I was a small child collecting rocks in jars, it was an omen of things to come? Of you and me meeting and falling in love?"

"All of life has its mysteries," Winter Raven

said, drawing her near to sit beside him. "But one true fact is that, from the beginning of time, you were meant to be my wife." He smiled at her as she gazed at him lovingly. "We have many blessings to prove it. I felt it at Spirit Bear Island, and I feel it now in the presence of the Rock People."

She snuggled closer and gazed into the flames of the fire. "I wish tonight would never end," she murmured. "It's wonderful to be here with you, alone. Tomorrow things will be very different. When we arrive at your village . . ."

"*Ho*, yes, tomorrow we return to the real world," Winter Raven admitted. "My father might have already started the long road to his afterlife."

"I hope not," Holly said. "I know how it leaves a gap in your heart if you are denied saying goodbye to a loved one, especially a father."

Suddenly the night air was filled with a coyote howling as it prowled the deep shadows of the forest. Another coyote returned the first one's cry with its *ki-hi*-ing.

"Hold me closer," Holly said, glad when Winter Raven reached for a blanket and wrapped it around her shoulders before drawing her more closely to him.

Silence fell between them as they listened to the night sounds and absorbed the tantalizing aroma of the bread and meat. Except for the music of the waterfall, it was serenely quiet again.

"I want to find a way to keep this moment and take it home with me," Holly said, giggling as she looked into Winter Raven's eyes. He smiled at her comment. "Wouldn't you like a piece of this moment each and every night?"

"Each night we are together we make new special moments," Winter Raven said. As if to prove it, he placed a finger beneath her chin and brought her lips to meet his.

Holly wrapped her arms around his neck and was lost in the ecstasy of his kiss. She could not help but think that at this moment nothing could ruin what they were sharing.

Nothing!

No one.

25

Not that I bid you spare her the pain,
Let death be felt and the proof remain;
Brand, burn up, bite into its grace!
—ROBERT BROWNING

Limping, his left arm dangling from having been yanked out of the socket by a blow from a warrior's club, Rudolph Anderson stumbled through the darkness of the forest.

He had stopped for the night in a hidden cove, but had been awakened by coyotes. Afraid that they were lurking in the dark in search of a meal, and knowing that he was vulnerable without a firearm for protection, he had decided to travel on tonight until he couldn't make it any further.

After the Gros Ventres' attack on the wolfers, he had played 'possum to make the warriors believe that he was dead. He had been the sole survivor of the Indian raid. Since that damnable day, Rudolph had wandered aimlessly in the forest, hoping to come across someone who might take pity on him and give him food and a blanket. Thus far, he had not found anyone.

And he had not been able to travel openly beside the river, afraid that a Gros Ventres warrior might ride by in a canoe and see him. The Indian would know that he had duped them into believing he was dead and would make sure this time that he was.

"I don't know how much longer I can last," Rudolph whispered to himself, his tongue like lead from thirst, his stomach gnawingly empty. He had survived on river water, berries, and roots that he had learned were nourishing from his relationship with Jake Two Moons.

Hearing the splash of a waterfall somewhere ahead made Rudolph's heart race. He had found waterfalls beneficial before for more than one reason. Usually there were caves behind them, and there he could make camp and even build a fire without worrying about being detected by redskins passing by.

Inside many of the caves he had found various mushrooms growing along the walls, which could be cooked with whatever small varmint he might catch on the tip of a sharpened stick. Even a baked mouse would taste good to him now, or perhaps a chipmunk or two.

Anything to stop this terrible gnawing. He could set up housekeeping in the cave until he got his strength back, and then he would make his way toward Three Forks, where he had left his personal belongings at the town's only hotel, including the remainder of the money that he had stolen from Holly and her mother.

His eyes gleamed, and he chuckled to himself as he recalled the last time he had seen Holly. He would have loved to watch her among the snakes, to see how frantically she would try to get them off her before she succumbed.

"For certain, she's outta my life for good," Rudolph said, sighing heavily as he found it harder and harder to take each step.

Then he stopped—and not because he couldn't walk any longer. It was the scent of meat and bread cooking somewhere up ahead that made his mouth begin to water.

"Surely the strangers will share with me, especially when they see that I'm almost on my last legs," he thought aloud.

He doubted that those who were cooking were redskins, since the bread smelled too much like what white women made.

He even recalled Holly's mother making it for supper, but not over an outdoor open fire. She used to make two huge loaves of bread at a time in her oven. He had enjoyed eating the fresh bread with gobs of butter and sticky, delicious honey.

Knowing that he was only making himself more hungry by thinking about such things, he forced himself to concentrate on walking to the campsite.

His pulse raced when he saw the glow of fire through the trees a short distance away. His knees almost buckled from excitement at being so close to humanity and food. He had never felt as alone as these past days after almost losing his life at the hands of those redskins.

If he ever had the chance, he would make them pay.

Once he had his strength back and made it to Three Forks, he would go to the sheriff and report the massacre. He would ride with the sheriff to the Gros Ventres village and laugh as he watched the warriors being arrested. He would tie the knot on their nooses, if he could, and laugh as each of the guilty redskins died. Why, he would even dance on their graves!

Realizing that it was best to take a close look at who was making camp before openly approaching them, he tensed up and walked stealthily closer to the fire's glow. He hunkered down behind bushes and studied the figures sitting on blankets beside the fire. His heart leapt into his throat, and everything within him went cold when he saw who it was.

"Holly?" he whispered harshly, in his mind's eye again seeing her as she dangled above the snake pit.

"Two Moons?" he choked out, confused that

he recognized the Indian. "How can it be? I left you dying from strychnine poison."

He wiped at his eyes with his fists. "Am I hallucinating?" he groaned, wondering if the lack of food and sleep was catching up to him.

Everything within him seemed to go numb and he turned with a start when he heard a noise behind him—a deep, low, threatening growl!

His eyes widened in disbelief and he swallowed hard. A great white bear with only three paws stood on its two hind legs, its teeth bared, ready to attack.

In a flash, Rudolph recalled another white bear, one that had threatened him not long ago as he rested from hunting. He had been bent over to get a drink of water from the river when the bear had come up behind him.

He managed to get the best of the beast and shoot it, but he had not bothered to take its hide. The wolfers were yelling for him to get back to the job at hand, so he had left the bloodied bear to die by the river.

But now he had no weapon! This bear was going to get the best of him.

"No, please," Rudolph begged in a strained whisper. He let out a loud scream of pain when the bear took one swipe with its good front paw and ripped open the side of his face.

Rudolph tumbled to the ground on his knees, his eyes pleading.

The bear emitted another loud growl before taking a fierce swipe at Rudolph, knocking him over onto his side. Then it settled down beside a berry bush and began its nightly feast.

Holly and Winter Raven had leapt to their feet at the sound of the first growl, followed closely by a scream of torment. Shocked, they listened intently. After a second scream, there was silence.

"Someone has been attacked by a bear," Holly cried as Winter Raven grabbed his rifle. "Who would be this close to us?" Her eyes filled with terror. "And where is the bear? Will it attack us? Will we be forced to kill it?"

"Come with me," Winter Raven whispered, indicating that they must move quietly.

Anxious not to be left alone, Holly nodded. She grabbed her rifle and walked with Winter Raven, stealthily and carefully, through the moon-splashed night until they found the person who had been attacked.

It was a man. He was still alive and writhing on the ground, moaning. The moon revealed his bloodied face, ripped open on both sides.

"Keep watch," Winter Raven instructed as he knelt beside the man. His face was unrecognizable. "Where is the bear? Why did it attack you?"

When Rudolph began trying to talk, Holly recognized his voice at once.

"Rudolph?" she said, stunned. She quickly knelt on his other side. "God. Rudolph? Is that you?"

"Damn it, Holly, how did you escape the snake . . . pit?" Rudolph gulped, getting weaker and more light-headed by the minute. The pain seemed numbed now. It was as though the good Lord above had granted him some mercy, even though Rudolph knew he didn't deserve any.

"Jake Two Moons, how did *you* survive?" he asked, his words becoming difficult to understand.

"This is . . . ?" Winter Raven started to ask, looking at Holly in disbelief.

"Yes. It's my stepfather," she said, her voice hollow. "He must have you confused with your brother."

"The bear," Rudolph rasped, raising a trembling hand to point. "It was a huge . . . white bear . . . only three paws. It . . . it . . ."

Rudolph's body trembled violently, and then his eyes stared straight ahead in a mask of death.

"He's dead," Holly said, shivering uncontrollably.

"Did you hear what he said about the bear?" Winter Raven whispered, slowly moving to his feet, his eyes searching around him. "The bear was white. It had three paws."

Holly moved to her feet beside him. She jumped with a start when suddenly a white bear cub bounded out into the open. It seemed to recognize Holly and Winter Raven, for it went straight to them and rubbed up against their legs.

"It's the lost cub," Holly gushed, kneeling and drawing it into her arms.

"Holly, do not trust so easily," Winter Raven warned, holding his rifle ready should the larger bear decide to attack again.

"I see him!" Holly pointed through a break in the trees at a large bear resting on the ground. It was licking blood from its paw, its eyes trustingly on Holly and Winter Raven. "That must be the cub's father, since the bear in the cave was its mother," she said.

Holly sighed when the cub reached up and began licking her face lovingly. She momentarily forgot the horror of her stepfather's death.

Winter Raven still didn't let down his guard. He kept his eyes on the papa bear as the cub romped over to him. He held his firearm steady until the two bears disappeared from view into the thick blackness of the forest.

"That bear with three paws was the cub in your father's dream, all grown up now," Holly said, "wasn't it?" She moved to Winter Raven's side.

"Although old, it is still alive and surely it has fathered many cubs by now."

"I can go to my father and share this news with a happy heart," Winter Raven said. "Hearing that the cub he wounded is still alive, and has grown up into a proud father bear, will give my chief much peace on his road to the hereafter."

Holly turned and stared down at Rudolph. "What a terrible way to die," she said. "Yet he died a far less painful death than my mother, whom he slowly poisoned."

"Her death has now been avenged," Winter Raven said, "and so has my brother's." He put an arm around Holly's waist, leading her away from the body. "Now let us break camp and move away from this unhappy place."

"I'm suddenly not so hungry for the bread," Holly said, smiling weakly at Winter Raven. "I'll make it again after we're home and all of this is behind us."

"I will make life good for you, so good that all of this ugliness will be erased," Winter Raven promised, stopping to draw her into his arms. He gave her a soft kiss. Then he went to bury Rudolph's body while Holly gathered their supplies.

After the fire was covered with dirt and the glowing embers were extinguished, they went to the canoe, loaded it, then headed homeward on the moon-splashed Missouri River.

"I wonder if we'll ever see the cub again?" Holly mused, looking over her shoulder toward the place where they had last seen the bears.

"No," Winter Raven said matter-of-factly. "The three-footed bear and the cub are also on their way home, to be among their own kind, where peace and love awaits them on Spirit Bear Island."

"I'm so glad the cub is all right," Holly sighed, feeling that tonight was the beginning of all of her tomorrows. The man she had followed to Montana was dead and no danger to anyone any longer.

She looked over her shoulder again. "Thank you," she whispered to the white spirit bear. "And keep that sweet cub safe, do you hear?"

26

All evil thoughts and deeds,
Anger, and lust, and pride;
The foulest, rankest weeds,
That choke Life's groaning tide!
—HENRY WADSWORTH LONGFELLOW

Long before Winter Raven and Holly reached the riverbank close by his village, the chanting and singing came to them.

The air was pulsating with the sounds of mourning, forcing Winter Raven to draw from deep within himself the courage that he would need to get through the next hours. He knew that his father had died. Winter Raven had not made it home in time to give his father all of the good news or to say a final good-bye.

Holly realized what was going on without him telling her, for nothing could sound as mournful as what she heard coming from his village.

She looked at Winter Raven, whose back still faced her as he powered the canoe. He had not slowed the movement of the paddle after realizing that their purpose in arriving home as quickly as possible was gone.

She thought back to the previous night and how she had snuggled next to Winter Raven as he had slept. He had been so at peace with himself, eager to carry the best of news to his father.

But she also recalled how he had said that if he did not make it home in time, he knew that his father would know, somehow, that everything had been achieved. If Winter Raven truly believed that, then he would not feel guilty about not arriving sooner.

She wanted to go to him, but she wasn't sure how to approach him now that his heart was burdened with such sadness. She understood sadness, having suffered enough losses to know how he must feel, but she thought he might want to be alone.

He began chanting as he guided the canoe closer to shore, his chants an extension of the voices coming from his village. Listening to the sounds gave Holly chills.

"Heyay, hoyo-heyah," he sang, repeating the words over and over again, not stopping even as he beached the canoe and held out a hand for Holly.

She stepped over the side onto the rocky beach, then took his hand and walked with him into the village. She flinched when everyone suddenly became quiet and broke away from one another to make space for Winter Raven to walk to his father's lodge.

Holly knew that his people were staring at her, especially since Winter Raven still clutched her hand so tightly that her fingers ached. It was as though he was drawing strength from her, and his people may have sensed this, for as she looked from one face to another, she saw no true resentment. Their hearts were too sad to worry over a woman whom their dead chief's son obviously needed with him.

She then realized that they were staring more at her attire, than at her, and she felt very self-conscious about her breeches, shirt, boots, and hat. With her free hand she pulled off her hat. She winced when a low gasp traveled through the crowd, and she saw that the villagers were staring at her hair.

When she had entered their village before, when Winter Raven had brought Two Moons home for burial, she didn't remember having removed her hat. They may not have realized that she had short hair.

She remembered an Indian custom that she had read about once, about how when Indian women mourned a loved one, they cut their hair. The Gros Ventres might think that she had cut her hair because of Yellow Knife's death.

Finally reaching his father's tepee, Winter

Raven grew quiet and stopped to take a deep breath before entering.

Holly moved closer to him and rose on tiptoe so that she could speak into his ear. "Are you sure you want me with you as you . . . as you . . . ?" she stammered. But she didn't need to say anything else, because his hand tightened and he nodded.

He pushed aside the entrance flap and led her into the lodge with him.

Holly swallowed hard when she saw the body at the far side of the tepee, and the woman—who she knew was Winter Raven's mother—kneeling beside it, her head bowed and her chants low and mournful.

Only then did Winter Raven release Holly's hand.

Holly took a step away from him as he walked toward his mother. He touched her gently on the shoulder. Tear-streaked eyes turned to look up at him.

He beckoned his mother to come to him. She rose and fell into his embrace, sobbing harshly.

"He is gone," she cried. "Last night, son. He took his final breath last night."

As he held his mother and comforted her, Winter Raven gazed down at his father, dressed in his finest buckskins, his face painted for his journey to the place where his ancestors awaited his arrival. Yellow Knife wore no feathers on his head, but his large feathered headdress lay on the floor beside him along with his other precious belongings.

Winter Raven was deeply touched by the smile on his father's face, evidence that he had died peacefully and with the knowledge that Winter Raven's quest had been successful.

Holly, standing in the shadows, realized that Winter Raven's mother had not noticed her yet. And Holly was glad, for it seemed appropriate for Winter Raven to have this time alone with his mother and father. She saw the gentle smile on his father's lips and wondered about it.

"Your father had one of his dreams just before he died," Prairie Blossom said, as if in answer to Holly's unspoken question. She stepped away from Winter Raven and gazed down at her beloved husband.

"What did his dream tell him?" Winter Raven asked, standing at her side, also looking at his father.

"It told him that all was well with the Spirit Bear People," she murmured. "They came to him in his dream. They told him they forgave him for his actions and thanked him for sending you to their island with the offerings. They said that the bear that he had wounded was still alive and had fathered many cubs. They also told him that they made peace with you, my son."

"All of that is so," Winter Raven said, reassured that his father's dream had revealed everything that Winter Raven would have told him.

"He did die in peace," Prairie Blossom said, choking back a sob. "Still, I miss him. My mourning will go on and on."

"Knowing that he died the way he wished to die, with a peaceful heart, and knowing how much he was loved, should make your mourning easier," Winter Raven said.

He put his hands on his mother's shoulders and turned her to face him. "Mother, do not mourn so much that I will have someone else, soon, to mourn," he said. "You are not strong. You cannot allow your heart to ache so deeply for long."

"I'm so glad I have you," Prairie Blossom said, flinging herself into his arms.

"Yes, you have me, always and forever," Winter Raven said, then carefully released her.

He turned to Holly and extended a hand to her. "You also have the woman who will soon be my wife to help you in your time of sorrow," Winter Raven said, watching his mother turn slowly around to see Holly emerge from the shadows.

Holly came to stand stiffly before Winter Raven and his mother. Prairie Blossom had not taken her eyes off Holly once she discovered her there.

"I'm so sorry about your loss," Holly murmured. "I wish we could have returned sooner, so that Winter Raven could have been here for you when . . ."

"He is here now," Prairie Blossom said, her voice and eyes friendly. "And I welcome you. Soft Eyes talked about you. She made me know you and like you."

"Truly?" Holly asked, softly blushing.

Prairie Blossom smiled, then reached a hand to her son's face. "Soft Eyes is awaiting your arrival in your lodge," she said. "Go to her. She needs your comforting arms. Then, my son, prepare yourself for the burial. It will be soon. Your father has his walk to take to his ancestors."

"I will not be long," Winter Raven promised.

He watched, in awe of his woman, as she leaned forward to embrace his mother. Then Holly took his hand and they started to leave, but Prairie Blossom lightly tapped her on the shoulder.

Holly turned, eyes wide as she saw what his mother held in her arms.

"I knew that you would be with my son on his return home, and I knew that you would want to wear the proper clothes of mourning, so I went through my dresses and found one that I wore when I was close to your age," she said softly. "Take it. It is now yours. Wear it for the burial."

"Thank you," Holly said, accepting the dress. "I shall wear it proudly."

Carrying the dress, Holly again took Winter Raven's hand. They left the lodge and walked through the milling crowd until they reached his large tepee.

Just as they stepped inside, the chanting outside began again, low and mournful, but soon all their attention was on Soft Eyes, who lay curled up on a thick pelt before the fire, sobbing.

Holly noticed that the child had on a beautifully beaded doeskin dress. Her hair was braided, with beads woven through each braid, and she wore lovely moccasins. And when Soft Eyes turned to look up at Winter Raven, Holly saw that the young girl's face was smudged with something black, which looked more like ash than paint.

Holly stood back as Winter Raven broke away and went to his daughter. She could hear him speaking in a low voice to Soft Eyes, who clung to him but nodded, as though listening intently and understanding.

When Soft Eyes stood up and saw Holly standing there, she wiped her eyes and went to her.

"Father wants me to help you get ready for the burial services," she said, swallowing a sob. "Come. As I did, you must change from your breeches to a dress."

"Yes, I know," Holly said, surprised when the child flung herself into her arms and hugged her.

Winter Raven found himself a little choked up by the scene. He was relieved that the woman of his heart was so readily accepted by not only his mother but also his daughter. Soon his people, as a whole, would also show their approval. But first, he had his father's burial to see to. Then he would begin the new phase of his life, as chief to his people and as husband to his love.

His thoughts were interrupted when Soft Eyes came to him and touched him gently on the arm. "Father, Brave Heart wants to join our people in mourning Grandfather," she said, her eyes quietly begging him. "Please say yes. Grandfather liked Brave Heart, and he deeply respected and admired Grandfather. He feels that he owes so much to Grandfather, because he was the one who found him injured and wandering aimlessly, with death not so far in his future. It was Grandfather who brought him here to see the shaman and even invited him to live among us, since the white man no longer could remember who he was, or if he had family. We're his family now."

It was true. Winter Raven's father found the man wandering in the foothills, alone and blind, with a wound that must have been inflicted by a war club only half healing at the base of his skull. Yellow Knife had taken the white man to the Gros Ventres village and had seen that he had received medical attention. Nothing had helped this man's blindness or his memory, but, otherwise, he had healed well enough.

He had stayed only after a personal, heartfelt invitation from Winter Raven's father, and was now a part of their lives as though he had been born a red man. He was the person who had proved to Winter Raven's people that not all whites were bad.

Soft Eyes interrupted Winter Raven's thoughts. "Please?" she asked again. "Grandfather even gave him the name Brave Heart," she reminded him, "because he saw the white man as brave and of good heart. Can I go and tell him that he can join the burial ceremony?"

"*Ho*, yes, but only after you prepare Holly for the rites," Winter Raven said, stooping to place sweet grass in the flames of the fire, over which hung a big, boiling pot of meat and dried corn. "Then take Holly with you. It will be good for Brave Heart to know that a white person will be living among us. Even though he does not remember much of his past, he must miss some ways of his white world."

Holly was listening with interest. "You have a white man living among you?" she asked, raising an eyebrow.

"For many moons now, yes, he has been among

us," Soft Eyes said. "And he has a wife now. He married my cousin Curly Hair, who is with child. Soon they will be parents."

"I look forward to meeting the man," Holly said, watching Winter Raven char a stick with fire, then blacken his face with it.

"The man is blind, but he sees well enough now with his fingers," Soft Eyes said, taking Holly behind the blanket that partitioned her place to sleep and dress away from the rest of the lodge. "Do not feel uneasy when Brave Heart wants to feel your face. That is his way of knowing one person from another."

"I see," Holly said. She laid the dress aside and unbuttoned her shirt, looking toward the blanket when she heard Winter Raven begin to chant, "You, Who Live Without Fire, hear my prayer . . ."

"He chants his medicine song to the Mysterious Ones," Soft Eyes explained.

Holly could now hear the sound of many drums pounding out a steady beat as the chants continued outside the lodge.

After she was dressed in the beautiful garment and had on a pair of butter-soft moccasins, she stepped out from behind the blanket and saw that Winter Raven was gone.

"He is with the others singing, dancing, and chanting, which will continue up until the time for the burial rites," Soft Eyes said, taking Holly's hand. "Come. We must hurry to Brave Heart's lodge and tell him he has father's blessing to join the burial ceremony with our people."

Holly stepped outside with Soft Eyes. She stopped short at the sight of Winter Raven dancing among thirty or forty warriors to a monotonous chant. They were all shuffling, bowing, and turning as the women watched in a wide circle, also chanting and singing.

As Soft Eyes led Holly around them, Holly still watched. Some men had stripped to their breechclouts. Others wore leggings adorned with brass and silver ornaments, paint, and feathers. The women all wore long, flowing doeskin dresses like Holly and Soft Eyes. Only a few of them had colored their faces with black ash or paint.

"Hurry," Soft Eyes said. She gave Holly's hand a pull.

Holly turned away from the dancers and rushed on with Soft Eyes until they came to a smaller tepee at the far end of the village, flanked on all sides by cottonwood trees.

Soft Eyes stepped up to the closed entrance flap. "Curly Hair? Brave Heart? It is I, Soft Eyes," the child called. "A friend and I have brought word from my father. Can we enter?"

Soon a lovely, very pregnant Indian woman, who appeared to be perhaps thirty years old, held the flap aside and smiled at Soft Eyes. She looked at Holly with a keen questioning in her eyes.

Holly looked at the woman's hair and understood how she had acquired her name. All of the other women in this village had straight hair, but this woman's black hair was thick with curls. And not only was her hair different from the hair of the others, but she had blue eyes, suggesting that she had white ancestry somewhere in her past.

"Curly Hair, this is my father's future wife," Soft Eyes said, stepping inside the tepee with Holly. "And, *ho*, yes, she is white. That is why I brought her. We think it would be nice if she and Brave Heart became acquainted."

"My husband is outside behind the lodge getting wood," Curly Hair said. "But he should not be long."

Holly felt herself being closely scrutinized by the other woman, but before long she heard a movement behind her as someone came into the lodge. Holly turned with curiosity to see the white stranger who was comfortably making his home among the Gros Ventres. She was eager to make friends with him, since it would be good to have someone from her own world to talk to occasionally.

The man's back was to Holly as he entered the lodge, his arms filled with firewood. "Wasps had made their home in one of our logs," he said, chuckling. "I heard them, but I shooed them off before any stung me."

"That voice!" Holly thought, her heart skipping several beats. Oh, Lord, she knew that voice!

"Curly Hair, you are so quiet," Brave Heart said, turning and squinting his sightless eyes as he seemed to sense a presence. "Is someone here with you? I thought I heard voices a moment ago, just before I came in."

When Holly saw the face of the man, her knees buckled beneath her.

"Papa!" she whispered. "Father!"

She then fainted dead away and crumpled at the man's feet.

27

Were I with her, the night would post too soon;
But now are minutes added to the hours;
To spite me now, each minute seems a moon!
                                    —WILLIAM SHAKESPEARE

"Holly!" Soft Eyes cried.

She bent down beside Holly and lifted her head from the mats on the floor, where she had fallen.

Soft Eyes stared at Holly for a moment, then slowly looked up at Brave Heart, who stood stiffly, staring sightlessly past her.

Soft Eyes wasn't very familiar with Holly's past, but she thought that Holly's father had died. Yet Holly had called "father" before she passed out, and only after seeing Brave Heart. Since Brave Heart had no memory of his past, Soft Eyes knew that she couldn't get answers from him as to whether or not he might be Holly's father. But perhaps her father hadn't died.

Soft Eyes watched Brave Heart go to the fire pit and bend low to put down the logs in his arms.

"Who's here that I do not know?" he asked, his voice wary.

"A woman, and she is white," Soft Eyes said, dabbing a damp cloth across Holly's brow that Curly Hair brought to her. "She is not just any woman. She will soon marry my father."

Brave Heart, dressed in buckskins, came and knelt beside Holly. "She has fainted?" he asked.

He reached a hand out to find Holly's face. And when he did, he slowly let his fingers roam over her features.

Soft Eyes set aside the damp cloth as she watched Brave Heart's hands study Holly's face. "When she saw your face she seemed to recognize you. She said the word 'father' and then fainted."

Soft Eyes bent her face closer to Holly's. "Brave Heart, do you feel anything familiar about her?" she asked softly. "I know that you can see things with your hands that sometimes people do not even see with their eyes. She called you 'father.' Surely that means . . ."

"That she is my daughter and that I am her father," Brave Heart said, his voice drawn.

Again he passed his fingers over Holly's face, and then he reached up and ran them through her cropped hair.

"Is she in mourning for your chief?" Brave Heart asked, raising an eyebrow. "Her hair is short, as though she has cut it for the purpose of mourning."

"One might think so, but she wore short hair the first time I saw her, and that was before my grandfather died," Soft Eyes said.

She looked nervously toward the entrance flap, then back at Brave Heart. "I must go and be with Father during the rites," she murmured. "But what about Holly? She still hasn't come to."

"Go. We will stay with her until she regains consciousness," Curly Hair said, her eyes on her husband. "My husband and I will care for her."

"I will go and explain her absence to my father," Soft Eyes said, rushing to her feet. "Yet if I do, and tell him that Holly has fainted, it will disturb his last moments with Grandfather." She frowned as she gazed down at Holly.

"Tell him that we will care for her so he can focus on his duties to his father," Brave Heart said, getting to his feet.

He walked Soft Eyes to the entrance flap. "Take our prayers with you and give them to your grandfather for us," he said solemnly.

"Yes, I shall," Soft Eyes said. She reached up and gave Brave Heart a big hug, then took one more look at Holly before running out of the tepee.

Curly Hair sat down on one side of Holly as Brave Heart sat on the other.

"Has nothing of your past come back to you

since hearing this young woman's voice?" Curly Hair asked tentatively.

She was afraid that if her husband did regain his memory, he might want to resume the life he had known before becoming a part of the Gros Ventres' village.

Yet what was to be, would be. She had no control over how destiny arranged this particular obstacle in the path of her future happiness with the man she adored.

"Husband, perhaps you *are* this woman's father," she said, a part of her hoping it wasn't so. But it had to be said, for as soon as Holly awakened, the truth would come out. The white woman could be mistaken, but she had no reason to make up such a thing as this.

"I remember nothing," Brave Heart said. Wishing that he could recall who he was and who had attacked him, he reached up to the scar on his skull. But, as always, nothing came back to him.

The way this woman reacted convinced him that she must be right, he must be her father. And it ate away at his heart to know that he had a daughter, only because he must have caused her much pain by his absence.

"When my chief found you, you were alone and there were no identifying papers on you," Curly Hair said. "Whoever downed you took all of your belongings, including your horse and weapons."

"Worst of all, I was robbed of my past, which must have included a daughter," Brave Heart said, "and a wife."

Curly Hair's spine stiffened. "But you do not recall having either, do you?" she asked. Her pulse raced waiting for the response that might tear her heart apart.

If this was, by chance, his daughter, and her presence caused him to slowly remember, could it be that he had a wife who would draw him back into her world? If so, where would that leave Curly Hair and the child that would soon be born to them?

She had always known that someday her husband might recall his name, his past, and remember having a family that he would want to seek out. Yet Curly Hair had hoped that their love was so strong that Brave Heart would never want to leave her for anything, or anyone.

"A wife?" Brave Heart asked, squinting as he tried desperately to remember such a woman, or a daughter.

He hung his head and slowly shook it back and forth. "No. I remember nothing," he said, resigned. "If this is my daughter, her voice did not stir anything within me."

He took his hands away from his face. "To me,

this woman is just another stranger, no more, no less," he said.

"What if she says things to you that make you remember your past?" Curly Hair asked, her voice breaking. "Tell me that will not take you away from me or our child. Please tell me that your devotion to me is for always."

He turned to her and reached out to touch her face. "I could never live without you," he said, drawing her into his arms. "Rest your troubled thoughts. I love you, now and forever."

He cradled her there, but his thoughts were on the white woman. He listened to her breathing change, which meant that she was waking up.

Just as Holly's eyes opened, she winced, for the first thing she saw was her father sitting there holding Soft Eyes' cousin.

Holly was stunned that her father was alive and that she had found him, but he seemed to be a total stranger to what and who he was. And, she realized, he was no less a stranger to her.

He was dressed in buckskin. His dark hair had grown out and hung to his waist in two braids. On his face were streaks of black paint, indicating his mourning of Chief Yellow Knife.

Looking at his sightless eyes and knowing that he could not see her, and did not even know her, caused a lump to rise in Holly's throat.

When Curly Hair moved out of Brave Heart's

arms, she gave Holly a look of resentment. Holly slid her gaze down to the beautiful woman's belly, now knowing that Curly Hair was carrying her father's child. It made Holly feel alien to everything around her.

But there was a part of her that rejoiced over knowing that her father was alive. Yes, even though he was blind and knew nothing of his past, he was alive! And that was enough for Holly. She would find a way to accept her father's new world, one that no longer included her.

Then a thought came to her that made her heart pound. Her mother! He didn't know about her mother, who had for so long been his dutiful wife. But Holly sensed that even if she told him about how her mother had died, and where she was buried on a hilltop beneath the willows, it would mean nothing to him. If he didn't know Holly, he most certainly wouldn't remember his beloved first wife.

Even though he and Holly had been so close, and she had grown up under his guidance and love, he still did not know her.

"You are awake?" Brave Heart asked. He reached out and found Holly's arm, then touched her cheek. "You are sitting before me. You are going to be all right?"

"Yes, I'm going to be all right," Holly murmured. She felt as if she were dying a slow death, knowing that if she reached out to hug him it would be meaningless to him. So she refrained, even though every fiber of her being wanted to be in his arms, to be held by the familiar arms of the father who had always been there to comfort her through the years.

She had to let the fact that he was alive be enough. And, no, she wouldn't talk about her mother. Not even if she was asked about her. She could tell that Curly Hair resented Holly enough for who she was, without her bringing another woman into the picture.

"I'm sorry for having come like this and . . . and fainted in your lodge," Holly managed, suddenly understanding what she must do. It surprised even herself, but she saw it as the only way out of this strained situation.

"And I'm sorry for having mistaken you for someone else," she blurted out, causing both her father and his wife to gasp.

This was the only way things could work out, she thought, especially since her father was contentedly married to another woman.

Even though he was blind, his happiness was obvious. And if this woman, this woman carrying his unborn child, could make him so happy, then Holly would do everything within her power to see that nothing interfered with his new life.

She would not hurt him, no matter how much

being denied his love hurt her. She was no longer a child, and now she had someone else to turn to. She would be happy that her father had someone to love in the same way that she and Winter Raven loved one another.

Yes, it would be enough for her to know that he was alive and happy, and to know that she would be seeing him every day. She would even be able to enjoy his new family, since she would soon marry into it.

"You mistook . . . ?" Curly Hair started to ask, unable to hide the joy that she felt at this news. "He isn't your father?"

"No, he's not my father," Holly lied, trying to pretend that the words didn't cut into her heart like knives.

But she knew she was doing the right thing, at least until her father could remember his past himself.

She gazed at the scar on his head and realized how much the blow that had caused it had taken from him, even though it spared his life. She doubted that he would regain his memory, if he had not done so by now.

"You know now that I am not your father?" Brave Heart asked, taken aback by her change.

"Yes, I was mistaken," Holly said softly. "It's just that there is so much about you that reminded me of him. It was a shock to see you, but you

couldn't be him. I know that my father is . . . dead.
I just never wanted to accept that as fact until
now."

"Why now, when not before?" Brave Heart
asked, taking one of Curly Hair's hands in his.

"Because I know it was wishful thinking,"
Holly answered, smiling at Curly Hair. "Look
how distressed I got, over nothing. I must never
do that to myself again. And I'm sorry I caused
you so much trouble."

A lie came to her that she felt was necessary.
"You see, I do this all the time," Holly said, slowly
hanging her head. "Often, I have seen men and
so badly wanted them to be my father, the same
as I did today." She swallowed hard. "I now realize that I must stop this or . . . I might never get
over his death, as I should have long ago."

"Where is your mother?" Brave Heart asked.

Holly looked intently at her father, wondering
why he would ask such a question, since it was
apparent that he didn't remember that he had a
previous wife. She glanced at Curly Hair, who
was also stunned by the question. She was pale
as she stared at her husband in disbelief, wondering if he had suddenly remembered something.

"My mother?" Holly said guardedly. "Why do
you ask?"

"Because you must be far from home," Brave

Heart said, his expression impossible to read. "Where are you from? And why are you here in the Gros Ventres village? I know that you are planning to marry Winter Raven, but is that the only reason you have come here?"

Holly suddenly felt trapped, for she had truly wanted to put all of this in the past for the sake of her father and his happiness.

"I came to Montana for reasons I would rather not discuss," she said weakly. "And while here, I met Winter Raven. We fell in love. I am putting my past behind me and will live from now on for my husband and his people."

"But what of your mother?" Brave Heart persisted, making Holly ache with longing. "Did you leave her behind? Where did you travel from?"

"My mother, she . . . is dead," Holly finally found herself able to say, hoping that would be answer enough to stop his questions. If she had to tell him about her mother's death and her stepfather, it could only lead down a road her father surely would not want to travel. She would have to tell him about how she tried to be a bounty hunter like him, and once she started explaining, she knew she'd end up trying everything in her power to make him remember her. It was all best left unsaid.

"I'm sorry," Brave Heart said, his throat dry.

"I am also sorry," Curly Hair said, putting a

hand on Holly's arm. "And I am grateful that you explained your mistake."

Holly's and Curly Hair's eyes met and at that moment Holly knew that Curly Hair sensed the truth. She understood that Holly had lied, and why. Curly Hair *should* be grateful, Holly thought, since she was giving up her father to his new wife without a fight!

The wailing and chanting had been quiet for a while, but now it began anew, and Holly looked quickly toward the closed entrance flap.

"I must go and be with Winter Raven," she said in a rush of words.

Holly glanced at her father, then hurried outside. She ran hard until she was finally at Winter Raven's side at the burial grounds of his ancestors.

She took his hand and knelt beside his father's blanket-wrapped body just before it was to be lowered into the fresh grave. She closed her eyes and listened to Winter Raven's prayer, but she was thinking back to her lie about her own father just moments ago. She kept reminding herself how lucky she was that her dear father was alive.

She began a prayer of her own, speaking it to herself, praying to her God to give her the grace and will to be thankful and accept things as they were. She prayed that she would always believe that her father's happiness was the most important thing.

When Winter Raven slid an arm around her waist and drew her closer to him, she felt the blessing in having him. Winter Raven was all that she needed.

And would it not be the same were her father to know who she was? Would she not still be with Winter Raven, soon to marry him, as her father would be with the woman of his desire?

No, she had not lost a father today after all. She had found one, and discovering that he was alive could only be a miracle!

She listened as Winter Raven prayed aloud. "You, Who Live Without Fire"—his impassioned words flew heavenward, growing stronger as his father's spirit rose and began its long journey to the Sand Hills.

Holly seemed to feel spirits all around her, as though they had come to assist Chief Yellow Knife on his final passage. She raised her eyes to the sky and inhaled sharply when she actually saw many apparitions there, like ghostly clouds floating upward. Today was a day of many miracles, she thought to herself, at peace.

28

I've got an arrow here;
Loving the hand that sent it,
I the dart revere.
      —EMILY DICKINSON

Holly felt as though she were walking on clouds. It was her wedding day, and she had already become Winter Raven's wife.

The celebration was in high gear now. Holly sat with Winter Raven on a blanket at one end of the crowd. Dusk was just beginning to fall. Fires had been lit inside all of the buffalo-skin lodges, their blurred lights marking the perfect circles of the tepees. Drums were beating as painted warriors with eagle feather headdresses danced around the huge outdoor fire, their sharp, exultant yelps wild like coyotes.

Through the previous night and the long day today, buffalo meat had been cooking in the ground for the feast, which was a big part of the wedding celebration. A hole had been dug for the fire, and ribs that had been prepared with *minnesquea*, salt, and wrapped in a piece of green hide, had been placed on the live coals. Coals had been drawn over the wrapped meat, and then dry earth had been packed over all of this.

When the hole was opened tonight, after the ceremony, the cover would be removed and the steaming meat would be revealed, juicy and brown. Holly had learned to love the taste of buffalo. It was sweet and good. She envisioned how everyone would attack the choice roast, for no food had been eaten the entire day in order to ready everyone for the delicacy cooking in the ground.

Holly was taken with the way the people swayed and sang to the rhythm of the drums and dancers. Yellow Knife had asked for no more than one day and night of mourning, since his son would become chief and deserved a celebration upon being given the holy honor. Yellow Knife had not wanted grief for him to cloud the very first moments of his son's reign. Out of respect for their departed chief's wishes, the village had stopped the mourning, and the celebration of life—and of their new chief and of his taking a bride—had begun.

The scene before Holly moved her. Tears of happiness pooled in the corners of her eyes. It was so hard to believe that this was happening to her, that she had found a man who loved her as much as she loved him.

Holly looked around the crowd until she found

her father sitting with Curly Hair. Seeing him so close, yet so far, was the only thing that diminished her joy. She was thankful that at least he could be at her wedding, even though she longed to share with him just how happy she was.

When Winter Raven reached over and took one of her hands, she looked at him with adoration and reminded herself again that he was all that she needed to be fulfilled. And she was so very much fulfilled.

"My husband," she murmured, gazing into his eyes.

"My wife," Winter Raven responded, his eyes devouring her. She looked so heavenly in the new white doeskin dress that his mother had given her, the colored shells and beads on it picking up the shine of the fire. He reached out and touched her hair, where his daughter had placed a wreath of wild red roses that she had made for her new mother.

He was touched deeply by the way Soft Eyes had taken pains to please him today. She wore a fringed buckskin dress with beaded designs of forest flowers gracing the front. Roses had been woven into her thick braids, which hung down her back. And the smile she gave him when she caught him looking at her made his insides melt.

He turned back to Holly and found Holly's eyes slowly moving over him. He had dressed especially fine for her, and he could tell that it was appreciated.

All day Holly had hardly been able to take her eyes off her new husband. His waist-length hair was braided and wrapped in strips of otter skin. Around his neck he wore brass ornaments and a necklace of pink shells. His shirt, breechclout, and leggings were fringed and decorated with bead-work. The same as Holly, Winter Raven wore nothing on his feet.

Suddenly Holly was aware that the drums were no longer being played, nor were the people singing. The dancers had stopped as well and were now sitting with their loved ones around the circle.

She gave Winter Raven a questioning look. "Is it time now to uncover the roasted meat?" she asked, although she was too enraptured even to feel hunger.

He only smiled, and then she felt a presence at her side. She looked over and found Soft Eyes kneeling beside her, holding out Holly's har-monica.

"Please play your music?" she asked softly. "I told my people about it, how mysterious it is, how beautiful. Will you share this with them and allow it to be a part of today's ceremony?"

Stunned that Soft Eyes would ask this of her, she realized just how in awe of the harmonica the child had been. Holly gave Winter Raven a quick glance.

"Fill the air with your music only if you wish to," Winter Raven said. "My woman, today is yours. Do with it what you wish."

Wanting to do everything possible to strengthen her bond with her new stepdaughter, Holly turned to Soft Eyes and held out her hand for the instrument.

She lifted it to her mouth, then lowered it slowly when she found herself staring at her father again. She could not help but remember those times with him when they had played the harmonica together. A sadness washed over her to know that even if he heard this today, he would not recognize it.

She hung her head, for now she wasn't certain if she could play the harmonica in her father's presence, or should. All at once, she felt overwhelmed by memories of her past.

Soft Eyes's hand on Holly's arm made Holly turn and look at her. "Do not be afraid," Soft Eyes reassured. "My people will adore your music."

Glad to realize that her hesitation was taken for stage fright, Holly inhaled a quivering breath, smiled, nodded, and lifted the instrument to her lips again.

But she willed herself not to look at her father while she played, for if she did, and she saw only a blank look on his face, it would make her never want to play the harmonica again for the rest of her life. Instead, she looked at her husband as she chose the most romantic songs to play. The music reverberated softly in the air, like a bird's sweet song.

When she was done and everyone applauded, she still didn't look at her father. She handed the harmonica back to Soft Eyes. "I shall teach you how to play it soon," she said, smiling at the child.

"Thank you. I shall be a good student," Soft Eyes said, running her fingers over the instrument.

"Come," Winter Raven said, standing and offering Holly a hand.

She gazed up at him uncertainly. "But we haven't shared the feast with your people," she said.

"*Our* people," he corrected. "Now that you are my wife, my people are also yours. And they do not expect us to delay any longer our private moments together in our lodge."

He glanced at Soft Eyes. "Sleep with Grandmother tonight," he said, his voice quiet yet full of authority.

"Yes, I will," Soft Eyes said, smiling at Holly.

Holly rose and took Winter Raven's hand. She could feel the eyes of all his—*their*—people on them as they walked away from the crowd.

A warrior let out a loud chant, then announced that food would soon be served.

Holly heard the chatter behind her now and realized that everyone was too absorbed in digging up the roasted meat even to notice that their chief was taking his new bride into their lodge and securing the ties at the entrance flap to ensure their privacy.

Winter Raven reached out for Holly and pulled her into his arms. His mouth covered hers as he pressed his body against her and led her down onto a warm nest of robes that he had prepared for their first lovemaking as man and wife.

Holly stretched out on her back beside the fire. Winter Raven knelt beside her, still kissing her, his hands expertly sliding up inside her dress. Soon finding her wet and ready place, he plunged a finger inside her, the very act dazzling Holly's senses.

With his other hand caressing her tender, throbbing woman's center, a fever spread through Holly, and she could hardly bear another moment without touching him.

When he moved away from her, she reached up and drew his shirt over his head, tossing it aside. She untied the thongs at the waist of his breechclout and leggings, and, with a racing heart, she slid them downward. Her gaze lingered on the part of him that proved he was as ready for their lovemaking as she.

He kicked his clothes aside, then closed his eyes and sucked in a wild breath of pleasure when Holly wrapped her fingers around his thickness. She began moving her hand on him, watching his lips part as he moaned. She saw movement behind his closed eyes and knew that he was becoming lost in bliss.

As his hands reached out for her breasts, she moved even closer to him. She continued pleasuring him while both of his hands cupped her breasts, his fingers flicking the nipples.

Before long, he eased her hand from his heat, and he placed his hands at her waist and turned her so that he was blanketing her with his body. With one fluid movement he was inside her. She clung to him as their bodies tangled and he took her mouth savagely in his.

The hot, pulsing desire spread like wildfire through Winter Raven. Holly's answering heat and excitement fired his even more. Again he cupped her swelling breasts, his mouth searing hers with intensity, leaving her breathless and quivering.

The vibrations of her body matched his as they found heaven together at the same moment.

Holly smiled and lay quietly with him for a

minute, a whole night of lovemaking still ahead
of them.

Winter Raven kissed her gently, then rolled
away from her and wet a buckskin cloth in a
wooden tray filled with water. Tenderly he
washed her free of the traces of their passion.
Holly took the cloth and softly cleansed him, then
bent low and kissed him there, making him sigh
deeply.

He reached out and drew her down with him
again and they rolled and rolled over the pelts,
kissing, fondling, and caressing.

After a while, Winter Raven broke away and
got to his feet. "I have something I should have
done before we made love," he said to her.

Holly leaned up on an elbow and watched him.
She knew that whatever he was going to do involved a custom that she as yet did not know
about. But soon she would know everything
about him and all of his customs.

Winter Raven opened the drawstring of a small
buckskin pouch. He reached inside and filled his
fingers with sweet grass, then scattered it over
the flames of his lodge fire. Holly watched a
shadow of white smoke from the burning grass
curl upward and fill the lodge with its fragrance.

"Now I can set our dishes outside so that my
daughter will see them and know that we would
like some of the delicious-smelling roasted meat,"

he said, bending to brush a soft kiss across her brow.

"I can't deny how hungry I am," Holly said, only now realizing just how much she did want to eat. She had discovered that lovemaking always made her ravenous!

"Then you get two wooden platters as I untie the entrance flap," Winter Raven said, smiling at her over his shoulder as he went to the entranceway.

Holly wrapped a blanket around her shoulders and picked up the two wooden bowls that she knew had been placed beside the lodge fire for this purpose. As Winter Raven held the flap aside, she slipped the two platters outside.

"It won't take long for food to arrive," Winter Raven predicted. He reached for Holly and led her down on the blanket beside the fire again. "Until then? Let us make our hunger twofold by making love again."

"The ties are undone," Holly said nervously, glancing toward the entrance flap. The slight breeze shimmied the flap so that if someone came close enough, they could see inside at the corners.

"No one will look," Winter Raven promised. "We are assured of our privacy."

Not having to be talked into it, aching so badly for her husband a second time tonight, Holly moved into his arms and forgot everything but the way he skillfully made a delicious desire steal over her.

He entered her and a blaze of urgency swept through her. She wrapped her legs around his waist, her body turning to liquid as she traveled with him again on the road to paradise.

29

She found me roots of relish sweet,
And honey wild, and manna dew;
And sure she said,
I love thee true.

—JOHN KEATS

"Holly?"

A voice outside her lodge awakened Holly with a start. Winter Raven woke up as well. They both sat up and looked questioningly at one another.

"I didn't dream I heard my name?" Holly whispered, her pulse racing.

Again she heard it, and this time she knew that she was not dreaming. Her name *was* being called just outside the entrance flap, and she recognized the voice that was calling for her. It was her father! His memory had returned!

It was light enough in the tepee for Holly to know that it was morning. She drew on a robe and smiled anxiously at Winter Raven. "It's a miracle," she said, swallowing a sob of joy. "My father. He remembers!"

She didn't stop to explain or wait for Winter Raven's reaction. She went to the entrance flap and rushed outside. Overwhelmed with emotion, she flung herself into her father's arms. She was deliriously happy that her father now knew her.

"Papa, how?" Holly sobbed, still clinging to him. "What happened?"

"The harmonica," Brave Heart said. "Last night as you played, everything began coming back to me. I wanted to come to you then, but you were already in the lodge with Winter Raven. It was your wedding night. I thought it best to wait until morning."

He stepped back from her and touched her face, remembering how she had looked the last time he had seen her. He held her hands tightly. His little girl had changed so much, but he still loved her fiercely. "Your mother," he said, his voice drawn. "How can I tell your mother about . . ."

Holly realized that her father still knew nothing of her life, or her mother's, since he had disappeared. He didn't know that his wife had thought that he was dead and had married another man, who had turned out to be a villain. She had so much to tell him.

"Everyone thought you were dead," she blurted out. She quickly filled him in on the happenings of the last few years. When she revealed that his beloved first wife was dead, a pained expression crossed his face. He looked heartsick when she went into the details about the man who had duped her mother out of all of their money and even their home. She had to tell him, for that was what had brought her to Montana.

But she didn't tell her father about the terrible way her mother had died. She thought it might be too much for him to bear. Holly still could not stand the thought that her mother had been poisoned and she herself had not been able to do anything about it.

"I came to Montana searching for my stepfather," Holly explained. "And to pay my passage on the boat, I . . . I had to become a bounty hunter."

"Since I've been gone, you've had to go through so much, as did your mother," Brave Heart said, his voice breaking. His anger flared at the thought of the injustice they had endured. "Did you find the man? Has he paid for his crimes?"

"Yes, and he won't be causing anyone else any harm," Holly said.

She did not want to have to tell him how she had achieved her goal, and she was glad when her father didn't pursue it, but what he did say made her heart ache.

"I feel as though I let you and your mother down," Brave Heart said. "I shouldn't have left that last time on a bounty hunt."

Holly flung herself into her father's arms again.

"Oh, Papa, I have missed you so," she cried, her body racked with deep sobs. "And so did Mama. I should've looked out for her and never allowed that man to take advantage of her. But . . . but she was lonely, and that made it easy for her to be fooled by him. Only she told me often that she never stopped loving you. Never!"

As Brave Heart embraced her he could not hold back the tears any longer. He cried until there were no more tears for either of them. Then Holly eased away from him and moved over into Winter Raven's arms.

"Everything will be all right now," Winter Raven said to Holly. He extended a hand to Brave Heart, placing it on his shoulder. "It is good that you remember your daughter, for she is someone special to know and love."

Brave Heart nodded, but Winter Raven frowned. "And your wife, my precious cousin?" Winter Raven asked warily. "What happens now that you remember the man you were before you met and married her?"

Brave Heart wiped a tear from his face with his sleeve. "I love her," he said. "I will always love her and would never leave her. And I can hardly wait for our child to be born."

"Then go to her," Winter Raven said. "I am certain she awaits your return with an anxious heart."

"No, she knows there is no need to be anxious about anything," Brave Heart said, smiling. "Before I came to your lodge, I explained everything to her, especially how much I love her and how proud I am to be her husband."

"It's good to see father and daughter reunited and happy," Winter Raven said. He chuckled. "And I have a father-in-law. The man my cousin adores is my wife's father."

"Papa, I love you so," Holly said, reaching out for his hand. "Because of our shared love for music, you have been returned, heart and soul, to me." She paused a moment before adding, "It is wonderful that you remember everything, but the past is behind us now. You and I are still alive. We have both found a new life. Let us feel blessed for it."

"We have much to be thankful for," Brave Heart agreed, squeezing Holly's hand. "In fact, before I return to my wife, I will go and say a prayer of thanks to the Heavens."

Holly gave Winter Raven a questioning glance. "Darling husband, would you miss me too much if I go with Papa to say my own prayer of thanks?" she asked.

"Go. Say a prayer of thanks, also, for your new husband, who has a wife who is his everything," Winter Raven said.

Laughing, smiling, walking side by side, Holly

and Brave Heart left the village. They made plans to go into the town of Three Forks the next day to clear up a few things about two wanted men.

Holly could hardly think about what it would be like to ride alongside her father again. Even though he was blind now, he still could skillfully handle a horse. It would be like old times, something that Holly had never dreamed would happen ever again! Yes, she had much to give thanks for.

She turned to her father. "Papa, now that you remember your past, what name should people call you?" she asked softly.

He turned his sightless eyes toward her and smiled. "Brave Heart, of course," he said proudly.

30

I made a garland for her head,
And bracelets, too, and fragrant zone;
She looked at me as she did love,
And made sweet moan.

—JOHN KEATS

It was June, "Moon of Roses" month, several years after Winter Raven and Holly's wedding night. The Gros Ventres had moved their village farther up the Missouri River, to a grand bottomland filled with cottonwood groves and grassy prairies. Where the shallows of the *Minnishushu* swept around a bend, thickets of tall willows grew, and deer and elk often visited in the heat of the day.

Holly was busying herself with raising the lodge skin off the ground, propping it up with sticks of firewood so that the evening breeze might cool it off for her two babies, who lay asleep in the wooden cradles their father had made for them.

Two heavy golden braids fell over Holly's shoulders as she knelt between the two cradles.

Her eyes filled with love and adoration as she gazed from one son to the other.

"Twins," she whispered, marveling anew at the surprise she had had when a second child came from her womb only seconds after the first.

She had known that she had gained a lot of weight during her pregnancy, but she had attributed it to her happiness. She giggled to herself, thinking about how ravenous she always was after making love, and since she and Winter Raven made love at any opportunity, she was always seeking some kind of food to satisfy her never-ending appetite.

"Two sons," she cooed.

She reached out and brushed a lock of black hair back from one baby's brow. They were both Gros Ventres in appearance, with their copper skin, dark eyes, and dark hair. They were truly their father's sons. And Holly couldn't be prouder.

She never allowed herself to think about how it had been between two other twins, Winter Raven and Two Moons, and how one had walked the good road of life and the other chose the bad.

She and Winter Raven had vowed to one another that they would do everything humanly possible to see that both of their sons remained good at heart, so that they would never go astray. He and Holly would give their children so much love that they would never have the need to seek fulfillment elsewhere.

Smelling the food cooking over her lodge fire reminded Holly that she should give the roasting venison another turn on the spit. She bent low, kissed one son and then the other, and then went outside where she had moved her cook fire because of the heat. She gave the spit a turn, and the drippings from the roast fell into the fire, giving off a tantalizing aroma.

Shortly afterward, just as she was adding a few sticks of cottonwood to replenish the fire, she heard someone step up behind her.

"You are driving your husband mad with the aroma of venison," Winter Raven said, grabbing one of Holly's hands.

He urged her to her feet and spun her around to face him. "My wife, are the children asleep?" he asked, his eyes smiling into hers.

"I think we might have a while longer before they will be crying for my milk," Holly said, glowing inside over how adoringly Winter Raven looked at her.

Wearing a beaded buckskin dress with her hair now grown past her waist, she knew that he saw her as beautiful. And she had gotten such a tan from being out-of-doors so often, her skin was almost the color of his.

"Then let us take a walk and marvel together

at the beauty of this summer day," Winter Raven said, pulling her close.

He looked over at Soft Eyes, who was sitting with friends beneath the shade of the cottonwood trees, making beaded necklaces. "Soft Eyes will come to us if the babies awaken and cry," he said.

Holly gazed past Soft Eyes at her father's lodge. He was inside with his wife and child. Holly had grown very fond of her half brother, who was no longer that much of a baby. He was learning early the art of shooting his bow and arrows.

As she and Winter Raven walked toward the bluff that overlooked their village and the surrounding land for miles, she thought back to the day when she and her father had ridden into Three Forks with the news to wire back to Sheriff Hawkins in Kansas City. They had told the sheriff that Rudolph Anderson and Jake Two Moons had died.

The sheriff had volunteered to send the reward money to her, but she knew that Winter Raven wouldn't want her to accept money that was earned, in part, from the death of his brother. She told the sheriff to give it to her friends Jana and Frank. They were poor, and giving the money to them would be a way of thanking them for being true friends to her for so long.

As Holly and her father started to leave the jail, Sheriff Chance Stone had told them that her stepfather's belongings had been brought there from the hotel. He had kept them for Holly. She could have what she wanted and he would give the rest away.

Among Rudolph's belongings was a good portion of the money he had stolen from Holly's mother, which in truth belonged to Holly's father. She had been happy to hand it over to him, and he had taken it to use for the betterment of his lodge and for pretty things for his beautiful wife.

"You are lost so deep in thought," Winter Raven said as he and Holly followed the worn path that took them up to the bluff.

"I was thinking about the day my father and I went into Three Forks," she said, smiling up at him. "Winter Raven, it was so wonderful being with him like that, on horseback. I had truly thought I would never see him again. And now to have him back in my life? It's almost more than a daughter could ask for."

"Being a woman with a good heart who always has kind words for everyone, you deserve to have good returned to you," Winter Raven said, stepping on the rocky ledge. He helped Holly up beside him, then they both moved to stand where they could see for eternity, it seemed.

"I could never be more happy," Holly said, as Winter Raven stretched out an arm and drew her closer. "And just look at everything. It's like we are a part of heaven on earth."

Down below, far in the distance, buffalo feasted on the thick grass. They had shed roll after roll of their winter coats. A close look at the land around them would reveal clumps of this soft down bobbing and bouncing over the green plains, occasionally to be caught by the sagebrush.

Beneath a sky of scudding clouds rode flocks of curlews, hundreds of them, circling above Winter Raven and Holly, swooping, darting, piping.

"I have gifts for our sons," Winter Raven told her. "While you were looking after the food over the outdoor fire, I took what I made inside and laid it on the floor beside their beds."

"The bows and quivers?" Holly asked excitedly. She had seen him sitting outside beneath the shade of trees, carving the gifts. "They are finished?"

"*Ho*, yes," he said. "Identical gifts for identical sons. The quivers made of otter skin are filled with tiny arrows with blunt ends."

"You are an eager father," Holly said, laughing softly. "Eager for sons to hunt with you."

"Yes, I have waited a lifetime, it seems, for a son, and now I have *two*," Winter Raven said, his chest puffed out proudly.

He turned her toward him. His hands moved gently over her face. "Did I ever tell you how beautiful you are?" he asked. "And that you fill my heart with joy?"

"I believe so," Holly replied, her eyes twinkling. "But, my wonderful husband, I never grow tired of hearing it."

"Even when you are gray and have grandchildren perched on your lap listening to your sweet harmonica music, I will still see you as nothing less than ravishingly beautiful," Winter Raven said. He drew her lips to his and gave her a long, deep kiss that sent a thrill through her, as though it was his first kiss, with the same promise of many to come.

She wrapped her arms around his neck and returned the kiss, and the meaning behind it, in kind. Oh, how fiercely she loved him!

And how she loved and adored her family. As her father had told her so many times, "Family is the true reward of life."

"How true," she thought to herself. "Yes, how true."

Dear Reader:

I hope you enjoyed reading *Winter Raven.* The next book in my Signet Indian Series, which I am writing exclusively for NAL, is *Midnight Falcon,* about the Powhatan tribe of early Virginia. This is my first book about the Powhatan Indians, and I am excited about the story—the intrigue, romance, and adventure. I hope you will buy *Midnight Falcon* and will enjoy reading it as much as I enjoyed writing about the interesting customs and lives of this tribe.

For those of you who are collecting all of the books in my Topaz and Signet Indian Series and want to read about them, you can send for my latest newsletter, as well as an autographed black-and-white photo and bookmark. Write to:

Cassie Edwards
6709 North Country Club Road
Mattoon, Illinois 61938
For a prompt reply, please send a self-addressed, stamped, legal-size envelope.

Or visit my web site at www.cassieedwards.com.

Thank you from the bottom of my heart for your support. I love researching and writing about our country's beloved Native Americans!

Cassie Edwards